DESTINY

DESTINY

STEEL BROTHERS SAGA

BOOK TWENTY-SEVEN

HELEN HARDT

WATERHOUSE PRESS

For everyone who believes in destiny.

PROLOGUE

Ava

Donny and Callie are hardly in the door when I pounce.

"I need to know everything you know about the future lawmakers club at Snow Creek High School."

Donny takes Callie's jacket from her and hangs it on the coatrack in the entryway. "Good evening to you too, cuz."

Michaela takes Donny's blazer once he removes it.

"Goodness, Ava," Mom says. "Let them get inside the house first."

I can't help myself. I'm starved for information. I've finally got a lot of the story behind my ancestors, and though it's nausea-inducing, I'm determined to find out everything.

"Don, Callie, what do you want to drink?" Dad asks.

"Just Diet Coke or water for me," Callie says. "Thanks."

"Water's good." Donny follows Mom into the kitchen and then the family room. "Something smells good."

"Michaela made rigatoni." Dad takes his place behind the bar. He pulls a can of Diet Coke out of the refrigerator for Callie and a bottle of water for Donny. Then he pours a glass of one of his reds for himself. "Ava, Ruby? Anything to drink?"

"I'll have some of the Ruby," Mom says, smiling at the mention of her namesake wine.

"Just water for me, thanks." I take a seat next to Donny and

Callie on the leather couch. "So . . . the future lawmakers . . ."

"Sounds like something from the past," Donny says.

"How much do you know?" I ask him.

"I know a lot, unfortunately."

Yes, he does. But I can't go there. The thought of what happened to him and Dale, to Uncle Talon . . .

"I can answer your question," Callie says. "The future lawmakers club didn't exist when Dale and Donny were in high school. But they did when Rory and I were there. It was a newer club, and I went to a meeting."

I drop my jaw and look to Donny.

"Callie and I don't have any secrets," he says.

"So you and she both know . . ."

"About the future lawmakers of the past? Yeah, we do."

"It was called the FLMC for short. I don't know who started the club when I was in school." Callie takes a sip of Diet Coke. "But as I've always been interested in law, I went to a meeting once."

"And . . . ?"

She takes another sip. "There was no discussion about the law or making law at all. It was all about"—air quotes—"*sticking it to the man.*"

"What's that mean?" I ask. "I mean, I know what it means. But what did it mean with regard to the club?"

"I don't know," Callie says. "I didn't stick around long enough to find out. Soon after that, the club became invite only."

"Oh?" I lift my eyebrows.

"Yeah, but anyone could get an invite. The FLMC members soon established themselves as troublemakers. They took credit for a lot of the crap that went on at school. When

Rory and I decided to try to figure out who had spiked the punch at the homecoming bonfire her senior year, the FLMC was where I was going to start investigating."

"What did you find?"

"Nothing, because I never got that far. I ended up overhearing Pat Lamone and Jimmy Dawson bragging about it, so I had my answer."

"Do you know anything else about the club?" I ask. "Was Pat Lamone a member?"

"Honestly, I have no idea. I don't even know if the club still exists."

"The question," Donny says, "is whether the reincarnation of the club had anything to do with the club our grandfather belonged to. And I sure hope not."

"I hope not as well," I say, "but with everything else that seems to be reappearing..."

"So Brock told you."

"He did. It made me sick. A lot of things have made me sick lately. It's getting easier to stomach each time I learn something new... which in itself is disturbing."

"I know. I hear you, Ava."

"You know about... Wendy?" I ask.

Donny nods. "Yes."

"So you know I'm not a full-blood Steel."

Donny frowns slightly. "You're more of a full-blood Steel than I am."

"I didn't mean—"

Donny nods, though he doesn't smile. "I know you didn't. Blood doesn't matter. Dale and I were fathered by a man who sold us into slavery for five thousand dollars."

I drop my jaw.

"I guess you don't know everything," Donny says.

"Donny, go easy on her," Callie says. "This is difficult for all of us."

"I know. I'm only saying that blood doesn't matter. Our ancestors don't matter. What matters is who we are. Who we want to be."

I nod, swallowing. "I'm so sorry for everything you and Dale have been through."

"It's ancient history, Ava. It sucked. I won't lie. But it was so long ago, and we've had amazing lives here on the ranch."

"I know. So have I."

"So our true parentage doesn't matter. We've all got major skeletons in the closet."

I take a drink of water. "How can we find out what this FLMC is up to now?"

"I don't even know if they still exist," Callie says. "I graduated eight years ago."

"Our family doesn't have anyone at that school anymore," Donny says.

"True. Maybe it's nothing."

But even as I say the words, I don't believe them. The FLMC, whether they're related to the original or not, are still around.

The question is what they're up to, and whether it's good or bad.

CHAPTER ONE

Brendan

The bar is busy for a weeknight, and hours pass before I remember to check my phone. Hmm. No text from Ava yet. I text her quickly and stuff my phone back into my pocket . . . just in time to see Pat Lamone walk into the bar.

Lord.

Did his mother tell him?

It's not my problem, but man . . .

He walks to the bar and takes an empty seat right in front of me.

"What can I get you, Lamone?"

"Answers," he says.

"Look, I'm sorry about your birth mother, and—"

"I can't talk about that." His tone is robotic. "Not yet."

"So she told you."

He nods.

"What can I get you?" I ask again.

"Scotch. Neat."

I pour his drink and slide it in front of him.

He downs it in one gulp and slides it back to me. "Another."

I pour another, set it in front of him. "If you have another after that one, I'm taking your keys."

"No problem. I walked over here."

"You still living at Mrs. Mayer's place?"

He nods, takes a drink.

I don't want to get into his life any more than I already am, but I'm a bartender. This is what I do.

"Spill it," I say. "Tell me what's on your mind."

"My grandmother," he says.

"Dyane Wingdam. Also known as Wendy Madigan."

"Yeah. I went to see her tonight. At the hospital in Grand Junction."

"I see."

"I wanted answers. I needed answers. Answers my birth mother couldn't give me. Answers about my grandfather. The man who made me a Steel."

"I understand, but how did you expect to get answers from a comatose woman?"

"I don't know, but my trip turned out to be in vain."

Now my curiosity is piqued.

"What's that supposed to mean?"

"It means ... the very day that I met my birth mother and learned the circumstances of my birth ... my grandmother ... "

He stares at his drink, picks it up, swirls the scotch in the glass.

"For God's sake, Lamone, what? What are you trying to say?"

"She's gone. Her hospital bed was empty." He slides the glass toward me once more. "Another."

I hide my surprise. Ava's grandmother ... gone? A comatose woman ... gone? Something's fishy. Ava will be affected, and not in a good way.

"I see."

Mrs. Mayer doesn't live too far away, so Pat should be able to make it home all right, even if he's stumbling most of the way.

I pour another drink. "Didn't the nurses say anything to you?"

"They just said they discharged her."

"How did that happen? A doctor would have to—"

"They wouldn't tell me. I'm her grandson. A DNA test proved that. But technically, I'm nothing to her. Not her next of kin, not anything. So they wouldn't give me any information."

"But you've been visiting her all this time."

"Apparently that doesn't matter in the medical world."

"Yeah, they're really careful. The HIPAA laws and everything. But still…" I shake my head. "I don't understand what could've happened. Do you think your mother had her discharged?"

"From what I understand from my talk with my mother"— he clears his throat, shoots the drink I just poured—"they weren't on speaking terms when my grandmother went into the hospital. So I doubt she had anything to do with it."

"Did you call her? Ask her?"

"How the hell can I do that? She just told me I was the product of a brutal gang rape. The last thing she needs is me bothering her."

"I see."

He shoves his glass toward me again. "You know what to do."

Damn.

I pour him another. If anyone ever needed a drink, it's Pat Lamone at this moment.

"I was hoping," he says, "that maybe you and your father could find out what happened to her."

"We're not related to her, unlike you."

"Yeah? Well, when my birth mother looks at you, she

doesn't have to relive a traumatic experience."

He's got me there. Plus . . . my father and I may well have a connection to the Madigan family through Lauren's son Jack. Though that seems pretty farfetched.

I sigh. "I don't think I'll get anywhere, but I know someone who might be able to."

"Who's that?"

"You leave that to me."

I'm thinking of Ryan Steel, of course, but I can't say this to Pat. He doesn't know about Ryan's connection to Wendy Madigan. He doesn't know that Ryan Steel is his uncle, and Ryan may not appreciate me telling him that.

While his connection to the Steel family is through his paternal grandfather, he has another connection through his mother. His mother and Ryan Steel.

This man is Ava's cousin.

Knowing what I know about him—what he did to Diana Steel and to Rory and Callie Pike—my sympathy for him is limited. But it does still exist. He didn't have the best start in life for sure.

I have no idea what his adoptive parents were like, and since they're both dead now, there's no way to ever know.

But I *am* a bartender—a makeshift therapist.

"What else is troubling you?" I ask.

"Does there have to be something else?" He shoots the fourth drink. "My birth mother was raped by three masked men, all of whom are now dead, so there's no—"

I hold up a hand. "Wait, wait, wait . . . How do you know they're all dead? Does that mean . . . "

He shakes his head. "No. I don't know who they are. My mother told me they're dead. At least that's what *her* mother told her."

"Hmm..."

Wendy could have had them taken care of. It's certainly on brand for her from what I know. Or...Wendy may know who they are, which means...

Fuck. I need to keep my head on straight.

"Hmm...what?" Pat lifts his eyebrows.

"Nothing. Go ahead."

"Right. Anyway, there's no way for me to know for sure which one fathered me." He closes his eyes for a moment, exhales. "Does it really matter? Genetics are genetics, right? Maybe there's a reason I'm a bad seed. Maybe there's a reason why I got involved with the likes of Brittany Sheraton. Why I did what I did to Diana Steel and the Pike sisters."

I scratch an itch on my temple. "What are you talking about? How are you involved with Brittany Sheraton?"

"So Ava hasn't told you the whole story."

"I'm not sure Ava *knows* the whole story."

"Brittany Sheraton is kind of screwed up. Plus, her dad blames the Steels for the loss of his business. It's a long story. Talk to Brock Steel. He knows all about it."

"I see." I wipe the bar down with a cloth. "How about you? Tell me about your adoptive parents."

"What the hell business is that of yours?"

I hold up a hand. "Hey, man. I'm just trying to be a friend."

"Right." Pat narrows his eyes. "And I'm just that gullible, Murphy. I know you're almost engaged to Ava Steel. You'll be a Steel before I will."

"I don't know about that." Though admittedly, the idea makes me happy. "Currently you're already a Steel."

"Descended from the bastard half brother. I don't even know who his mother was."

"I don't think anyone does."

"And there's no way to find out, short of finding his grave, exhuming his body, and doing a DNA test." He sighs, rubbing his forehead. "And even then, what would it yield? Without knowing who the DNA belongs to . . . "

"Nothing," I say. "It would yield nothing. You're going to have to get used to the fact that you'll never know."

"Just as well. I sure as hell wish I didn't know about my birth father."

"You don't want to tell me about your adoptive parents, then?"

"Why the fuck do you care, Murphy?"

"I'm a bartender. It's what I do. I listen."

"Right."

"Ask any bartender, Lamone. They'll all tell you the same thing."

He sighs. "My birth parents were okay. They didn't think they could have kids, so when they adopted me, it was a big deal to them. They were great parents up until the time I was about nine or ten years old."

"What happened after that?"

"A damned miracle," he says. "My mother got pregnant."

I nearly drop the cloth I'm holding. "Oh?"

"So once they realized they could actually have their own biological child, they stopped caring so much about me." He taps his fingers on the bar.

"I'm sorry to hear that."

"Yeah, whatever. The problem is, the baby was . . . "

"What?"

He inhales, lets it out slowly. "The baby was stillborn. A little girl. They named her Patricia Rose."

"Patricia? After they named you Pat?" Man, that's weird.

"Yeah." He frowns. "Except I don't think my name is actually Pat. According to some PI, my birth certificate says Baby Boy Wingdam, which makes sense. But apparently I wasn't adopted by Peter and Julie Lamone and named Patrick John Lamone. I was adopted by some family named Clark who named me Daniel. Which is another question I have. Why did my birth parents change their names and mine? It's got to have something to do with this Wendy Madigan and Steel stuff."

He's babbling now. Too much information. "Wait, wait, wait. Back up a minute. Your baby sister was stillborn."

"Yeah."

"So your parents . . ."

"They never stopped mourning her. They didn't give a shit about me anymore."

Man, no wonder he's so screwed up.

They changed his name from Daniel to Patrick. And then, when they had a baby girl, they called her Patricia.

It could mean nothing. Maybe they just like the name in its masculine and feminine form.

He shoves his glass at me.

"I'm going to have to cut you off, Lamone."

"Really? After that sob story I just gave you?"

"Yeah."

"Fuck you, then." He opens his wallet, lays down a hundred-dollar bill. "Will this help you?"

Pat Lamone works over at the hotel. He rents a room at Mrs. Mayer's house. Why the hell is he carrying around hundred-dollar bills?

I slide the bill back toward him. "Afraid not."

"Well then, fuck you to next Sunday." Lamone rises and

then stumbles, falling to the ground.

A couple of guys at a table nearby help him up. "You okay, buddy?" one of them asks.

"Hell no," Lamone says. "I'm not sure I've ever been okay."

I shake my head, clearing away his empty glass. He stumbles out the door just as Donny Steel and Callie Pike walk in and take a seat at the bar.

"Pat Lamone looks in a bad way." Callie rolls her eyes. "Not that I give a damn."

"The man's a derelict," Donny agrees.

I simply nod. After what he did to Callie, the two of them will never see part of Lamone deserves sympathy.

"What can I get you two?"

"Just Diet Coke for me," Callie says.

"Margarita," Donny says.

I hold back my chuckle. It cracks me up that one of the big and burly Steel men likes sweet drinks.

"Frozen or on the rocks?"

"On the rocks."

"What was Lamone doing in here anyway?" Callie asks.

"He's got some troubles."

"Good," she says.

"We were just talking to Ava," Donny says. "She was asking us about the future lawmakers club over at Snow Creek High School."

"Oh?"

"Yeah. We're going to look into it. Apparently, back in the day—I'm talking Brad Steel's day—they were a pretty bad organization."

"So I've heard."

"How much do you know?" Donny asks me.

"Not a lot, mostly because Ava doesn't know a lot. At least not yet. Ava and I don't have secrets ... unless someone else asked her to keep a secret, in which case I respect that."

"Tell you what," Donny says. "Why don't you and I look into this? It would mean a lot to Ava."

I slide Callie's Diet Coke in front of her. "I'll do anything for Ava. You can take that to the bank."

CHAPTER TWO

Ava

"I want to spend the night here," I say to my mother.

Donny and Callie have been gone for an hour, and Mom and I have been talking. Dad went to bed. He's still exhausted from his episode at the party.

"Don't you have to open the bakery early?" Mom asks.

"Yeah...but I can get up early."

"I wish you'd get someone to help you. You shouldn't have to be there so early every single day."

"We've been through this, Mom."

Mom rubs her temples. "I know we have. But even if you won't accept any monetary help, can you have Luke or Maya open up for you sometimes? Why do you always have to be the one to get up early and get everything started?"

"Because it's my business, Mom. It's my bakery. I'm the baker. I have to make all the bread."

"You could teach them—"

I shake my head. "I can't. My baking is a source of pride for me. When people walk into that bakery, they're looking for Ava Steel's bread. Not Maya's bread. Not Luke's bread. *My* bread, Mom. It's important."

"I know." She sighs. "It's just that you've been through so much."

Mom doesn't know I had a panic attack of my own after Dad had his. I'm not about to tell her. I'm not sure how I let myself go there. I usually have more control over my body than that. I won't have another attack. No matter what happens. I just won't.

Still … there are times when I wish I could stay at home. Let my mother take care of me. But I chose my own business. I chose to put my whole self into my baking, and I don't regret that choice.

I let out a yawn.

"See?" Mom pounces. "If you insist on being the one to open the bakery at the asscrack of dawn every day, you need your sleep. You should get home."

She's right. I am completely exhausted, both physically and emotionally. It's better to get home now and get a good night's sleep in my own bed at my own place. Before I go, though—

"Dad mentioned a ring," I say. "A ring that the future lawmakers wore."

"Yes. Both your grandfathers had one."

"Who has them?"

She pauses a moment. Then, "Actually … *I* have one of them—Brad Steel's."

"You?" I lift my brow. "How do you have it? And why wouldn't you have your own father's ring?"

"I don't know what happened to my father's. He stopped wearing it at the end of his life, and we never found it. Brad Steel's ring was left for me once, as a clue. Your father found it in my couch in my old apartment before we were married. We never found out who planted it there, but it led him and Uncle Talon to me."

"Wait . . . " I blink, trying to make sense of what my mother just said. "What?"

"Ava, there's so much more to the story. About how your father and Uncle Talon took down the trafficking ring, or so they thought. About how we found out Brad Steel was alive—the first time. And about how Dale and Donny came to our family."

"I'm not going anywhere until you tell me more."

She sighs and looks at her watch. Why is she so concerned about the time? "All right. You may as well know. My father had me drugged and abducted."

I drop my jaw open.

"It was horrible, but no one hurt me. My father wouldn't let them hurt me. Which was odd in itself because he's the one who tried to hurt me in the first place, which resulted in my running away and living on the streets."

"I don't understand."

"You see, when we found Dale and Donny, they were on an island in the Caribbean. A private island."

"I still don't understand."

"Your grandfather, Brad Steel, owned a couple of islands in the Caribbean. He sold one to a corporation. And it was used . . . Well, you can guess what it was used for."

"Yes." I swallow.

"Anyway, somehow, your grandfather's future lawmakers ring ended up at my apartment, beneath the cushion of my couch. When I disappeared, your father came to my apartment to search for clues, and he found his own father's ring. Engraved inside the ring were GPS coordinates for the island."

"So someone left the ring for Dad to find? So he could find *you*?"

"Yes. I never found out who. It had to be either my father or your dad's. And the more I thought about it . . . the more I believed it was *my* father."

"But your father was—"

"He was. He was a horrible human being who did horrible things. He hurt so many people, myself included. But in the end, he saved my life. It was because of him that we found out Brad Steel—along with Daphne, at that point—was alive. We found Dale and Donny, and we found an old girlfriend of your father's—"

"Wait, wait, wait. What?"

"Yes. Your father had a girlfriend before me." She smiles. "Why does that surprise you? I mean, look at your father. Sometimes I still can't believe he chose me."

"Because you're beautiful, Mom." I shake my head. "Of course he had other girlfriends. I just never knew."

"Her name was Anna. Anna Shane. She and her family used to own or rent—I'm not sure which—some of the land that now belongs to the Pike family. It was originally owned by the Steel family at some point. Honestly, I don't know all the logistics. But your father dated her, and his mother—Wendy Madigan—didn't think she was good enough for him. So . . ."

"She had the woman taken." I hold back puke.

"Yes."

"My God. What if the same thing had happened to you?"

"There was a time when I thought it had. When I ended up on that island. But no one harmed me. Other than drugging me and abducting me, of course." She lets out a huff.

"I can't believe everything you've been through."

Mom nods, closes her eyes for a few seconds. "In the end, I think my father tried to atone for his sins. It certainly would never have been possible, but I think he tried. He did save my life. He led your father and Uncle Talon to me and, consequently, to the island. So maybe it was Wendy who had me taken. The FBI was after them as well. Dad and Uncle Talon hired a man they thought was a Jamaican guide to take them to the island, but he turned out to be an FBI agent."

I rub my forehead against an ache that's beginning to form. "I'm not following all of this."

Mom squeezes my shoulders. "I know. We just don't have all the answers, Ava. Either Wendy or my father had me abducted. And someone, most likely my father, planted Brad Steel's ring at my place as a clue."

"Which led Dad to the island. And to you."

"And to Dale and Donny. And to Anna Shane, Dad's old girlfriend. And myriad others they saved that day."

"But the trafficking ring was never broken up."

"Apparently not."

"And are they now?"

She frowns. "We just don't know. We got them off our property, and we erased all evidence that could implicate our family. But we don't know if the traffic ring is still working."

I massage my forehead again. "I can't deal with all of this."

"I know, Ava. It's too much for anyone to deal with."

I wipe a tear away before it falls. "I want to see the ring. Do you still have it?"

She nods. "I offered it to your father, to both of your uncles, but of course none of them wanted it. It represented evil to them. It represents the same to me, but still... It *is* an heirloom. I couldn't bring myself to part with it."

"Where is it?"

"It's in one of the safes."

"Could I see it?"

"Do you really want to go there?"

"I can't shake the feeling that this future lawmakers club that has sprung up at the high school has something to do with all of this."

"How could high school students have anything to do with our family? We don't have any students at the school anymore. Besides, the original club was at a completely different high school. Tejon Prep in the city."

"I know." I tug on my lip ring. "It's just... You know me and my intuition."

"I have intuition too," she says. "And I'm not feeling that at all."

"You're not feeling it because you don't see any hard evidence to back it up. We've been through all this, Mom. You and I share many things, but we differ in our use of our intuition. You use it to find facts. If it doesn't lead you to facts, then you discount it. I see it in a different way."

Mom sighs and checks her watch again. "All right. I'll get it."

A few minutes later, she returns to the kitchen. I take the ring from her. It's large and heavy. The center stone is black, probably onyx. On one side are the initials B and S, but on the other...

"What the hell?"

I examine the strange symbol. An oval and an X, with one corner of the X touching the elongated part of the oval.

"Uncle Joe and Uncle Talon asked a Freemason who specializes in symbols to look at it when they found Tom Simpson's ring. He theorized that it was a twisted version of the symbol for female, which is also the symbol for the planet

Venus ... and for Lucifer."

"The devil?"

"Yes, but some scholars believe that Lucifer, at least in this context, has nothing to do with Satan. The name literally means light bringer, which coincides with the planet Venus being the morning star."

"Okay ... "

"But"—Mom sighs—"*we* know for sure what it means. Your father told you when he relayed the whole story. Wendy admitted to it. It's a symbol for an evil woman. A symbol for Wendy Madigan."

CHAPTER THREE

Brendan

I go with Donny the next day to Snow Creek High School. He's the city attorney for the town, so he'll be taking the lead. We didn't make an appointment. As the city attorney, he has every right to visit the school whenever he wants.

We walk through the metal detector and then stop at the office, where we're allowed to bypass the security check with IDs because of Donny's position with the city. The receptionist on duty gives us each a visitor tag.

"What can I help you with, Mr. Steel?" she asks.

"We need to see the principal."

"Do you have an appointment?"

"No, we don't, but it's very important that we see him right away."

"All right. I'll let him know you're here." She taps on her computer and then speaks into her headset. "Darrell? Donny Steel and Brendan Murphy are here to see you."

Pause.

"I don't know."

Pause.

"All right."

Then she turns back to us. "You two can go right in."

Darrell Hutchins is the principal at Snow Creek High

School. He and Hardy Solomon were both in Dale's and my class. He was on the quieter side, but a nice guy.

Donny knocks.

"Come on in," Darrell says through the door.

When Donny opens the door, I walk in before him.

"Brendan, Donny. What can I help you with today?" Darrell asks.

Donny closes the door behind him, and we both remain standing while Darrell sits at his desk.

"We have some questions for you, Darrell," Donny says. "About a club here at the school."

"I'm afraid I don't understand." Darrell furrows his brow. "The two of you no longer go to the school, and you don't have any children in the school. In fact, we have no Steels on our roster at all this year."

"I am still the city attorney," Donny says.

"Yes, which is why I allowed you to come in without an appointment. But I have to tell you, Don, I don't see how our extracurricular activities are any of your business."

"It's certainly my business if there are illegal activities going on."

Darrell frowns. "Now you wait just a min—"

Donny holds up his hand. "No accusations. We're just curious about a club."

Darrell clears his throat, his eyes narrowed. "If there were anything illegal going on at my school, I'd contact the proper authorities. Eventually it would be your business, but the first order of business would be for the police to investigate."

"Are you saying there may be some illegal activities going on?" Donny pushes.

"Don't twist my words, Steel. Tell me what you want.

What club are you concerned about?"

Darrell's etiquette seems to have vanished. Is he hiding something?

"The future lawmakers club," Donny says.

"What about them?"

"So they do still exist," I say.

"They do. The club was here when I took over as principal a couple of years ago."

"Our concern is that it may have some relationship to a club with the same name at Tejon Prep about fifty years ago."

"Fifty years ago? At a private school in the city?" He lets out a scoffing laugh. "Why in the world would that be a concern?"

"Because..." Donny clears his throat. "The club in question was into some nefarious activities."

"But it was a different school. Why would it have any relation to the club here?"

"Darrell, we don't know that it does," Donny says. "But we want to take a look at it. My fiancée, Callie Pike, says it was around when she was a student here and that it had nothing to do with future lawmakers. That it was a club by invitation only, and when she went to a meeting, they didn't talk about the law at all. All they talked about were ways to stick it to the man. Apparently, during those years, the club took credit for some bad stuff that went on."

"Can you elaborate?"

"Pranks. Things like spiking punch at dances, stuff like that."

"Things like that happen at every school, I'm afraid." Darrell sighs.

"We understand that, Darrell," I say. "But here's the issue.

The future lawmakers club at Tejon Prep all those years ago turned out to be involved in some illegal activity."

"Again, I'm just not sure what—"

Donny holds up his hand. "We're not accusing you of anything, Darrell. We're not accusing your students of anything. We just want some information. Could you tell us who on faculty is the advisor to the club?"

"That would be me," he says.

I stop my jaw from dropping.

"You," Donny says. "And you didn't think it was important to tell us that right off the bat?"

He places both hands on his desk and leans toward us. "I didn't think it was any of your business, Don. I can assure you the club is not involved in any illegal activities, nor are we involved in sticking it to the man in any way."

"What *is* the club involved with?"

"Charitable work, mostly. The members support nonprofits that are working on legislation at the state level."

I wrinkle my forehead. "Exactly how do members of your club help with legislation at the state level? We're in a little one-horse town here."

"We take field trips into Denver sometimes, work with the nonprofits there."

"And what types of legislation are you trying to help get passed?" I ask.

"Usually bills that are important to ranching communities like Snow Creek. The club is what it says it is, gentlemen. It's a club of future lawmakers."

"So no one's sticking it to any man, then?" I say.

"Not since I've been the advisor to the club."

"Why did you take on this advisory job?" Donny asks.

"Because I'm interested in it." Darrell leans back in his chair. "I'm interested in helping the community I live in."

Donny shakes his head. "But you're not a rancher, Darrell."

"My parents are ranchers. Have you forgotten, Steel?" Darrell lets out a sarcastic scoff. "You don't own *all* the ranch land on the western slope."

Donny draws in a breath. Inside my head I can hear him counting to ten.

"Last I checked, Darrell, the Steel Trust has a lien on your family's property."

This time Darrell draws in a breath. Yeah, now *he's* counting to ten.

I'm not sure where Donny's going with this, but I don't like it. All those rumors appear to be true. The Steels *do* own the damned town. Even though I'm in love with one of them, I'd like some answers just as much as Darrell would.

"I was not aware of that," Darrell says.

"Oh, come on, Darrell. You've heard the same thing the rest of us have our whole lives. That my family owns this town."

"So you're saying it's true?"

"I'm saying the Steel Trust has a lien on your family's property. Nothing more than that. Take what I say at face value, Darrell."

"What the hell does all this have to do with the future lawmakers club?" Darrell asks.

I can't blame him. It's a good question.

"Brendan and I would like to attend your next meeting," Donny says.

"There won't be any more meetings until after the first of the year. We're going on holiday break soon, as you well know. None of our clubs meet in December."

"Fine. January, then." Don turns to me. "You ready, Brendan?"

"I suppose. Darrell?"

"Yeah?"

"Do you keep minutes of your club?"

"Not really. The kids take notes."

"Donny and I would like to see those notes."

"You don't have any right to see those notes."

"Darrell, you, Dale, and I went to school together. I'd like to think we were friends."

"You and I might've been friendly. Dale Steel wasn't anyone's friend."

Donny goes rigid next to me. "You might want to watch how you talk about my brother."

Darrell nods. "I didn't mean that in a bad way, Don. Dale didn't talk to anyone. None of us really knew him."

"Anyway," I continue, "I'm asking a favor, Darrell. From an old classmate. Humor me."

Darrell rolls his eyes. "All right. I'll talk to the students. Get what I can for you."

"When?"

"Sometime this week. Or next. We go on break after that."

"Good."

Donny stands, pulls out his card, and hands it to Darrell. "You know where I am, but in case you don't know the number, here it is. Call me when you have something." He walks out the door without so much as a thank-you.

I stay for a moment. "Listen, Darrell. Donny's doing his lawyer thing, but this could be very important. So please. We need those notes."

Darrell rises and gestures to the door. "I said I'd get them to you, Brendan. I'll be in touch."

I nod. "Thank you. Thank you very much."

I leave the office, joining Donny out in the reception area.

"I really think we're barking up the wrong tree here, Don," I say. "Just because the name of the club is the same doesn't mean this club has anything to do with the club fifty years ago at a different school altogether."

"You know, in a normal world, I'd agree with you, Brendan." Donny shakes his head. "But I've come to find out just recently that the Steels don't live in a normal world."

CHAPTER FOUR

Ava

I'm getting ready for the lunch rush when Brendan walks through the bakery door.

"Hey," I say from the counter. "What can I get you?"

He grins. "How about a kiss, for starters?"

My cheeks warm. I wipe my hands on my apron, walk out from behind the counter, and give him a peck on the lips. "What have you been up to today?"

"Donny and I went over to see Darrell at the high school to ask about the future lawmakers club."

"And?"

"It exists, but he said it doesn't have anything to do with sticking it to the man, like Callie said. Darrell himself is the advisor, and he's going to get us some notes. There aren't any official records from the club, but according to him, it's a simple club that works with nonprofits to get legislation passed that helps the ranching communities here on the western slope."

"He sure makes it sound legit."

"Honestly, Ava, I don't have any reason to think it's *not* legit at this point. But Donny..."

I nod. "Yeah. Donny's another story. But you have to see this from his angle, Brendan. He was a victim of—"

Brendan holds up a hand. "You don't have to say it. I

understand. And I understand that your family history is full of skeletons. I mean, whose isn't?"

"Most families have skeletons in their closet, Brendan. But we have entire *graveyards* in ours."

He doesn't respond.

"I have to run. The lunch rush will be on us soon, and I've got some orders I need to fill."

"I understand." He grabs one of my gloved hands. "Can I see you tonight?"

"Of course. Are you off at the bar tonight?"

"Yes, ma'am, I am. And I would love to take you to dinner."

"Sounds great. But you know I can't be out late."

"I know. I can make you dinner at my place."

"That's fine with me." I smile. "I love your hamburgers."

"Good thing. Because it's about all I can make."

"Would you rather come to my place for dinner?"

"No. I invited *you*, remember? I'm not going to invite myself over for dinner and make you cook for me."

"I don't mind, Brendan."

"Actually . . . What if we go out?"

"Sure. Lorenzo's sounds good."

"I was thinking we go into the city. To a real restaurant."

My cheeks warm again. "Sure. But that's awfully expensive."

"I can afford to take my girl out every once in a while," he says. "Say yes."

"All right. Yes."

"Good. I have some things I want to talk to you about."

"Like what things?"

"It can wait, Ava. I love you. Have a wonderful day." He kisses my lips, and then without another word, he turns and walks out the bakery door. The bells cling.

I head back behind the counter.

★ ★ ★

I've heard of Fortnight—Grand Junction's newest restaurant. Dale and Ashley have been here, as have Donny and Callie. Probably Brock and Rory also, though I don't know. The wine list features many of my father's and Dale's wine's.

But the prices...

Normally, they wouldn't matter to a Steel. But I'm on my own, and Brendan is a bartender.

Still, he doesn't seem bothered by the amounts. I'll order something inexpensive. And by inexpensive I mean slightly less than fifty dollars.

"Would you like to order a bottle of wine?"

"No." I hold up the wine list. "Most of these wines are from my dad's winery, Brendan. I can get them for free. Why should I pay these pumped-up prices?"

"Because I want you to have what you want, Ava. You deserve a dinner out, and I'm happy to treat you to it."

"Brendan..."

"Look." He grabs my hand across the table. "I wouldn't have invited you if I didn't think I could afford it. I can handle a nice dinner every so often. This means a lot to me. I want you to enjoy it."

"All right. But I don't need a bottle of wine."

"That's fine, but I want you to order whatever you want."

I scan the menu for a moment.

Our server arrives. "Good evening, I'm Adrian, and I'll be taking care of you this evening. Can I start you both off with something to drink? A cocktail?"

"Ava?" Brendan raises his eyebrows.

I smile. "I'll have a pink squirrel."

Brendan chuckles, his fair skin blushing. "It won't be as good as mine."

"Probably not. But that's what I'll have."

"I'll have Peach Street bourbon on the rocks," Brendan says.

"Good enough. I'll be right back with those drinks, and I'll get your appetizer order then." Adrian whisks away.

I look back down at the menu. The appetizers are so expensive.

"So what are you thinking?" Brendan asks.

"I don't know. Probably a green salad and then maybe the vegetable linguine."

Brendan raises an eyebrow. "You're not a vegetarian, Ava."

"That doesn't mean I don't like eating vegetarian meals sometimes. When you grow up on a beef ranch, sometimes it's nice to stay away from meat."

He gives me a stern look. "Ava, order whatever you'd like."

"That *is* what I'd like, Brendan."

He narrows his gaze, looking even sterner. "If you could order anything on this menu, what would it be?"

I look down. I do like vegetables, and I'd enjoy the vegetable linguine. But if I'm being honest… "The grilled Rocky Mountain trout. With the lobster risotto."

"Then that is what you'll have," Brendan says. "And I am going to have the New York strip, rare."

I lean toward him, lowering my voice. "It's probably our beef. You can come eat dinner at my house and have it for free."

He laughs. "You're not getting it, are you? I want to take my lady out. I want to pay for a nice dinner. I don't care that I can get the wine and beef for free if I eat with your family, and I'm not interested in what this will cost. I want to treat you to dinner at a nice place because I love you."

My cheeks warm once more. "Okay, Brendan. But next time, I treat."

He smiles. "Absolutely. I am fine with that."

Adrian returns with our drinks.

"Hmm," I say. "This looks different from the pink squirrel you made for me."

"Probably because I had to improvise that night. The drink calls for heavy cream, which I didn't have, so I used melted vanilla ice cream."

This pink squirrel is in a martini glass, with pink-tinted granulated sugar—I assume—around the edges. The drink itself is a lighter pink than Brendan's.

"Is that why it's a lighter pink?"

"Probably not," he says. "Most likely they used a little less crème de noyaux."

Adrian clears his throat. "Can I get you anything for an appetizer?"

"Yes," Brendan says. "I would like the tuna tartare. Ava, what would you like?"

"Can I just share yours?"

"If that's what you'd like," he says.

I look down. I've got to stop this. I don't want to insult Brendan. If he truly wants to treat me, I need to let him and stop worrying about the cost. I look up then, meeting Adrian's gaze. "I'll have the calamari."

"Very good. Are you ready to order your dinners now?"

"We are," Brendan says. "The lady will have the Rocky Mountain trout with the lobster risotto, along with a green salad."

"Is the house vinaigrette all right?" Adrian asks me.

"Yes, that would be perfect."

"And I will have the New York strip, rare, with a baked potato, loaded. And broccoli."

"Wonderful. I'll get these orders in. Your appetizers should be out soon. Would you like wine with dinner?"

Brendan looks to me.

"No, thank you," I say. "I think I'll stick with my drink and then water with dinner."

"I'll have another bourbon with my dinner," Brendan says.

"Very good. Thank you." Adrian whisks away again.

"So?" Brendan points to my drink.

I smile and pick up the pink squirrel, swirl it around in the glass a little, watching as the creamy pink sticks to the glass. Then I taste it. It's creamy, for sure, and I let it flow over my tongue and coat my mouth.

"Does it rival mine?" he says.

I lick the cream from my bottom lip. "It's... It doesn't taste as...*pink* as yours did."

He chuckles. "It doesn't?"

"It's not as sweet, I think? I don't know. It's good. Not as good as yours, but I like it. You want to taste it?"

"Not even a little bit, Ava." He laughs and takes a drink of his bourbon. "So... last night Pat Lamone came to the bar."

I lift my eyebrows.

"Apparently, his grandmother—your grandmother—is no longer at the hospital."

I part my lips, and some of the pink squirrel dribbles onto my chin. I hastily wipe it away with my napkin.

"What?"

"Yeah. He went to see her last night to get answers to some questions."

"How did he expect to get answers from a woman who's in a medically induced coma?"

"I don't know that he was actually *looking* for answers, Ava. I think . . ."

"What *aren't* you telling me, Brendan?"

"I will tell you everything, but I wanted to let you know that your grandmother is no longer in the hospital. I don't know where she is, but I'm sure your father can find out."

"I'm honestly not sure my father wants to know."

"Who could blame him?" Brendan takes another sip. "But I thought maybe we should talk to him."

"I saw him last night. I was exhausted, and I wanted to spend the night in my old room."

"You did?"

"Yeah. I was a mess. But my mom talked me out of it, said I'd be too tired in the morning to make the drive to the bakery on time. She was probably right."

He wrinkles his forehead. "That sounds odd, coming from your mother. If you were tired, she should have wanted you to stay."

"Right? It *was* weird, but that's not the main thing I want to tell you. I was talking to my mom about the future lawmakers club, and she gave me this." I grab my purse and pull out my grandfather's future lawmakers ring.

Brendan takes it, gazes at it. "That's a lot of gold. And what is that? Onyx?"

"Probably. Mom didn't know. I'm surprised my dad and uncles didn't have it analyzed. But check out the symbol."

He turns the ring over. "Nothing I've ever seen before."

"Me neither. Apparently my grandmother designed it. It's a long story, but it represents an evil woman. Which she, of course, was. Or is. Hell, I don't even know what tense to use."

"Do you want to leave, Ava? Go back and talk to your parents about this?"

I shake my head. "No, I don't. I want to enjoy my pink squirrel—which is not nearly as good as yours—and I want my rainbow trout. I'm looking forward to it, Brendan. Thank you for this nice dinner."

"You're absolutely welcome, Ava." Then he jerks. "Sorry, my phone buzzed." He pulls it out of his pocket. "Do you mind? I have to take this."

"I don't mind, Brendan." I take another sip of pink squirrel.

CHAPTER FIVE

Brendan

I rise and walk to the front of the restaurant. "Hey, Dad," I say into the phone.

"Hi, son. I just heard from Jack. He'd like us to go to a clinic in the city tomorrow morning to have our blood drawn for the DNA test."

"Okay. I can make that work. As long as I'm back by around two to get the bar ready to open."

"I'm at the bar now," Dad says. "I came to see you, but Laney said you're off tonight."

"Yeah, I'm in the city. I took Ava to dinner."

"Ava . . . That's good."

"I thought so."

"Yeah, it is, but that's not what I mean." Dad pauses a moment. "The thing is, I'd like this clinic checked out. You never know who you can trust these days, so I thought maybe you could ask Ruby—"

"Dad, I'm on a date."

"Yes, you are. With Ruby's daughter."

"Fine." I sigh. "I'll see if we can stop by Ryan and Ruby's place after dinner. It's on the way back anyway."

"Thanks," Dad says. "I'll text you the name and address of the clinic. If Ruby says it's okay, then we'll go."

"Dad, Ruby and Ryan don't know everything yet. About Lauren and Jack and Wendy Madigan."

"They probably know by now."

"If they do, I don't think they've told Ava."

"Then you need to bring Ava up to speed."

"Yeah, I guess I do."

I end the call and head back into the dining room. I just wanted a nice dinner with Ava tonight. I know all hell is about to break loose, but I was hoping we could have one enjoyable evening. Who knows when I'll be able to afford another one like this?

I have some money left over from the huge insurance settlement I got to renovate my place, but that won't last long.

When I return, our appetizers are on the table, and Ava is done with her pink squirrel and is sipping water.

"The calamari is to die for," she says after swallowing. "I only ate one piece. I hope you don't mind that I started without you."

"Of course not." My tuna tartare looks amazing on a bed of greens with fried wontons, green onions, and a little wasabi. But I'm no longer hungry. I meet Ava's gaze. "That was my dad."

"Everything okay?"

"Yeah. But I have a lot to tell you."

"Okay." She spears another calamari ring with her fork. "I'm all ears."

"I met your . . . Well, I guess she's your aunt."

"Oh?" She pops the calamari into her mouth.

"You know, Pat Lamone's birth mother. Anyway, she has another son. A son named Jack Murphy."

Ava's eyes widen.

"I know, right? His father is apparently a man named Sean Murphy. He was conceived via donated sperm."

"Not your dad . . . "

"No, not my dad." I shake my head. "God, that would be too weird. My dad swears he never donated sperm and that he's been faithful to my mother since their marriage. Jack is a year younger than I am. He's thirty-one."

"Okay . . . "

"Anyway, he *does* kind of bear a familial resemblance. His hair isn't quite as red as mine, but we share some characteristics."

"So you think you're related to this guy?"

"I don't know, Ava. Sean Murphy is a pretty common name for an Irish guy. But Jack asked my dad and me to submit our blood for DNA testing to see if we're related."

"Oh, okay. I'm sure he'd like to know. And I'm sure *you'd* like to know."

"I would." I fidget with my napkin. "Though it seems doubtful. I may be imagining the characteristics we share. I don't know any other Sean Murphys in our family, other than my great-uncle, and he can't be the father since he died over fifty years ago."

"Right. So go get the DNA test."

"My dad wants to check with your mom first. Run the clinic by her."

"Oh, of course. She knows all the best places in the city from when she was on the force."

"She was on the force a long time ago."

"Oh, I know, but she keeps up with these people. She still does investigative work from time to time, and she's got a lot of contacts."

"Good. So do you think it would be okay if we went to your place after dinner? Your parents' place, I mean?"

"I don't see why not. Unless they're out tonight."

"Would you mind checking?"

"Not at all." Ava pulls her phone out of her purse.

And I realize I'm still holding her grandfather's ring. I hand it back to her.

She takes it, and then— "Mom? Hey, are you and Dad home?"

Pause.

"Brendan and I are at dinner in Grand Junction, and he was wondering if we could stop by on our way back to town."

Pause.

"Why not?"

Pause.

"Mom, you're acting really strange."

Pause.

Ava huffs. "Fine. We won't stop by." She ends the call.

"Is something the matter?" I ask. "We're not stopping by tonight?"

She shoves her phone back into her purse. "Oh, we're *definitely* stopping by tonight. My mom was acting so strange on the phone. Just like last night."

"What do you mean, strange?"

"She's good, my mom. I mean, she was a detective. She's good at masking her emotions, but I'm also good at seeing them anyway. Maybe it's because I'm an old soul."

"Maybe . . ."

She lifts her wrist and jingles some gold bracelets at me. "My mom gave me these. They belonged to her mother. Who apparently was also an old soul. Suffice it to say, my mom is not acting like herself. And quite frankly, I can't think of one other time in my short life when I've asked my parents to come to their house and they said no. Whether they're home or not, I'm always welcome there."

"And tonight they said you're not welcome?"

"No, my mom would never say that. She just said tonight wasn't a good night. My father isn't feeling very well."

"Maybe she thinks he's coming down with something and she doesn't want you to catch it."

"That's crap. Our house is huge. If my father has germs, he can stay far away from me. We're definitely going over there, Brendan. Definitely."

"All right, if you say so." I take a bite of my tuna tartare. It's delicious, but my appetite has gone on hiatus.

Something's rotten.

And I don't think it has anything to do with the future lawmakers club, or Jack Murphy, or the clinic where he wants us to get our blood tested.

I think it's much closer to home than that.

CHAPTER SIX

Ava

"Are you sure about this?" Brendan asks me as we begin the drive up the long winding road to my parents' house.

"I'm very sure," I say. "Something's going on, and I'm done being left in the dark."

"All right. I suppose we may as well tell your father that his mother is missing tonight too."

"Yes, we will tell him that. And we will ask my mother about the clinic in Grand Junction where you and your dad are going to get your blood tested. We'll do all of that. But the first thing we're going to figure out is why my mother told us not to come over tonight, and why she wouldn't let me stay last night either. I don't think for a minute that it's because my father's not feeling good. I just saw him last night. He's fine. He's never been sick a day in his life except for that panic attack."

Brendan simply nods as we continue the drive.

I wish I were home. I'd draw a card. Perhaps three cards. Hell, perhaps I'd even do the whole Celtic cross spread—which I almost never use—because right now I need guidance.

Or do I?

Already I know my mother is lying to me.

Perhaps I don't need the cards after all.

Perhaps all I need is my own brain. My own intuition. My own emotion.

After all... the cards are simply a tool to access those parts of me.

Still, once I'm back at my place, I'll draw some cards.

For now, I'll rely on what's inside me. Ava Steel. Ava Steel has always been Ava Steel. I may not have known my true genetics, but that doesn't change who I've always been.

Brendan pulls up next to one of my parents' cars and stops the engine. He turns to me. "Ready when you are."

I clutch the door handle. "Let's roll."

We walk to the door, and Brendan raises his hand to knock, but I whisk it away.

"We're going in."

"What if the door is locked?"

"I have a key. I know all the codes."

"All right."

I open the door, which turns out to be unlocked anyway. No dogs greet us, so they must be outside.

"Mom?" I call.

No reply.

"Dad? Michaela?"

"Is Michaela still here?"

I nod. "She has a room on the other side of the house. She lives here."

"Michaela?" I yell again.

But no one comes.

No Mom, no Dad, no Michaela.

"Come with me," I say to Brendan.

"Okay."

Brendan follows as we walk through the foyer, glancing into the living room and dining room, and then to the back of the house where the kitchen and family room are.

Everything is vacant.

So we head down the hallway to the main wing of the house. We pass my own room, where I wanted to sleep last night. It's empty, of course, as is Gina's, and as are the various guest rooms. Finally at the end of the hallway is the master suite.

I knock.

No reply.

So I open the door. "Mom? Dad?"

The sitting room—including the two armchairs where I learned the truth about my parentage—sits empty, and I walk into the bedroom. Also empty.

"Strange," I say. "All the cars were in the driveway."

"What about the other hallway?"

"Yes, the small wing of the house where Michaela lives. No one else lives there, but it's the only place left to check."

I lead Brendan back through the main hallway and into the second one. I have to key in a code, as this is considered a private area for household staff.

I tap in the numbers, open the door to the hallway, and head to Michaela's room. I knock. "Michaela?"

No response.

I try her door, but it's locked.

I knock again, this time more loudly. "Michaela? It's Ava. Are you okay?"

Brendan nudges me. "Ava..." He gestures to one of the other doors.

"What?"

There are three other doors in this hallway. All rooms for household staff, but the only one currently in use is Michaela's.

Which is why it's very strange that a sliver of light shines from under another one of them.

My heart jumps.

Brendan takes my hand, leads me to the doorway, and knocks.

No response.

"Mom, Dad. I know you're in there. It's me, Ava. Open up. Open up, or I swear to God I'll call the cops."

"No!" Mom's voice.

The door rustles a bit and then opens.

This is a large room. It's a master suite, complete with a sitting room, bedroom, and en suite bathroom. As far as I know, it's rarely been used. Only when we had extended family in town.

"I told you not to come tonight," Mom whispers harshly.

"Yeah, you told me Dad was sick." I take a tentative step into the room. "Funny, he wasn't in his room or in his bed, which is where he'd be if he were sick."

"You have to leave, Ava."

"Are you kidding me?" I respect the hell out of my mother, but I hold my ground. "No way. Both of you are done keeping things from me. What's going on?"

Mom sighs and holds the door open. "All right. Come on in, both of you. But you're on your honor not to tell anyone what you see in this room."

"For God's sake, Mother." I rub my arms against a sudden chill. "You're scaring me."

"No need to be frightened, Ava. Nothing will harm you here."

I follow my mother through the sitting room and into the bedroom. My father stands over the bed, Michaela at his side along with two others.

And in the bed—

I gasp.

"You," I say. "*You* two took her."

In the bed lies Sabrina Smith. Dyane Wingdam. Wendy Madigan.

My fucking grandmother.

"So this is where she disappeared to," Brendan says.

"You knew?" Mom asks.

"Pat Lamone came to the bar last night. Said he went to see his grandmother, but she was no longer at the hospital."

"Last night?" I shake my head, trying to comprehend. "Last night I wanted to stay here, Mom. You told me it was better to go home. I knew something was up. You would never say that to me."

"I did ask you to go home." Mom lets out a heaving sigh and rubs her forehead. "And I'm sorry."

"You were bringing her here. You didn't want me to be here to see what was happening. To ask questions."

"Ava," Dad begins, ushering us back into the sitting area and leaving Michaela and the others by Wendy's bedside.

"Oh, no. You had this all planned, didn't you? From the time you told me your story. You were going to bring her here. In fact, you—" I shake my head.

"We need the answers, Ava," Dad says calmly. "There's nothing wrong with my mother. She's been kept in sedation at her own request. I got all the medical records."

"How?"

"I'm her next of kin."

"Not on paper you're not. Her daughter, Lauren, is."

"I was able to get the records," Dad says calmly.

"You tossed our name around, didn't you?"

"I do what I have to do," Dad says. "I made peace with that a long time ago."

I love my father. And my mother. Truly I do. But this reliance on the family name is something I've never understood, and it's a big part of why I chose to open my business on my own, without my family's help.

Sure, I have my trust fund. I've considered signing it over to some charity that I love, but I haven't because quite frankly, it's mine. I'm still a Steel, and I know I may need that money someday. It's my birthright.

Or is it?

My father is illegitimate.

Not on his birth certificate, of course, which I've seen. His birth certificate lists Daphne Steel as his mother.

Daphne Steel is *not* his mother. Not biologically. Not genetically. This woman—this frail old woman—is his mother.

My grandmother.

I do what I have to do. I made peace with that a long time ago.

Interesting words from my father.

Brendan hasn't said anything for a while, so I turn to him. He simply takes my hand and squeezes it.

"Why?" I ask my father. "Why did you bring her here?"

"She's my mother," he says.

"But you don't think of her that way. You never have. And all this time you thought she was dead. You have no love for the woman. So why bring her here?"

"Ava, you already know the answer to that question."

I nod. I do. "To protect us."

"No. *Not* to protect us. You and I aren't in any danger."

"To protect your brothers and sister. Your nieces and nephews."

"Bingo," Dad says. "This woman tried to destroy my brother once, and now that I know she's alive, I'm pretty sure I know who was behind his shooting and attempted poisoning. I'm also pretty sure I know who was behind setting up the human trafficking on our land."

"But what about Doc and Brittany?"

"They had a hand in it for sure. But Doc is not an inherently evil person. He was angry at Joe and Bryce for not giving him the veterinary contract for our ranch. Brittany is another story. She has some issues."

"What issues?"

"She's responsible for her mother's death," Mom says.

My skin goes cold.

"She was just a child," Mom continues, "and according to Melanie, she was probably suffering from some kind of personality disorder that went undiagnosed. But still, she was a child."

I clamp my palm to my forehead. "What is it with this town? How do we attract all these freaks?"

"I don't know all the answers," Dad says, "but this woman lying here knows a lot of them, and by God, I'm going to get them out of her."

CHAPTER SEVEN

Brendan

When I was a kid—probably around seven or eight years old—my father took me on a camping trip. Neither one of us were that outdoorsy, but he said it was a rite of passage. That every father should take his son camping at least once.

We ended up enjoying it, and we went often after that. It was always something he and I did together while Mom stayed home.

That first time was special. Just Dad, me, and the outdoors. We didn't bring any food because Dad decided we should live off the land.

Of course he somehow forgot that he didn't know how to fish or hunt. It was by sheer luck that we found an apple tree growing in the wild, and Dad said it was probably an offshoot from the Steel apple orchards.

"The Steels," he said. "They own this town. They do what they want."

I never quite understood what that had to do with a lone apple tree growing seemingly in the wild. Later I realized that it was probably the result of someone else camping and then throwing an apple core and the seeds taking root. Dad and I ate many apples from that tree through our years of camping. Of course we also started to bring food of our own and eventually learned how to fish in the nearby creeks.

But that apple tree was always our spot.

We always ate those apples.

And every time we ate one, Dad made some comment about the Steel family.

"*The Steels. They do whatever they want.*"

"*They're even taking over the wilderness with their damned apples.*"

"*They own this damned town.*"

I never believed it. Not until I found those timeworn documents under my floorboards. Not until I found out the Steel family had a lien on my property.

And now, looking at Ryan and Ruby Steel—two people I've known my whole life—I can't help but wonder.

Would this town even *be* a town without the Steels? Is there a reason they think they can do whatever they want? Why Ryan Steel felt he could take a woman from the hospital, bring her here to his home?

My father has always been convinced that the Steel family had something to do with my great-uncle's death. He could never say anything negative about any of the Steels we know, but he was always certain their family was behind Uncle Sean's overdose. *The apple doesn't fall far from the tree*, Dad always said.

I never believed him.

Never . . . But now? I'm wondering.

I'm in love with Ava. In love with a member of the Steel family. And I think for the most part they're good people. But the words that just came out of Ryan's mouth simmer in my brain.

I do what I have to do. I made peace with that a long time ago.

"Ava, let me get you home."

"No," Ava says adamantly. "I'm not going anywhere."

"It's getting late."

"It's barely nine thirty," she says. "I'm used to not getting any sleep anyway. I'm waiting. I'm waiting to find out everything this woman knows."

"She may never wake up," I say.

"Oh, she'll wake up." This from Ryan. "She *will* wake up, and she will answer to me."

"Don't you think you should call her daughter?" I ask.

"I already have. Her daughter doesn't want anything to do with her."

I say nothing more on that subject. I believe Ryan. Lauren clearly has no love for Wendy.

"That actually reminds me," I say. "The reason why Ava and I wanted to stop by tonight. Ruby, what do you know about the Foster Diagnostics Lab in Grand Junction?"

Ruby meets my gaze, her forehead wrinkled. "Why do you ask?"

"Jack Murphy, Lauren's son, has asked Dad and me to submit our blood for DNA sampling. Jack wants to find out if he's related to our family. That's the name of the lab he asked us to go to."

"I can give you someone to call," Ruby says. "Someone who can get the results done quickly."

"All right."

Except . . . right now I'm not sure whether to trust Ryan or Ruby.

Why would they care whether Dad and I are related to Jack Murphy?

Ruby pulls out her phone and taps on it. "I'm sending

you the info. Tucker Madden is a science geek. Genius, but never had it together enough to actually do anything with his microbiology degree. So he worked as a lab tech for years and now he's completely freelance. He works out of a private lab in the city. He's a wiz with DNA. He can pick out strands from samples that other techs can't make heads or tails of. The DA used to call him as an expert witness frequently, and then when I left the force, I continued to use him. He's the best in the state. Maybe the country."

My phone vibrates as the text message comes through. I take a quick look. Tucker Madden, and an address and phone number. "Great. Thanks, Ruby."

"You can text him now. In fact, if you want, I'll text him and get you in tomorrow."

"That'd be perfect. Thanks again."

"No problem." She taps on her phone again. "I'll forward you the time."

A pause.

Then, "He says just come by anytime tomorrow. He'll be there."

I nod. In the morning, Dad and I will drive to the city and see Ruby's contact. But we'll also go to the clinic Jack recommended.

Doesn't hurt for the results to be checked.

Michaela and the other two enter the sitting area from the bedroom. "Mr. Steel?" one of the women asks.

Ryan nods. "Yes?"

"She's not going to wake up tonight. Her melatonin is at work. It's nighttime. Her body isn't going to recognize that it needs to be awake."

Ryan sighs. "All right, Doctor." He turns to Ava. "Doctor,

this is my daughter, Ava, and her friend Brendan Murphy. This is Dr. Louisa Parks and her nurse, Jemima Landry. They'll both be staying here as long as Wendy is. Michaela will be moving into the family wing while our guests are here."

Guests? Interesting choice of words.

We shake hands all around. Leave it to the Steels to be able to hire a doctor and nurse to care for one patient at their home.

"If you don't need me for anything else," Michaela says, "I'd like to get to bed."

Ruby smiles. "Of course, Michaela. You've been a huge help today. Thank you."

Once Michaela is gone, Dr. Parks leaves as well, and Jemima returns to the bedroom.

"Ryan," Ruby says, "you heard the doctor. She's not going to wake up tonight."

Ryan's jaw goes rigid. "I'm not leaving this room until she stirs."

Ruby grabs his hand. "She can't go anywhere. She's in her eighties and strapped down. You need to get some sleep."

"Nope. I'm still not leaving, Ruby. I've seen this woman disappear into thin air before, and it's not happening on my watch. I'll be staying in here. I'll tell Jemima she can go to bed. In the meantime, if Wendy so much as flutters her eyelid, I will be here."

"I'm not going anywhere either," Ava says.

Ruby shakes her head. "Ava . . . this isn't your battle."

"Are you kidding me? Who got all the messages? Not you and Dad. *I* did. This woman turned *my* life upside down to let me know she was alive."

"You're assuming the messages came from her," I say, though I'm playing devil's advocate.

Ava turns to me, hands on her hips. "Brendan, where else could they have come from? Perhaps the end of her life is near, and she wants to know me."

"You don't want to know her," Ryan says.

Ava meets her father's gaze, frowning. "Who are *you* to say that?"

"For God's sake, Ava," Ruby admonishes. "You've heard the horror stories."

"I have," Ava says. "There's no doubt in my mind that she's a complete and total psychopath. But the messages came to *me*, Mom. Me. Not to you. Not to Dad. Not to Gina. To me. And I want to know why."

"We don't know that the messages came from Wendy herself," Ruby says. "Indeed, they most likely didn't. Her hospital records indicate that she's been in a medically induced coma for the last six months. The messages began to come after that."

"You're a detective, Mom. You know damned well that she could have put a plan for the messages in place before she went into this medically induced coma."

"Yes, she could have. But don't you think it's more likely that someone *else* wanted you to know?"

"Who else? She went to a lot of trouble to conceal the fact that she was still alive. She changed her entire identity. Wendy Madigan no longer existed on paper. She became Dyane Wingdam. She even forced Lauren to change her name."

"Maybe it's Lauren—or her son—who sent the messages."

I speak up then. "I don't think so. I've met Lauren and Jack."

"And I've talked to my sister on the phone," Ryan says. "She's not behind this. This is all Wendy."

"You're sure about that?" Ruby says.

"Yes, baby, I'm sure. You remember her as well as I do. She'll stop at nothing. She was ready to kill me and my father just so we couldn't be with the people we love. Just so we would end up with her instead."

"Except she didn't die," Ruby says.

"I've thought about that. I believe she *was* willing to die. And I believe she thought she killed my father. She was ready to kill me and then herself."

"But she *didn't die*," Ruby says again. "She was clearly wearing bulletproof garments. Clearly had—"

"I've thought about all of that, baby. I have. My theory is that she was going to shoot herself in the head after Dad and I were dead."

"I see." Ruby nods. "So she was protected if something went wrong. Which it did."

"Exactly," Ryan says. "That's how her mind works. She's an evil genius. She was ready to meet her maker as long as Dad and I went with her, but on the off chance that something didn't work out? She wasn't ready to go yet."

"This is still a theory," Ava says.

"A theory, yes," Ryan agrees. "But it's a theory based on what your mother and I know about this woman. We know a lot about her, about how her mind works. She stayed alive for a reason. A reason we haven't figured out yet, but believe me, there *was* a reason."

"Then there's a reason why she reached out to me and not to you and Mom."

"Ava," Ruby says. "Dad and I really want you to stay out of this. She's very dangerous."

"She's a comatose octogenarian. Lying on a bed in your heavily secured home. In fact, I'm surprised you don't have someone other than a nurse watching her right now."

"We've already arranged for that. Her security detail will be here first thing in the morning. For tonight, *I'm* watching her." Ryan purses his lips.

I sigh. "Ava, sweetie. We need to leave."

"Go right ahead. I'm not going anywhere."

"But your car's not here."

Ava pauses a moment, strokes her chin. "I'm going to do something I never thought I would do."

"What's that?" I ask.

She pauses again, closes her eyes, and then exhales before reopening them. "I'm going to close the bakery. I've been wanting to remodel anyway, and now is as good a time as any to get that started. While that's happening, I will be devoting myself full-time to figuring out what the hell my grandmother's doing. Why she reached out to me. And why she's still here when we all thought she was dead."

I drop my jaw. "Baby…"

"I'm serious," she says. "I'll be staying here at my parents' house tonight. I will be staying in this room with my father. I will be here when this woman wakes up, and I will ask her, point-blank, why she has gotten in touch with me."

I inhale.

Ava's stance is indignant, and her countenance serious. She wouldn't close the bakery if she weren't completely sure she needs to be here.

I'll step back for now.

But there's something else at work, as well.

Because while Wendy reached out to Ava and not Ryan and Ruby, she also reached out to *me*.

CHAPTER EIGHT

Ava

Saying goodbye to Brendan wasn't easy. We shared a searing kiss, and I waited outside until his truck was no longer visible driving down our winding driveway. Then I texted both Luke and Maya, telling them I was closing the bakery for remodeling and that they'd be paid for the time off. And no, I won't be dipping into my trust fund to do so. I have some money saved to use for the remodeling, and it's enough to take care of my people.

I wish I had my tarot deck. I do have a deck here, but I don't like to use it. The one I have at home is a simple Rider-Waite deck, but that's not what makes it special. What makes it special is that it's wrapped in my grandmother Didi's scarf.

The deck I have here—which is a fancier deck, no doubt, with intricate drawings of fairies on each card—doesn't speak to me the way the other deck does. It's more beautiful, to be sure, but these things don't always make sense. So even though I want to draw a card, I resist. It will have to wait until I'm back at my place.

Mom is in the kitchen, heating up some water in a kettle on the stove. "Would you like a cup of tea, Ava?"

I shake my head. "No, thank you."

"I'm fixing some chamomile for myself. I need to try to get

some sleep. I wish I could convince your father."

"No one will convince him until there's someone else watching Wendy."

She sighs. "I know."

"We could just lock her in," I say.

"No." Mom shakes her head. "That's false imprisonment."

I can't help a scoff. "Mom, isn't this false imprisonment anyway?"

"No. Your father, as Wendy's next of kin—"

"Not legally." I roll my eyes. "Don't say it. We've already been through this. The Steel name."

"You carry the Steel name too, Ava. I know you don't like to use it, and I commend you for that, but it will serve you well if you ever need it. Besides, your father didn't lie to anyone. He *is* Wendy's son."

"At the risk of repeating myself . . . not *legally*."

"He is now. Or he will be. Aunt Jade is working on that. At any rate, your dad was able to make the decision to have her discharged from the hospital. He had to sign an AMA."

"What's that?"

"A document saying that he was having her discharged against medical advice."

"But I don't understand something. If she was kept under sedation at her own request, how could someone else make these decisions for her? And how does someone get to decide to stay under sedation at her own request, anyway? Any hospital worth anything wouldn't—"

"Ava"—Mom gestures to me to quiet down—"if there's one thing Dad and I know about his mother, it's that she can get things done that others can't. She somehow managed to escape lockdown in a mental health facility twenty-five years ago. No one knows how she does it. She gets people on the inside to trust her, and she waves money around. That's my theory, anyway."

I lock my gaze on the tiled kitchen floor. "I can't help it, Mom. I'm still kind of disgusted about the way *our* family throws our name around to get what we want."

"We do what we have to do." Mom sighs. "It's not always pretty, Ava. We have to protect our own."

"From this woman? This sickly old woman?"

"Yes. Absolutely. You've heard the stories."

She's right. I have. But it's so far removed from me. The stories were horrendous. I cried. But still, it's difficult to believe that the frail old woman in that room is the same person responsible for so much horror.

"Yes, she was obviously awful in her day. But she's no threat to anyone in her current state. When I went to see her in the hospital—"

"You *what*?"

"Yes. I went with Brock."

"What the hell does Brock have to do with any of this?"

"He has everything to do with it, Mom, and you know it."

Mom sighs again. "You're right. I suppose we all allowed ourselves to become complacent. It's been clear, ever since Talon got shot, that things aren't over for the family. That the past is coming back to haunt us."

"Yes. And that trafficking ring... Brock and Uncle Joe may have gotten it off our property, but it may still be operating."

"I know. We've got our investigators looking into it."

"Well, you guys have the best."

"We thought we did. But then again, we had to change our security company. In fact, that's another long story, Ava."

"I'm not going anywhere."

"I know you're not, but I am." Mom pours a cup of tea, dips the tea bag. "I'm going to bed. It's time for this day to end."

I regard my mother—her pretty face, her beautiful blue eyes . . . and the dark circles under them.

She's tired. Tired and worried. Her brow is wrinkled, and her normally rosy cheeks are pale.

I lean toward her, give her a kiss on her cheek. "Go to bed, Mom. Try to get some sleep."

"I don't sleep well without your father next to me, but I have to try." She takes her tea and walks out of the kitchen.

I pour myself a glass of water, add ice, and then I head back down the hallway to the room where my grandmother sleeps. I walk through the sitting area and into the bedroom.

"Anything?" I say to my father as I enter.

He's sitting in a recliner next to the bed where his birth mother sleeps. "She's still out. I told Jemima to get some sleep. She and Dr. Parks are in the rooms across the hallway."

I nod. "I think Dr. Parks and Mom are right. I don't think Wendy's going to wake up. Not until morning at least."

"I know they're right, but I'm not leaving her side."

"Dad?"

"Yeah?"

I bite on my lip, twisting my lip ring. "Do you have any . . . feelings for this woman?"

"Of course I do."

I raise my eyebrows.

"They're all negative, Ava. I hate her. I hate the fact that I share her genes. I hate what she's done to my family. What she did to my brother all those years ago, and through him, what she did to my father. My father was no saint, to be sure, but he wasn't as evil as this woman."

"You told me yourself that he financed the club back in high school and then continued to do so."

"Yes, until they got into the illegal stuff."

"Are you sure about that? Are you sure your father wasn't still involved?"

Dad drops his head. "Ava, I'm not sure of anything anymore." Then he raises his head and looks up at me. "Except that I love you and your sister and your mother more than anything in this world. And after that, I love the rest of my family. As long as this woman is alive, the rest of my family is in danger." He nods to the recliner next to his. "Take a load off."

I take a seat. "Dad . . . one of the documents that Brendan found . . ."

"The deed. Yes, I know."

"What do you make of it?"

"I think it's obvious. This woman forced my father to sign it. She wanted everything to go to me—her son. She didn't want anything to go to Daphne's children."

"But it was never recorded."

"No, it wasn't, thank God. Knowing Wendy, there was some kind of contingency plan. But who knows what could've happened? All the property had already been transferred to the four of us the year Marjorie turned eighteen—after the first time my father faked his death."

"What if . . . What if all of it *truly* belongs to you, Dad?"

"It doesn't matter. I would never cut my brothers and sister out."

"That's what I figured."

"Would you want me to?"

"Of course not! Not ever. They don't deserve that. They're Brad Steel's children too."

He nods. "Exactly. In fact, they're Brad Steel's *legitimate* children."

I say nothing. He's right, of course. "Except in the eyes of the law ... "

"Yes. In the eyes of the law, we're all legitimate. Daphne's name is on my birth certificate. But we all know it's a crock. I had my DNA tested years ago. It shattered my world, Ava. But you already know that story."

"I do." I won't make my father repeat it, but still, I have so many questions.

"I don't know why she reached out to you," Dad says. "Or had someone else do it. Either way, she's behind it."

"So you understand my curiosity."

"Of course I do. For some reason, you, the Murphys, Pat Lamone ... "

"Yes. Obviously you were her pride and joy, Dad. I wonder why she didn't go to *you*?"

"She knows what I think of her. She was ready to kill me twenty-five years ago. It's only because of your mother that I'm alive."

"Do you think Mom is safe?"

"I do. In her twisted way, my mother loves me. She knows how much it would hurt me if anything happened to your mother."

"But still ... " Fear pulses through me. "Gina and I, we're your daughters. Your flesh and blood. But Mom ... "

"Yes, it's crossed my mind."

"But still, you feel she's safe?"

"I do."

"Are you sure about that, Ryan?"

I drop my jaw.

The words . . .

They came from my grandmother's lips.

CHAPTER NINE

Brendan

I'm surprised to see my father at the bar when I return.

"Hey, Dad."

He's wiping off some glasses. "Laney gave me a call. She had an emergency, so I came in."

"That's kind of you. Thank you. Is everything okay with Laney?"

"Yeah. Lulu spiked a fever and wanted her mom." Dad sets down the glass. "Where's Ava? I thought you had a big date."

"She's spending the night at her parents' house."

"Oh?" Dad furrows his brow.

"Everything's okay. Between Ava and me, I mean. But the Steels..."

"Always drama," Dad says.

"So it would seem," I say. "At least the last couple months, anyway. Ruby gave me the name of a different lab to go to tomorrow for the blood work, but I'm thinking we should go to both."

"Oh?"

"Yeah. I mean it doesn't hurt to get two opinions, right?"

"Opinions have nothing to do with this. Our DNA is fact, Brendan."

"Right. In a perfect world. But who knows who might tamper with it?"

"Why in the world would anyone care about our DNA?" Dad asks.

"I don't know, Dad. But if this is our connection to the Steels..." I shake my head. "I love Ava. That's not going to change. Her family..."

"Maybe they aren't who they seem to be," Dad says.

"I never believed it. I never *wanted* to believe it. I mean, the Steels do so much for the town. They're good people."

"I believe they *think* they are."

"What's that supposed to mean?"

"It means I have no reason to think badly about the Steel brothers or Marjorie. It's their father I have a beef with."

"Yes... The apple doesn't fall far from the tree..."

"It's not a saying I ever believed," Dad says.

"You said it. Remember that first camping trip we took, when we found that apple tree?"

"Yeah." Dad chuckles. "I'm surprised you remember that."

"How can I not? That tree fed us every time we went camping after that. But the point is, you made that statement, and you've said many times over the years that the Steels own this town."

"Everyone in town has said that at one time or another."

"Fair enough, but I don't think anyone really believed it. Do you?"

Dad sighs. "I don't know, son. The older I get, the less sure I am about any fucking thing."

I simply nod. What else is there to say?

"Tell you what, Brendan," he says. "I agree with you. We'll go to the lab Jack suggested, and then we'll go to Ruby's lab. We'll make sure these blood results are correct."

"Sounds good. What time are we meeting Jack tomorrow?"

"Ten. At the lab he chose."

"Good enough. Then we'll head over to Ruby's lab." I nod. "Pour me a shot of Peach Street."

"You got it, son." Dad prepares my drink and slides it toward me on a bar napkin.

"I had two of these with dinner tonight. Ava and I went to Fortnight. Dinner was delicious, but then we stopped by her house."

"Yeah, why was that?"

"It was Ava's idea. She said her mother sounded strange on the phone, so we went."

"And..."

"And... Ava chose to stay there tonight. That's about all I can say at this point, Dad. But I can tell you this." I lower my voice. "Things are developing. I just hope it's not all bad."

CHAPTER TEN

Ava

Wendy's eyes aren't open, only fluttering.

"Wendy?" Dad says.

She doesn't respond.

"Was that . . . her?" I ask.

"Yes. I recognize her voice. It's a little different from what I remember, since she's older now. But that was her."

"So she's awake."

Dad's lips tremble slightly. "So it would seem. Wendy?"

Again, no response.

"Are you sure she's awake?"

"I'm sure, Ava. She responded to me. She knows we're talking about her. She just made a threat against your mother because she knew it would get my attention." Dad nudges her. "Wendy, open your eyes. Speak to me."

And again no response.

"Let me try," I say.

"She doesn't know you, Ava."

"She does. She's been reaching out to me." I touch her shoulder. "Wendy?"

And again . . . no response.

I know she's in there. My father's right. She made a threat against my mother, and I'm not at all happy about that.

"Wendy . . . " This time I nudge her shoulder. "Wendy, talk to us."

Then the lightning bolt . . .

The same one that destroyed the tower on my card. It appears in my mind, and I know what I have to do.

I nudge her again. "Grandmother?"

Her eyes flutter.

That's it. Dad called her Wendy. I called her Wendy.

She doesn't think of herself as Wendy to us.

"Grandma, do you hear me?"

"Yes, child," she ekes out.

"You reached out to me," I say. "Why?"

No response.

"Grandma?"

Again, the eye flutter.

"Dad, you should try. You need to call her Mom. Mother. Something like that."

Dad's jaw clenches. "I will *not*. She thinks she can threaten my wife and then have me call her Mother? She can fucking think again."

I sigh.

I understand. He has all this history with her. But I don't. I know the stories, but I didn't live them. So it's up to me.

"Grandma, please don't hurt my mother."

Her eyes flutter again, but she doesn't speak.

"I know you would never harm Dad or me or Gina. But my mother means everything to me, everything to Dad. Please tell me she's safe."

"I never said she wasn't."

"But you did, Grandma. When Dad said he didn't think Mom was in danger, you said, 'Are you sure about that, Ryan?'"

More eye flutters. Can't she just open her damned eyes?

"Please, Grandma. Please spare us all."

"Do you think I'm some kind of monster, Ava?"

Her voice is stronger now, and when her eyes flutter, this time they open.

The fierceness of their blue color overwhelms me. The whites of her eyes are bloodshot, but the piercing blue of her irises...

Unreal, almost. Yet somewhat familiar...

She doesn't turn her head, doesn't turn to look at me or at Dad, but her eyes are open now.

"Grandma, why did you reach out to me? What do you want?"

"What I've always wanted," she says, her voice soft with a touch of gravel. "To be a family. With my children. My grandchildren."

Dad stiffens.

I nod to him, gesturing.

He doesn't move.

"Tell me what you need, Grandma."

"I just told you."

Her eyes close, and she says no more, even after I try speaking to her again.

"She's asleep," Dad finally says.

"Are you sure? She appeared to be asleep before."

"No, I'm not sure." He shakes his head slowly. "I'm not sure of anything where she's concerned."

I rise from my chair, grab Dad's arm, pull him into a stand, and lead him out of the bedroom, closing the door. "You need to talk to her," I whisper. "Call her Mom. It's what she wants. I think you're the only one who can get through to her."

"She has another child," Dad says.

"I know. But you're *Brad's* child."

He doesn't respond for a moment, but then he finally nods.

He gets it. But—

"I can't. I hate her."

"I know that, Dad. In my way I hate her too. But you're the only one who's going to be able to get any information out of her."

"I'm not sure that's true, Ava. As you say, she reached out to *you* for a reason. You. Not me, not your sister. You." Dad looks at me then. Stares at me, as if he's memorizing my face. "You know? I always thought you had your mother's eyes. But now I realize . . . They're hers. Wendy's." He takes a step back.

I swallow. I was thinking the same thing myself. My eyes are a brighter blue than Mom's.

They're just like Wendy Madigan's.

"But that doesn't make genetic sense," I say. "Anything from Wendy would come through you, and your eyes are brown."

"Genetics don't always make sense," Dad says. "Living on a ranch, you find that out quickly. Sometimes you put your best stock together for breeding, and the calf that results is substandard. There's no way of knowing."

"Right . . . "

"I think, Ava, that you might be the key to all of this."

I don't reply to Dad because I'm realizing that I've known this the whole time. I've only just now allowed the words to come together in my own head. Darth Morgen. Grandmother. The acrostic that says Wendy Madigan. Pat Lamone. The Murphys.

Brendan.

The woman inside that room is the key.

And perhaps I'm the key to *that* key.

Why did she choose me? I may never know.

But perhaps it's the same reason why my maternal grandmother thought I was an old soul. Maybe there's something about me that speaks to Wendy Madigan.

If I'm going to find out why she's come back into our lives now, why Uncle Talon was shot and then poisoned, we need to get her to communicate.

And yes.

I am that key.

CHAPTER ELEVEN

Brendan

When Dad and I arrive at the Foster Diagnostics at ten a.m. sharp, Jack is already there.

"Hello, Brendan, Sean," he says, holding out his hand.

Dad and I both shake Jack's hand, and then sit down.

"They'll be with us soon."

"Good," I say, "and after this, we need you to come with us to another clinic."

Jack raises his eyebrows.

"Ava's mother, Ruby Steel, is an ex-cop and a private detective. She has labs she works with that will get us the results within twenty-four hours."

"Why would we need two results?" Jack asks.

"Just to be sure," I say. "It doesn't hurt to be sure, right?"

"I suppose not." Jack fiddles with his phone. "That's fine. I'll go with you."

"I'll text the address to you."

He nods, and seconds later, we're called back individually for our blood draws.

"Do we have an appointment at the other place?" Jack asks.

"We don't need one," I say. "We'll see you there in a few."

★ ★ ★

Tucker Madden tightens the rubber band around my upper arm to get my veins to pop out. His lab, so to speak, is in the basement of his small house. A wine rack sits along the back wall, but other than that, it's all science geek stuff down here.

"How's Ruby doing?" he asks.

That's a loaded question. Ryan and Ruby are a big mess. "She's good," I say.

"I haven't talked to her in a while," he says. "She and I used to work together a lot when she was active on the force, and then we stayed in touch, but it's been nearly a year since we've talked."

"She speaks highly of you."

"She's the best." He grabs a clear cylinder. "So you think you're related to this other guy, huh?"

"It's possible. We don't know for sure. How does this testing work, anyway?"

"We look for similar strands of DNA, try to find a common ancestor up three generations or so. Past that, it gets kind of difficult." He pokes the needle into my vein.

The guy's good. I hardly feel a thing.

"Got it. Well, whatever you can find out, we appreciate it."

"Not a problem."

"What do we owe you?"

"Not a cent. Like I said, Ruby and I go way back."

I hold up my hand. "Let me pay something."

"I won't hear of it. You just give Ruby my best."

"Good enough." I shake his hand. "I appreciate it, man."

It's eleven a.m. by the time we're done, and my stomach is starting to growl. I skipped breakfast this morning.

"Dad, feel like some lunch?"

He looks at his watch. "It's a little early for that."

"Make it brunch, then. Do you want to join us, Jack?"

"Sure. Where do you guys want to go?"

"There's a Waffle House down the road," I say. "It's a little on the nose, but it's inexpensive and satisfying."

"Sounds good to me," Jack says. "My treat, for your trouble."

"You don't have to do that," Dad says.

"I'm happy to."

Fifteen minutes later, we're sitting at a table, drinking black coffee.

"There's something you should know, Jack," I say.

"What's that?"

"Apparently your grandmother is no longer in the hospital."

Jack nods. "Oh, yeah. I know that. Ryan Steel called my mother yesterday. Her number was listed on Wendy's medical records."

I nearly drop my jaw. "So you know where she is?"

"No. I don't. All I know is that my mother gave Ryan permission to do whatever the hell he wanted with her."

"So there's really no love lost there."

"Hell, no. My mother can't stand her own mother. You heard her when we were talking."

"Right. Family squabbles and all," I say.

"What happened with us goes way beyond family squabbles. My mother suspects that her own mother orchestrated the rape that resulted in my half brother."

My jaw drops. So does Dad's, but probably for a different reason.

Ryan's theory... That Wendy had her daughter raped by those three...

"I see that surprises you," Jack says.

Dad nods. "For sure it does. Do you believe it?"

"I don't know. I was only three years old, and I was staying with my grandmother at the time."

Our waitress comes by then, and I'm thankful to have the chance to stop talking about this.

Damn.

Ryan Steel seems to know his mother very well... and that's not necessarily a good thing.

CHAPTER TWELVE

Ava

I head home in the morning after security for Wendy is in place and the nurse Dad hired has taken over her care. I make some preliminary arrangements for the contractor to come in for my remodel, make sure Luke and Maya are taken care of, make a few calls to get the necessary permits started, and throw out all the deli meat that will expire in the next few days. Ugh. I hate wasting food. Then I put up a sign.

TEMPORARILY CLOSED FOR REMODELING

Then I head up to my apartment, take a quick shower, and text Brendan.

He doesn't respond right away, which is odd.

So I head to my cards.

I'm going to do a reading. My question is, why was I chosen by my grandmother?

I remove the deck from the scarf with the daisy print that belonged to my Grandma Didi.

And I feel . . .

I always feel a connection to Didi when I touch the scarf, but this time I feel something different. A connection, yes, but something more.

I feel my two grandmothers together.

It's an odd sensation, to be sure, because Wendy has nothing to do with this scarf. It was Didi's.

Perhaps I'm imagining it.

I remove the deck, shuffle them once, twice, three times, and then I hold them to my heart, infusing them with not only my own energy but also the energy of my paternal grandmother, Wendy Madigan.

I choose the three-card spread.

The first card is the hermit.

An old man with a walking stick holds a lantern.

It's a card I've drawn many times before, but it signifies something different this time.

The hermit usually implies some kind of healing or recovery.

Odd that I would draw it first, because I'm not getting a healing sensation at all. This represents the past for Wendy. Her mind.

She has certainly never done any healing or recovery in the past—at least not from what I know of her.

Yet . . . she did keep her distance from my father—her son. So much that he didn't even realize she was still alive.

But was she healing? Recovering? Unlikely, since as Dyane Wingdam, she committed many crimes.

Felony forgery, insider trading. What else did Brock say? The list is endless.

Yet Wendy didn't serve a second of time for any of those crimes. She's smart. She covers her tracks. She gets out of bad situations.

Then I understand.

The hermit. She withdrew. She allowed her son to believe she was dead. The hermit now makes sense to me.

She was thinking. Hiding. Waiting to strike again.

And she did strike.

She struck with *me*. She reached out to me.

The second card—death. The reaper.

Most people cringe when this card comes up, but I always tell them not to. It doesn't mean literal death.

It simply means change.

And God, does it make sense for both Wendy and me for the present.

Change is definitely coming.

And then the third card . . .

The wheel of fortune. A circle that constantly moves, flowing, always cycling. Perhaps a moment of clarity at the top, but before you know it, you're at the bottom once more.

It's inescapable.

It's . . . destiny.

Destiny.

My destiny or Wendy's?

Probably both.

What is *her* destiny?

She doesn't have much longer to live. She's in her late eighties now.

The reading makes sense, but something feels off about it. I gaze at the cards, looking for the connection. They're all from the major arcana. A tarot deck consists of seventy-eight cards. Fifty-six in the minor arcana—the numbered and suited cards—leaving only twenty-two in the major arcana. The chance of drawing three cards all from the major arcana defies the odds.

Something doesn't feel right.

"Oh!" I say out loud.

I'm not feeling negative.

I'm not feeling positive, either, but that horrific foreboding I felt with the tower card is not manifesting.

Perhaps because I know my heritage now. I've accepted it.

Perhaps because I don't see an old woman as a threat.

And perhaps I should.

Clearly she was a huge threat in the past. She put my family through hell. But she's an old woman now. A sickly old woman, at that. A woman who has been kept under sedation at her own request.

I don't know why.

But I do know—from talking to my father—that his mother does nothing without a good reason. Every move she makes is calculated.

A reason exists for her exile from her son.

A reason exists why she chose to stay under sedation.

And a reason exists for why she reached out to me.

I leave the cards on the table.

I need to give them some more thought, but then I jerk when my phone buzzes.

It's Brendan.

"Hi there," I say into the phone.

"Hey, I just got back into town from an appointment this morning, and I see you closed the bakery already. I didn't realize you'd do it so quickly. Is everything all right?"

"I need some time."

"That's so unlike you, Ava."

"Believe me, I know it. But Snow Creek will continue to go on without my homemade bread for a couple of weeks. I've been wanting to do some remodeling anyway. This will give me the chance to do it while also letting me deal with my grandmother."

"If you're sure."

"I'm sure, Brendan. It's honestly strange to be so sure about closing my business. But I am. There's a reason why she reached out to me. And to you."

"Don't forget Pat Lamone."

"I haven't. But I need to come to the end of this. There's a reason for *my* involvement in particular, and I need to find out why."

"You want some company? I don't have to open the bar for a few hours."

"Sure. Come on over. Have you eaten?"

"Yeah. I had an early lunch in the city. I'll be right over."

I go downstairs, open the back door, and within another minute, Brendan comes walking up the alley.

He kisses me on the lips. "I've missed you."

I smile. "You just saw me last night."

"I've still missed you." This time he kisses me again, a full-on tongue-filled kiss.

And I'm aching for him already.

Aching in a new way, to be honest. Now that I'm finally getting some answers. I feel—not whole, exactly—but stronger.

And I want Brendan.

I want him now.

I grab his hand and lead him up to my place.

Once we're inside, I wrap my arms around him, kiss him hard, let our tongues tangle.

He looks amazing. His hair is down, waving over his shoulders, and his light-blue shirt brings out the bright cerulean of his eyes.

I remove my shirt, and I'm standing topless, no bra.

He groans, turns behind me, gropes my breasts, squeezing

them and tugging on a nipple. I turn back toward him, fuse my lips to his, and we kiss as he massages and caresses my breasts.

A moment later, he breaks the kiss, leans down, and takes a nipple between his lips. He flicks his tongue over it, fluttering it, and then sucks it, chews on it.

Already I'm so wet, I slide my jeans down, turn and bend against the sofa, my ass bare.

Then he does something I don't expect. Instead of going for my pussy, he goes for my asshole. He tongues it, caresses it, and my God, it feels good.

I sigh. I moan. I cry out his name.

"You like that, baby?"

"God, yes . . ."

He slides his fingers to my pussy then, massages my clit as he licks my ass.

"So sweet . . ." he murmurs against me.

I revel in the velvety feel of his tongue, his fingers plucking at my clit. I lurch forward, higher, higher, higher, and then, when he thrusts a finger into my pussy, I explode.

"That's it. Come for me."

A flash later and he's inside me, fucking me as I lean against the couch.

He fucks me and he fucks me, but then—

He pulls out.

"Need to feel your mouth on me," he grits out.

His shirt is still on, and his pants are around his upper thighs.

His beautiful dick is sticking out, and I drop to my knees and take it between my lips.

I suck on it, using my hands to increase the sensation, until he cups my cheeks, brings me to him, and kisses me.

We kiss a long time, as I continue to massage his cock with my hands.

I've already come once, but I want to come again. Want to revel in the love I feel for Brendan. The physical sensations between our two bodies.

I break the kiss.

"Take off your clothes, Brendan. I want to see you."

He steps away, sheds his clothes quickly. I stare at him. At his raw beauty. The scattered auburn hair over his chest, his copper-coin nipples, his gorgeous ginger bush, and his big fat cock.

"Like what you see?"

"Always." I step toward him, into his arms, lift my lips to his.

The kiss is soft and gentle at first, and then hard and feral.

And then—he picks me up, sets me on his cock.

So strong. Those thighs of his, like a god's. He grips the cheeks of my ass as he lifts me up and down on his cock.

So good, so good, so good . . .

In a moment, I'm coming again, and this time he joins me, grunting as he pushes me down onto his cock.

My legs are clamped around his hips, and I feel every pulse as he spurts into me.

We stay clamped together for some timeless moments, until he lets me down and I slide off him.

I plunk down on my couch, the fabric tickling my bare ass, and he sits next to me.

"Wow," he says.

"Double wow."

"If you think I'm done, think again."

"I was hoping you'd say that."

"Hey..." He trails a finger over my cheek. "I love you, baby."

"I love you too."

He kisses my lips. "What would you say about...making this thing between us permanent?"

My heart races. "You want to live together?"

"Well, yeah." He pauses and then looks me right in my eyes. "But I was talking about marriage, Ava. I want you to be my wife."

I gasp without meaning to. "Brendan..."

He frowns slightly. "You didn't think that was where this was going?"

"Well, yeah. Of course." My voice sounds...stilted. "But not so soon. We haven't been together for long, and—"

He looks away. "I understand. You're so much younger than I am."

"That doesn't have anything to do with it."

"Of course it does. I'm older. More ready to settle down."

"No, you're totally misunderstanding me." I touch both his cheeks. "I do want to marry you, Brendan. I do. But I have to figure this whole thing out first. This thing with my grandmother. Why she chose me. What your involvement is."

He nods. "I may find out soon what my involvement is."

"The blood tests?"

"Yeah. If I'm related to Wendy's grandson, Jack, that would explain my involvement."

"It would. Maybe. Why would it matter?"

"I haven't quite figured that out yet," he says.

I stand. "That's my point. There's a reason. There's a reason both you and I are involved."

He pulls me back down next to him. "There's not always a reason, Ava."

"But with this woman, there is. Why did she reach out to me? Why not my father? He's her son. Or why not my sister? Why me?"

"I don't know, Ava."

I scoot a few inches away from him. It's not that I don't want to be close, but I feel... I feel like I need some space. "I have to know. I have to figure this whole thing out before I can be a good wife to you, Brendan."

He chuckles lightly. "I'm not saying we have to get married tomorrow."

"I know that. I just think..."

He inhales sharply. "You don't want to make the commitment."

I grab his hand. "No, that's not it at all."

"Then what is it, Ava? We just had some mind-blowing sex. It was incredible. I love you, and I know you love me. So what is it?"

Before I think better of it, I blurt out an answer. "It's... I need space, Brendan. I can't deal with anything more than my family right now. I closed my bakery, for God's sake. Something I'd never do."

Brendan stands, grabs his jeans and boxer briefs, and stumbles back into them.

"What are you doing?"

"What does it look like I'm doing? I'm getting dressed, Ava. And then I'm leaving."

"But you don't have to open the bar yet, you can—"

"I'm giving you space."

"Brendan..." I don't know how to make him understand. I'm not sure I understand myself. I don't need space from him. Except I do, sort of.

"You've made it pretty clear where you stand, Ava. Why don't you call me when you no longer need space from me?"

"But I . . ." I shake my head. "It's hard to explain."

"You're a smart girl, Ava. One of the smartest people I know, and one of the most intuitive. If *you* can't say what you mean, then who can?" He grabs his shirt, shoves it over his shoulders. "I love you, and because I love you, I'll give you the space you require."

He leaves.

And I let him leave.

I hate myself for it, but I let him go.

Because I have so much else on my mind. The mystery I need to solve.

I am the key.

And I need to figure out why.

CHAPTER THIRTEEN

Brendan

I'm not angry with Ava so much as frustrated. I get that she wants answers. That she wants to figure out why her grandmother came to her. What I don't get is why she won't let me help her.

I head back to the bar and up to my place. I still have another hour before I need to get everything open. I think about Ava and the dinner we enjoyed last night at Fortnight. The dinner cost me a fortune, but I was glad to pay for it because she's my lady—at least I hope she still is—and she deserves the best.

Perhaps she's just not ready for a proposal of marriage.

Indeed, it wasn't my intention to propose today. My God, that lovemaking was so amazing. We were together in a way we haven't been before. Maybe that's because of everything going on in Ava's life as well. She's finding herself. Not that she didn't know who she was before, but now she's been forced to recognize the fact that things were never what they seemed, and she's finding herself within.

In the back of my mind, though, a sliver of fear erupts.

Ava is somehow connected to Wendy Madigan, and I'm not just talking about her genetics.

She's right. There's a reason why Wendy chose her, and it

frightens me—not why Wendy chose Ava, but how it's affecting her.

My phone buzzes.

My insurance company. Now what the hell do they want?

"Yeah, this is Brendan Murphy," I say into the phone.

"Hey, Mr. Murphy. This is Nigel Wilson from Silverthorne Insurance. How are you today?"

I hate when businesspeople start the call with small talk. I don't care how he is, and he doesn't care how I am. We both have things to do, so isn't it better to get right to the point?

Yeah, I'm in a mood.

"Fine. Could you tell me what this call is regarding, please?"

"Sure. I just want to apologize for the delay in processing your claim."

"Delay?"

"Yeah, there were some clerical problems. It just got onto my desk this morning."

"But...the claim is already processed. You made a payment already."

A slight pause. "Are we talking about two different claims here?"

"No. I've had only one claim. For the vandalism of my apartment over my bar."

"Yes, that's what I'm looking at right here. You have a deductible of two grand, correct?"

"Which you guys waived," I say.

A longer pause. "Sir, we never waive deductibles. I don't have the authority to do that."

"Then there must be some mistake. Check with your supervisor or something. You must've received a duplicate claim. I've already been paid."

I hear tapping on the computer from the other end of the line.

"I'm showing that this claim is still outstanding. Let me do some checking, Mr. Murphy. I'm sorry I bothered you."

"Not a problem." I end the call and throw my phone down on the table.

I need to go down and get the bar ready for opening. But damn, I could use a drink myself right now.

If only Ava had said yes to my proposal. Talk about shitty timing. What was I thinking?

I believe she loves me. I believe she loves me as much as I love her.

But... I'm worried for her.

Worried enough that—

I pick up my phone. My first instinct is to call Ryan, but I can't.

So I decide to call Donny.

"City of Snow Creek," says a bright feminine voice that I don't recognize. Did they get a new receptionist?

"Hi. Brendan Murphy for Donny Steel, please."

"I'm sorry. Mr. Steel is out of the office. Would you like to leave a message?"

"Yes, please let him know I called." I end the call.

Maybe I'll call Ryan after all.

Except my phone buzzes again—Silverthorne Insurance.

"Yeah?" I say, not nicely.

"Mr. Murphy, Nigel from Silverthorne again. How are you?"

"The same as I was ten minutes ago."

"Seems we've got some weird things going on with this claim," he says. "I checked with the higher-ups, and they say there's only one claim and it hasn't been processed yet. Plus, we have not waived the deductible. We only do that in extenuating circumstances."

"Well, you did it for me. If you want to pay me again, I won't complain."

"The point is that we *haven't* paid you yet. And I found out why. We were waiting for the results of the investigation."

"What investigation?"

"There seemed to be some question about whether"—he clears his throat—"*you* caused the damage yourself."

"Are you kidding me? You think I trashed my own place?"

"No, we don't think that, which is why your claim is on my desk now. Our investigation indicates that your claim is valid and your damages are covered."

"Which you guys already paid, very handsomely."

"I'm not sure how you think we could've paid it yet, sir, since we haven't sent out an adjuster yet to look at the damages."

"Yeah, you did. I talked to him myself."

Another pause. "Do you happen to remember his name?"

"No."

"Did he give you a card?"

"Not that I recall."

"Mr. Murphy, our adjusters always give an insured a card. That way you know how to get in touch with them."

"I don't have time for this. You guys already paid me. I appreciate it. Now goodbye." I end the call.

More and more red tape. Just because someone screwed up, and now they're harassing me.

I suppose I should be grateful. My insurance company thinks I haven't been paid, and they want to take care of it.

That's great. But they'll eventually realize their error and they'll want the money back.

Red tape, red tape, red tape.

I don't have time for this.

I head down to the bar to make sure things are ready for opening.

I was half hoping to find Ava waiting for me. Then she'd jump into my arms and tell me she doesn't need space, that she wants to be with me forever.

But that's not Ava's way.

I'm checking the stock when someone knocks at the front door.

I go to it.

Donny Steel stands there with Callie.

I open the door. "I was just trying to get ahold of you."

"Yeah, I know. I called Nell to get my messages. Callie and I were walking by, we saw you in here setting up, so I thought I'd see what you wanted."

I open my mouth to comment on my concern about Ava, but I think better of it. Ava wouldn't appreciate my interference.

So I tell him something else.

"Yeah. I don't know if you're the person I should talk to or if it's Hardy, but apparently there's been some weird mix-up with my insurance."

"Oh?"

Callie looks down at her feet.

Strange.

"Yeah. They just called me, said that they had held off on processing my claim pending an investigation."

"An investigation into what?"

"An investigation into whether I trashed my own place. I

didn't even know an investigation was ongoing. No one asked me any questions. Not one phone call."

Neither says a word.

I go on, "You know, I guess they thought I'm the arsonist who sets his own place on fire just to get the insurance money or something."

Donny clears his throat. "I don't know why they would think that."

"I don't either, but apparently they did an investigation, determined that I did *not* trash my own place, and now they're ready to send an adjuster over and process the claim. Except... they refused to admit that they already did all that and that they already paid me and waived my deductible, which this guy who I talked to today—Nigel something or other—claims they never do."

Donny glances at Callie and then flicks his gaze to the floor. Sheepish doesn't look good on him. Donny Steel is not known for looking sheepish. None of the Steels are.

"Donny..." Callie says.

Donny looks up and meets my gaze. "Can we sit down for a minute, Brendan?"

"Yeah. Sure. Why?"

"I need to tell you something."

"Is it bad?"

"Not at all. Though you may take it that way."

Great. Just what I need. "I'm not sitting. You can tell me what you need to tell me right here, while we're both standing."

"Okay, have it your way." Then he clears his throat. "The fact that your place got trashed is my fault."

My mouth drops open, and I'm sure I look like an idiot about to drool. "You've got to be kidding me... *You* trashed my place?"

He shakes his head. "No, of course not. But Dale and I . . . We wanted to do some more investigating, see what else may be hidden in your place. So we . . . Rather *I* . . . "

"Let me guess. That gas line was never an issue, was it?"

"No. I felt terrible about it, so I ended it. But all it took was that one night for you to be out of your apartment for someone else to come in and . . . Well, you know the rest."

"And Hardy couldn't find out who did it. Neither could you."

"No," Donny says, "but now that Wendy Madigan has resurfaced and we shut down the human trafficking on our property, I'm pretty sure I know who was responsible for trashing your place."

"Who?"

"The mastermind behind everything that has ever befallen our family. Wendy Madigan herself."

"None of that is explaining—" I shake my head. "Two plus two equals four. Always."

"Look, Brendan . . . Brock was supposed to take care of the insurance company. Make sure they didn't call you. I know he did, but . . . Well, you know corporate red tape and all. Something didn't get done on their end, and—"

"Save it. You paid my"—air quotes—"insurance claim. I should've known no insurance company would ever waive the deductible. Or pay so quickly and give me the amount I got. My bad."

"We would've just paid you, Brendan, but we didn't think you'd take it."

"Damn right I wouldn't have. And you can have it all back."

"But it's our fault your place was vandalized. If you had been there, it wouldn't have happened. You weren't there because we made up the gas line lie."

"I will never be beholden to a Steel."

Donny sighs. "You sound like your old man."

I raise my eyebrows. "When has my old man ever said anything like that?"

Donny cocks his head slightly, but his voice is steady. "Your old man has made it very clear over the years how he feels about the Steels. He's nice to us, acts respectful, but it's clear he still thinks our family had something to do with his uncle's death."

I stare Donny Steel straight in his hazel eyes. "Yeah? Frankly I haven't ruled that out either."

"You do know that none of us were alive when that happened, right?"

"I've told my father that ad nauseam. I always thought he was chasing his own tail on that one. But now? With you people having a lien on this property? A lien, by the way, that you promised to lift."

"Yeah, you're right. Except ... "

"For Christ's sake. What now?"

"Nothing. I'll take care of it."

"And I will pay you back every cent you gave me to fix this place up."

"You're cutting off your nose to spite your face, Brendan," Callie says, turning to me. "I don't condone what Donny did. I really don't."

Donny eyes her.

Callie crosses her arms. "Well, I don't. My family is proud too. Your uncle and your father offered to pay us off when our vineyards were destroyed in that fire, but did we take your handouts? No, we didn't."

I've always liked Callie Pike, but I like her a whole hell of a lot more in this moment.

"But," she continues, "it *is* Dale and Donny's fault that you weren't here that night to defend your property. It was open and ripe for the picking. Obviously, someone knew it, and someone trashed it, taking whatever else might've been hidden under those floorboards."

"I never found anything else."

"I understand that," Donny says, "but you probably didn't look that hard either."

"I looked."

"But did you look at all the places the thieves looked?"

I hate to admit that he's right. "No, I didn't. It didn't occur to me that someone might've hidden stuff in a couch cushion."

"I'm not even talking about that. That couch probably hasn't been there for fifty years. I'm talking about inside the drywall, underneath the joists. All the places they trashed."

"You're right," I say. "I didn't."

"That's what Dale and I planned to do, but in the end, I couldn't do it. I'm an ethical lawyer, and I breached my ethics. I couldn't live with that, so I put an end to it. Because I breached my ethics in the first place, your place got trashed. So yeah, I believe it was my family's obligation to restore it."

"You know you paid me way more than my policy limits."

"Yeah, and what we gave you allowed you to get it done quickly, just the way you wanted it. Better than any insurance payout would've been."

"True, but it still wasn't your place."

"That's what I'm trying to tell you, Brendan." Donny taps his chest. "It *was* my place. The whole thing was my fucking fault."

Callie nods. "I love him, but he's right. He screwed up, and he knows it."

My hands are already curled into fists, and anger has slithered up my spine.

I'm not going to get into a fight with Donny Steel. I could take him, but it'd be tough. He's one big muscle, just like his brother. Besides, what am I really angry about here? Is it the fact that the Steels paid my bills? Yeah, but I'm more angry about...

Ava...

Ava, Ava, Ava.

Does she know about this?

"What am I supposed to do about this? The insurance company thinks my claim is still outstanding."

"Simply call them and withdraw the claim."

"And say what? Some anonymous benefactor took care of it?"

"It doesn't matter what you tell them," Donny says. "They'll be happy as clams that they don't have to pay you."

"He's right," Callie says. "I've told you, Brendan, that I don't agree with what he did. He and Dale made a huge mistake, but they tried to fix it. They've tried to make you whole."

She's not wrong. They have. In fact, they went above and beyond—though the amount it took to fix up my place is only pennies to the Steel family.

"Please take the money," Callie says. "I won't say it's their generosity, although they are generous people. But this isn't generosity. This is just righting a wrong."

I roll my eyes, shaking my head. "Righting a wrong? Maybe. You know I could have you disbarred for this."

"You could," Donny says. "I wouldn't blame you."

Callie gasps. "Brendan, please..."

"For Christ's sake, I'm not going to go to the bar association.

But you realize, don't you, that if there was anything else to find at my place, it's long gone now?"

"Yeah, I know," Donny says. "And yes, I know it's all my fault. Not my finest hour."

I sigh. I can't give this man any more shit. The first seven years of his life were horrific. He was doing what the Steels always do—looking out for his family.

"I'm going to pay you back."

"That's your choice," he says, "but I don't expect it. I don't need it. I don't want it. No money you can pay me will bring back whatever may have been found at your place. We've done what we can. I don't know how much Ava has told you, but there was some serious shit going down on our property without our knowledge. We put an end to it, but there's still stuff going on."

I nod.

"What exactly *has* Ava told you?" Donny asks.

"That's between her and me."

"I understand." He nods to Callie. "You ready?"

"Yeah. We should get back to the office."

I nod again. I don't open my mouth because I'm not sure what will come out. The two of them leave, and I check my watch.

Two o'clock. I open the bar at four.

I have time.

Time to go see Ava...and find out whether she knew about this all along.

CHAPTER FOURTEEN

Ava

Someone's pounding on my door. I mean really pounding. I hear it all the way up at my place.

Then the yelling.

It's Brendan. And he's angry . . .

Why did he come back? He made it clear where he stood. He's no doubt angry that I didn't accept his proposal.

I sigh, scurrying to my clothes, which I haven't bothered to put on since our lovemaking earlier, and hurry down the stairs to the back door of the bakery.

I open it. "Would you cut out all that racket?"

He walks past me into the bakery. "You've got some explaining to do."

I scoff. "No, I don't. I'm just not ready—"

"That's not what I'm talking about." He runs his fingers through his hair, and it almost looks like a lion's mane—a red-blond lion's mane.

"What now?" I set my hands on my hips, trying to maintain a strong stance even though my whole body is throbbing in his presence.

But I don't feel strong in front of him. I feel . . . small. Not weak, but small. He is so big, so tall, so muscular . . . My God, my pulse is racing—and it's not out of anger or fear.

It's out of arousal.

"I just had an interesting chat with your cousin."

I can't help a smirk. "You'll have to tell me more than that. You know I have many cousins."

He doesn't reply.

"I hope you're not talking about Pat Lamone."

"For Christ's sake, Ava. I'm talking about Donny. Donny and Callie were just at the bar because I had some questions."

"What kind of questions?"

"About the insurance claim on my place. You see, I got an interesting phone call once I left here. Seems my claim hasn't even been adjusted yet. They were calling to apologize for the delay."

I bite my lip, fiddle with my lip ring.

"Stop doing that. You know how that makes me—" He grabs me, crashes his lips to mine.

I open for him. It's instinct, pure and simple. Our bodies speak to each other. Even when our minds are angry, our bodies speak to each other in passion and desire.

He breaks the kiss almost as suddenly, wiping his mouth. "Fuck it all."

"Brendan..."

"I just have one question for you, Ava. Did you know? Did you know that your fucking family paid for my so-called insurance claim?"

"I..."

"Just answer, damn it."

"I did, Brendan. I did—"

He opens his mouth, but I hold up my hand to stop him.

"Wait just a minute. I only just found out. Brock told me." I let out a breath. "Good old Brock."

"And I told him how much you would hate it."

"I do hate it, but here's the question, Ava. Why didn't you tell me? As soon as you found out, you should've told me."

I bite my lip again, fiddle with my ring, and then I stop. He's going to accuse me of turning him on again.

Hell, what do I care? So I fiddle with my lip ring. If it turns him on, good.

He stands rigid beside me, clenching his jaw.

"I don't know why I didn't tell you."

"Did Brock tell you not to?"

I rack my brain. Did he? Right now all I can think about is that kiss.

"Honestly, I don't remember, Brendan. Maybe he did, and maybe he didn't."

"It's irrelevant. You should've told me when you found out. How are we supposed to have a relationship when you keep secrets from me?"

"I . . . I knew it would upset you, and—"

He drops his gaze and turns away from me. "So you decided, unilaterally, not to tell me. Great."

I grab his shoulders and force him to turn around and face me. "It's not that simple, Brendan, and you know it."

"It's every bit that simple, Ava. Every bit. I love you, damn it. I love you, and I want a life with you. I would put a ring on your finger right now, and, thanks to your family's meddling in my insurance claim, I can afford one."

"Brendan, I already told you that—"

"Yeah. You told me, didn't you? You told me you had to deal with your family first. Before you could make a commitment to me. I get it. I do . . . but this new development that you didn't tell me about . . . " He shoves his hands into his pockets. "I don't know where I fucking stand anymore."

"Brendan, no. You know where you stand. I love you!"

"Do you? Do you fucking love me, Ava? Because you show it in a really strange way."

I run to him then, grab on to him, melt my body into his.

His arms don't go around me. He's stiff as a board.

I pull away, and I do something that I know I'll regret later. I purposefully tug on my lip ring, run my tongue around it. Knowing that it will arouse him.

It does just that.

He stalks toward me like a wolf, grabs me, smashes his lips to mine again.

It's an open-mouthed kiss. An animalistic kiss. Tongues and teeth everywhere, passion and desire exuding.

And anger. Anger overshadowing it all.

Not just on his part but on mine as well. He's accusing me of keeping things from him. He's right, but he doesn't understand the need I have to figure this out for my family.

So I'm angry too. Angry that he can't wait for me. That he's pushing me, prodding me.

Our mouths still fused, he pushes me against the wall, grinding his hard cock into my belly.

The melting. The melting of my body, permeating between my legs. I'm wet. Always so wet for him.

He breaks the kiss, takes a step backward, his blue eyes blazing into mine.

"Take off those clothes, Ava. All of them. Now."

I obey him without question. I don't even consider not complying. I strip myself. It's easy, as I'm only wearing sweat pants and a T-shirt.

I stand before him naked, my nipples hard and protruding, begging for his touch.

He narrows his eyes, never wavering from my gaze. He unbuckles his belt, unzips his jeans, and shoves them along with his underwear over his hips, letting his cock spring out.

Then he comes toward me, pushes me against the wall, lifts me, and sets me down on his cock.

My back is cold against the wall, but only for a moment. Because in that moment, I blaze. I become flame. I'm on fire.

On fire as he shoves his cock into me, burning through me.

It's the middle of the day, and though the lights in the bakery are off, anyone could walk by, look through the window. We're in the back, but if they look hard, squint, they will see us.

Brendan, fucking me up against the wall of my own bakery.

He grunts with each thrust, a grunt of anger, of passion.

I'm not even thinking about coming—I don't care about coming.

That isn't what this is about.

This is...

Pure instinct. Pure primal instinct. We are animals, Brendan and I. Animals fucking.

Because that's who we are.

He grunts again, this time harder, and as he shoves himself so deep within me, spurting, I join him in climax.

How am I coming? He hasn't touched my clit. I haven't touched my clit.

But because of this angry passion, I'm coming. I'm shattering, right here in front of the whole town through my window.

The orgasm is explosive.

As if our anger, our passion, the whole main street of Snow Creek laid out before us made it even more arousing.

We stay there for a moment, our bodies locked together,

and then he withdraws, and I slide down the wall onto my feet.

Without a word, he buckles his pants. I stand naked, watching him.

"Brendan . . . "

"I don't want to hear it," he says.

"You're going to hear it. I'm going to—"

He turns, walks away.

"Damn it! Do not walk away from me!" I grab my sweats, stumble into them. I run after him, still topless.

He opens the door, and my nipples harden against the cold.

"Brendan, don't go."

"There's nothing more to say, Ava. You get in touch with me when you're ready to own up to what you did."

The door closes.

And I stand there, my nipples still hard, straining, aching for him.

But inside, I'm as angry as he is. *Own up?* It wasn't my idea to compensate him for his losses. How dare he?

Except that's not what he means.

He thinks I lied to him. He thinks I'm putting him off in favor of dealing with my family issues.

So I'll show him. I'll figure this whole thing out about Wendy Madigan and my family. Then I'll go back to him. And I *will* commit. I'll commit to him, and there will be no more secrets between us.

But I owe my family. And . . . in some small way, which may well be warped, I owe my grandmother.

But for her, I wouldn't exist.

So I need to do this.

I need to do it.

I just hope it doesn't cost me everything.

CHAPTER FIFTEEN

Brendan

By the next morning, my anger at Ava has dissipated. Now I feel only remorse. Sadness. I miss her. I don't want to lose her, and I shouldn't have told her to own up. I will apologize, but not just yet. I can't face her right now.

The phone buzzes.

"Brendan Murphy."

"Hey, Mr. Murphy, this is Tucker. I've got your DNA results."

"Already? Ruby told me you were quick, but damn."

"I have the best tech out there."

"So . . . what did you find?"

"You're definitely related to the other Mr. Murphy. I'd like all three of you to come into the city this morning if you can so we can discuss the results."

"I can probably get my dad. As for the other Mr. Murphy, I can't be sure."

"Not a problem. You guys come on down, and I'll go ahead and give him a call."

"All right. I'll be there soon."

I quickly call my father.

★ ★ ★

Sure enough, Jack is at the lab when Dad and I get there.

"Seems we're related after all," Jack says to Dad and me.

I nod. "Sounds like it. Let's see what Tucker has to say."

We walk into the lab together, and Tucker greets us. "I'm glad you could all make it."

"So I guess we're third or fourth cousins, huh?" I chuckle.

"You're related much more closely than that," he says. "Let me show you my findings."

He leads us over to a table where he's printed out some documents. "This will all look like a mess to you, but these are the DNA strands that show the relation. Normally in situations like this, I expect to find that you shared a grandparent maybe three or four generations up. That's not the case here." He shuffles his documents and then slides a page in front of us. "Do you see the strand?"

We all nod, though it looks like nothing to me.

"Mr. Murphy," he says to my father. "You and Jack share grandparents on the patrilineal side."

Dad wrinkles his brow. "Say what?"

"It means," Tucker continues, "that you have the same paternal grandparents."

"My father had two siblings," Dad says. "The one who I was named after, Sean Murphy, passed away without having children. The other, my father's sister, was married and had three children, all by her husband."

"She'd be a nonissue anyway. We know who Jack's mother is, and this concerns the patrilineal line, not matrilineal."

"Maybe it's a grandparent on the other side," I say. "No, wait. You said paternal side."

"Right," Tucker says.

"Well . . . my father's name *was* Sean Murphy," Jack says.

"That's what your mother tells you," I say.

He turns to me, his jaw rigid. "Hey, my mother's a good woman."

I nod. "I apologize. That's not what I meant. It wasn't a dig on your mother. It was a dig on your grandmother."

Jack nods. "I see what you mean."

Dad shakes his head. "None of this makes a lick of sense. I might believe you if you said Brendan was the key. That *he* and Jack shared a great-grandparent. But Jack and me? It doesn't add up."

"I only read the DNA, sir," Tucker says. "And I can tell you, almost for certain, that you two"—he nods to Dad and then to Jack—"share paternal grandparents. It's clear as day."

"I'd say it's about as clear as mud," Dad says.

"You have another set of results coming," Tucker says. "They're not going to be as quick as I am. But let me know what they say."

Dad stands. "Good idea. I know Ruby Steel recommended you and all, but you got this one wrong."

Dad walks out.

Jack and I sit there, staring at each other.

Jack shakes his head. "I've got to agree with your dad," he says. "None of this makes any kind of sense."

"Dad seems a little weirded out by it." I inhale. "Is there a way to see whether this could've been a half-sibling or something?"

Jack nods. "I'm surprised your father didn't think to ask that. It would make more sense if it were a half-sibling situation. The product of an affair, or . . . "

"A rape. A child given up for adoption," I say, thinking of Lauren and Pat Lamone.

"Yes, exactly," Tucker says. "But that's not the case here. The two of you—Jack and Sean—are full-blooded first cousins on the patrilineal side. There is no indication of a half-sibling situation."

I shake my head. "Doesn't make sense."

"Sure doesn't," Jack agrees. "Although, apparently I'm your uncle."

"Crazy." I meet Tucker's gaze. "You must've made a mistake."

Tucker shifts in his seat. "I don't make mistakes. But like I said, see what the other clinic tells you."

I rise. "Thank you for your time." I hold out my hand.

Tucker shakes it. "Not at all. Anything for Ruby."

Jack and I leave, and we find Dad waiting for us in the parking lot. He's smoking a cigarette, something he almost never does.

"What the hell?" I say.

"I keep a pack in the car. For emergencies."

"So being related to me sent you to smoke," Jack says.

"Not at all," Dad says. "You're a nice young man. I'd be proud to be a relation. But this doesn't make sense."

"I agree," I say. "Something's rotten here."

"You heard Tucker," Jack says. "He doesn't make mistakes."

Dad flicks his ashes on the asphalt. "Yeah, but he was recommended by the Steel family."

"My grandfather was a Steel."

"An illegitimate Steel," I say. "No offense."

"None taken."

"How long have you known about your ancestry?" I ask.

"Pretty much my whole life," Jack says.

"And you never wanted a piece of their pie?"

Jack shrugs. "I never *needed* a piece of the pie. Mom and I came into some money not long after . . . "

"Not long after what?"

"Not long after she was raped. After she gave away my brother."

"Really? Where did the money come from?" I ask.

"I was a kid, so I didn't ask a lot of questions. But as I understand it, when my father passed away, he left a pretty sizable estate to my mother. But that's according to my grandmother. Everything came through her."

Dad rubs his jawline. "So William Elijah Steel . . . Maybe he did have some money."

"It's possible that his father, George Steel, knew about him," Dad says. "Probably made arrangements. Siphoned off the money to give him a small estate."

I nod. "That does make sense."

"There sure are a lot of questions we need answered," Jack says.

"There sure are." I hold out my hand to Jack. "But I can't say I'm unhappy that you're related to us. It's nice to have a new uncle."

"Son," Dad says. "Don't be counting those chickens until we get the additional results."

"Dad, you and I both know what those results are going to say."

Dad shakes his head again. "How can this be?"

"I don't know," Jack says, "but I think between the three of us, we can put our brainpower together and figure it out."

"You bet we will," Dad says. "If it's the last thing I do, I'm going to figure out what the fuck is going on here...and what the Steel family has to do with it."

CHAPTER SIXTEEN

Ava

Dad sits with me at my grandmother's bedside. I asked him to leave me alone with her, but he won't.

"Don't you need to go to the winery?"

"Have you forgotten I'm retired now?" Dad shakes his head. "I'm allowing you to do this because you're my daughter and I love you, Ava. But no way am I leaving you alone with her."

I gesture to Wendy, who's asleep. "She is not any danger to me."

Jemima enters the room, checks the monitors on the machines that she set up for Wendy. "Everything looks good. Her heart rate is normal. Blood pressure's good. Pulse ox is good. For a woman her age, she's in excellent health."

"Which doesn't explain why she kept herself in a self-induced coma," Dad says.

"Only she can answer those questions," Jemima says. "Dr. Parks is on rounds at the hospital now, but she'll be back when she can. You know where I am if you need anything."

Since Michaela has moved into the normal wing of the house, staying in one of the guest bedrooms, until this thing with Wendy is resolved, the staff wing has become the hospital wing.

"I don't know what you think she's going to tell you," Dad says. "She's lied her whole life. Spent most of her life in disguise. She's a mastermind criminal. The woman won't tell you the truth."

Wendy's eyes flutter open. "I've always told you the truth, my son."

Dad doesn't react to her waking up. Was he expecting it?

"Oh? Have you?" He scoffs. "All those years when you were an investigative journalist, all those years knowing you were my mother, but you never said anything. Not until it suited you to do so."

"I wasn't lying, was I?"

"Lying by omission is still lying, Wendy," he says.

Lying by omission. The words strike me in my gut. That's why Brendan is so angry . . . and I don't blame him. I lied by omission when I didn't tell him that my family paid for his damages.

Dad continues, "Plus, you knew my mother and father—"

"Your father and Daphne," she says. "*I'm* your mother, Ryan."

Dad narrows his eyes. "Only genetically. All those years you knew my mother and father were alive, living on that island. You knew what was happening on the adjacent island as well. The island that my father sold to that horrid corporation. Which turned out to be . . ." Dad shakes his head. "How can one individual be so sick?"

"Everything I've done, I've done for my children."

"Why didn't you ever tell me I had a sister?"

"You never asked me, Ryan."

"This is all such bullshit. My daughter here"—he looks at me with love in his brown eyes—"this very sweet soul, thinks there's something of value we can learn from you. I've tried to tell her that's ridiculous, but she's her own person, my Ava. She wants to give you the benefit of the doubt despite everything she knows about you. And she *does* know everything. Ruby and I told her the truth about what happened twenty-five years ago."

Wendy's lips curve slightly. "Then that says something for me, doesn't it?"

"Why did you reach out to me?" I ask.

She turns her head, looks at me. "Because you're my granddaughter, Ava."

"Okay, but why? You have another granddaughter. You have Gina. You have Lauren's son, Jack. You have Pat Lamone."

"I reached out to Pat also."

"Yes, but you reached out to me first. Me...and the Murphys."

"It will all become apparent soon."

"Why don't you just tell me?"

"Ava, I'm an old woman. There's a reason why I checked myself into the hospital and a reason why I revealed certain things to Pat so he would come visit me."

"Are you ready to tell me why?"

"I am. First I need to tell you a story."

"For God's sake, Wendy." Dad huffs.

"Will you ever call me Mother, Ryan?"

"I did once. Don't you remember?"

"You did." She turns her gaze to my father. "You did it because you wanted information from me. You want information now, don't you?"

"Yes, I want information, but I don't want to experience the sickness I felt the last time I called you Mother. You're *not* my mother, Wendy. You never were. Daphne Steel was my mother in every way that counted."

"Daphne Steel was crazy."

"Daphne Steel was the product of her childhood. She was . . ." He shakes his head. "I don't need to tell you all of this. I'm sure you know."

"Yes, I do know. I know her half brother, Larry, assaulted and raped her, along with Tom Simpson and Theo Mathias."

"My guess is you orchestrated it."

"I can see why you might think that, but I didn't, actually. That was all Theo's doing."

I shudder.

Theo Matthias was my grandfather as well. On Mom's side.

"He was obsessed with Daphne."

"Here's what I don't understand . . . Grandmother," I say.

Dad seethes.

But I'm going to get the truth out of her by any means necessary.

"You all went to high school together. You, my grandfather, Daphne's half brother, Tom, and Theo. How did Brad Steel not know Daphne then?"

"Brad wasn't involved in the club as much as the four of us were. He and Theo weren't close, not in the way Theo was close to Tom and Larry. He knew Larry had a sister, but that was it. They didn't live together. Larry lived with his mother here on the western slope, and Daphne lived in Denver with her parents."

"So Brad knew of Daphne but never met her."

"That's right, Ava. And Daphne didn't know the identity of her rapists until . . ."

"She knew. She just kept it compartmentalized, in the head of her other personalities."

"Ava . . ." Dad says.

"I'm sorry, Dad. But I need to know the answers to these questions. I just don't understand how all of this could've happened."

"You're talking about things that happened fifty years ago. Wendy may not even remember everything. She's an old woman, Ava."

Wendy's eyes narrow. "I'm an old woman with a mind as sharp as a tack, Ryan. Do you even doubt that for a moment?"

Dad says nothing.

I know what he's thinking. He's thinking about Wendy and her genius IQ.

"Did you know I used to paint, Ava?" Wendy says.

"No, I didn't."

"Your sister's talent clearly comes from me. Your father's creativity also. How is he able to make wines that no one else in the world can make?"

"Dale can make them."

"Only because he learned from your father."

"That's not fair, Wendy," Dad says. "Dale is a huge talent in his own right."

"If that's what you need to tell yourself, Ryan."

I brace myself. Time to get back on track. "I guess what I want to know, Grandmother, is how you could've been involved in such horrific things. Child trafficking. How you could . . . I mean . . . Uncle Talon . . . Dale and Donny . . ."

"First of all, Ava, I had nothing to do with Dale and Donny. Their father sold them into slavery, for a mere five thousand dollars."

"I know the whole story, and it makes me want to be sick. But Uncle Talon? When he was just a boy?"

"Oh, Ava, I don't expect you to understand." Wendy's gaze darkens. "Know only that I had no choice at the time."

"That's crap," Dad says.

I look at Dad. *Please, let me talk. Let me get the information.* I hope he understands my mental message.

"I'm trying to understand, Grandmother. How could you allow a ten-year-old boy to be taken and abused by those three monsters?"

"It wasn't my fault," Wendy says. "It was Brad's. Brad broke a promise to me."

"What promise?"

Wendy closes her eyes for a moment. "I see, Ryan, that you haven't told her exactly everything. That's the story I want to tell you, Ava. About two soul mates who were torn apart."

I lock eyes with my father. "Dad, what is she talking about?"

Dad's jaw tightens. "For Christ's sake, Wendy. You still did it. He broke some stupid promise to you. A promise he never meant. You and I both know it."

"It was a promise between soul mates."

Dad turns to me. "Apparently, my father, after I was born, promised Wendy that he would never sleep with Daphne again."

"But Marjorie ... "

"Exactly, Ava," Wendy says. "Aunt Marjorie. Proof that Brad did not keep his promise to me. When Daphne ended up pregnant, Brad paid for his betrayal."

"Dad didn't pay," my father says. "Not like Talon paid. Talon, and in our own way, Joe and I paid too. And our mother."

"You were spared that day, Ryan."

"Joe and I didn't go through what Talon went through for sure. But we paid in our own way. Joe paid with guilt for not going that day with Talon. For not protecting his brother. And I paid with guilt too. I was spared. Talon saved me."

"You *thought* Talon saved you. You know the truth."

I grab Dad's arm. "What the hell is she talking about?"

"I was with Uncle Talon that day when the men took him. Uncle Talon told me to run, so I ran. For the first thirty-two years of my life, your uncle was my hero. I thought he had saved me that day. He's still my hero, Ava. He's a military hero, and my hero anyway. But it turns out . . . "

"What, Dad?"

"It turns out I was spared because I was Wendy's son."

I swallow.

I don't know what to say.

And I don't know if I can handle trying to get this information out of my grandmother any longer.

I rise. "Please excuse me."

I leave the room as calmly as I can, run all the way down the hallway through the next hallway to my own bedroom, close the door, enter my en suite bathroom, and throw up in the toilet.

CHAPTER SEVENTEEN

Brendan

"You think the bar could use some remodeling, Dad?"

"Why the hell would it need remodeling?"

I sigh. "I need some time off."

Dad steps toward me. "Does this have anything to do with Ava shutting down her bakery?"

"Yes and no. Ava and I ..." I pause. "Well, I guess we're taking a bit of a break. She has some stuff to work through, and frankly, so do I."

"You know, Brendan"—Dad rubs his chin—"I like Ava. But it wouldn't bother me if you stayed far away from the Steels."

"I'm in love with her, Dad. Right now, I'm not sure where her head is in the whole thing. So we're taking a little time. She has some family stuff to deal with. The reappearance of her grandmother is the biggest part. I think she feels ... I don't know. She feels some kind of kinship with this woman. This woman who, by the way, was a complete psychopath, so I'm a little bit scared for Ava. But I can't be with her right now."

Dad exhales. "I can't believe I'm saying this, since I just told you I wouldn't mind you staying away from the Steels, but perhaps she needs you now more than ever."

I clench my hands into fists. "If it comes to anything like that, if she's in danger or anything, I will be there in a moment to protect her with my life. But that's not what I'm feeling. This is just some stuff she needs to work out."

"All right, son." Dad looks around. "So why do you need to shut down the bar?"

"I want to figure out the whole thing with my great-uncle once and for all."

Dad raises an eyebrow. "Brendan?"

"I know, Dad. I know I've told you to let it lie. But this thing with Jack. We need to figure out where he came from. How it's possible that the two of you share grandparents."

"I thought you said you wanted to wait until we got the rest of the DNA results."

"You and I both know they're going to say the same thing."

Dad nods. "I know. I've given that some thought, and I believe you're right."

"I don't want to sacrifice the income, but I see Ava's point. She needs to figure this out, and I'm feeling the same thing about our situation. I need to devote some time to this."

"We could hire people. Laney, Johnny, Marianne, the Petersons. They could all take extra shifts. They might like that."

"They might. Plus I suppose we could bring in some temporaries too."

"Tell you what. I'll help you get it all set up." Dad takes his phone out and begins scrolling. "We don't need to close the bar, Brendan. You just need to take a week off. You and I will figure this out together."

★ ★ ★

Turns out Dad was right. All the employees were more than

happy to take extra shifts, all except the Petersons, of course, who have to work their liquor store the rest of the week. I filled any gaps with the temp agency, and now I have a week off.

Feels strange—very strange sitting in my apartment, which was paid for by the Steels.

In my heart, I know Ava had nothing to do with that, but she did keep it from me. Now I know, and somehow I will pay back every cent, but in the meantime, I need to figure out my own family's involvement.

It will be a few more days before we get the DNA results from the other lab, but as of now, Dad and Jack Murphy are cousins, which makes Jack my first cousin once removed.

It also means we have a link not only to the Steels but also to crazy Wendy Madigan.

At least our link isn't genetic. Only Jack is that unfortunate.

Jack...and Ava.

But Jack will be fine, just as Ava is fine. Ryan is fine and Lauren, although I only met her once, seems fine as well—as fine as anyone who was brutally raped thirty years ago *can* be.

I sigh.

To think... How much I loved this new place. Especially how quickly it got done, and now? It's tainted. Tainted with Steel money.

It's so obvious as I think about it. No insurance company pays as quickly as mine did, and no insurance company waives a deductible. I just didn't want to see what was right in front of my face. I was anxious to get back to my place, anxious to stop living with my parents.

So I chose not to see.

Never again. Never fucking again.

I will never have a blind spot—not when it comes to the

Steels. Not when it comes to anything.

My phone rings. Speak of the devil. Ruby Steel.

"Yeah? This is Brendan."

"Brendan, it's Ruby Steel."

"Hi, Ruby. How's Ava?"

"She's hanging in there. She's with her father and her"—throat clear—"*grandmother* at the moment."

"You're not with them?"

"No. It's best that I'm not there. But that's why I'm calling. I wanted to check to see if Tucker was able to help you."

"Yes, thank you for the recommendation. He already got the results back to us."

"And?"

"What the hell, I guess you know everything anyway. It seems that my father and Lauren's son, Jack, share a grandparent. Which makes absolutely no sense at all."

"I see." Her tone is odd, almost robotic.

"My grandfather's brother, as you know, died at Brad Steel's wedding."

"Yes. I've been thinking about this. And I have a working theory."

"I have a working theory too," I say. "Although I haven't even allowed myself to think about it."

"I'd like to meet with you and your father. I think we have some digging to do."

"Whose side are you on, Ruby?"

"There's only one side here, Brendan. The side *against* Wendy Madigan. She may be Ryan's mother and Ava's grandmother, but she is the enemy. We would all be wise never to forget that."

"I haven't forgotten that. Do you feel Ava has?"

Ruby pauses a moment before she speaks. "No, I don't think Ava has, but Ryan and I are concerned. Ava seems to want something from Wendy. She seems to feel some kind of connection to her. And I'm not just talking genetically."

"Yes, I got that feeling as well. Especially when she was reading some cards, and when she figured out exactly who Wendy was."

"Ryan doesn't want to leave Ava's side right now, and I don't blame him. I think Ava would like to be left alone with Wendy, but Ryan won't allow it. However, I don't plan to be anywhere near the woman. And I just have a feeling that . . . a lot more is going on here."

"Yes."

"I know you're busy—"

"Actually, Ruby, I'm not. I'm taking a week off from work. I've got all my shifts covered with the addition of some temps."

"So you're pulling an Ava? Very strange indeed."

"Stranger for her than for me. But yes, I suppose I'm pulling an Ava. My father and I . . . We want to figure out this thing with his great-uncle once and for all."

"I do too, Brendan. Can the two of you meet me later today?"

"Yeah. I think he'd appreciate that."

"Actually, I'd like to meet Lauren."

"I can probably arrange that. I'll call Jack."

"Great. If the three of us could go over there sometime today, I think that would be helpful."

"Yeah. I'll arrange it if I can and get back in touch with you as soon as I know anything."

"Thank you, Brendan. And for what it's worth, I hope you and Ava work things out."

"I do too, Ruby."

"I wasn't born a Steel, and I know better than most that they're not always the easiest people to love. But they are worth it in the end, Brendan. Trust me on that."

"I do love your daughter, Ruby. That's not in question at all. I'll call Jack and get back to you."

"Very well. Thank you, Brendan."

CHAPTER EIGHTEEN

Ava

I need a break.

Why am I doing this again?

Why do I feel like I need to know something from this woman?

Because she makes up a quarter of my DNA? She makes up half of my dad's, a quarter of Gina's as well.

Does it even matter?

I don't have to be anything like her.

But I feel something about her. Some kind of bizarre link.

I wipe my mouth and then rinse it with water from the sink. Then I walk out of my room.

My mother's in the kitchen. "Ava, do you need anything?"

I shake my head.

"You look a little ... green."

"Just things."

Mom touches my arm. "You don't have to do this."

I meet her gaze. "Mom. I *do* have to. There's a reason why she reached out to me. Not to Dad. Not to her other daughter. Not to Gina. But to *me*, Mom."

"Ava, you can't try to make sense of anything a crazy person does."

"But is she truly crazy?"

Mom's gaze darkens. "You know what she's done. How can you even ask that?"

"Evil doesn't necessarily mean crazy, Mom. I get the feeling she knew what she was doing every step of the way."

"You know, it's funny," Mom says. "You can look back at our history. People like Adolf Hitler, Joseph Stalin, even more recent as Osama bin Laden, Timothy McVeigh. Each of them knew exactly what they were doing. They were sociopathic, yes. Psychopathic, even. In fact, Aunt Mel says there's not a lot of difference between the two. But Aunt Jade says the insanity plea wouldn't have worked for any of them. So you have to ask yourself... What is *true* insanity? Is there even a valid definition? Aunt Jade and Aunt Melanie look at it two different ways—as an attorney and as a psychiatrist. Aunt Mel has studied these things, and so has Aunt Jade, from a completely different angle. But they both agree that an insanity plea would not work for Wendy Madigan."

"I'm not sure what you're trying to say," I say. "Is she insane or not?"

"My point is, Ava, that you may never get the answers you're looking for. Yes, she is insane, but so was Daphne Steel, in a completely different way. Wendy is not insane the way Daphne was. She's mentally competent, although deranged, and you can't trust anything she says."

"But you and Dad both say how brilliant she is. An evil mastermind. Which means logically she has a reason for everything she does."

"Yes, but remember that logic to *her* may not be logic to us. Psychopaths don't see things the same way we do. To her, it was logical to punish your grandfather by abusing his son. How is that even remotely logical to a normal person?"

I look down, fiddle with my fingers. My mother is right, of course.

"Take my father, for example. To him, it was perfectly logical to try to rape me. That's what he knew. How he lived his life. But normal fathers don't try to rape their daughters, Ava."

I wipe a tear from my eye before it falls. "For God's sake, Mom. I know that."

Mom pulls me into a hug. "Exactly. But my father would never have been able to use a plea of insanity in a trial for his crimes."

"So there's insanity . . . and there's *insanity*," I say.

"I suppose so." Mom sighs and lets me go. "I just don't want you looking for something in your grandmother that isn't there. She's not a good woman. She never was and never will be. The doctor says she's in perfect health, but she's nearing ninety. She will not live forever. Especially not without sunshine and exercise."

"I'm not asking her to live forever."

"I know you're not, Ava, but you *are* asking for her to tell you something. To tell you why she reached out to you. I just wouldn't hold your breath, sweetheart. The answers may not come."

"But Mom . . ."

She grabs my hand. "I'm thinking only of you, Ava. I don't want to see you doing this to yourself. This could take you to a dark place, and I've been to those dark places. I don't want that for you."

"I'll be careful, Mom."

"I know you will. That's not what I'm concerned about."

"It might help if . . ."

"If what?"

"If Dad lets me talk to her alone."

Mom shakes her head. "That will never happen."

"Why not? She's no threat to me. She's an old woman."

"Don't ask your father to leave you alone with her. He won't do it. Your father hates saying no to you, but he will."

I sigh. "All right."

"Now, before you go back in there—because I know I can't talk you out of not going back—tell me what's going on with you and Brendan."

"He's angry."

"Why?"

"Because he found out that Dale, Donny, and Brock arranged for him to be paid for the vandalism of his place."

"I see." Mom looks to the floor.

"You knew?"

She frowns. "I did. Joe finally leveled with Ryan and me about what's going on. They tried to keep it from Ryan because of his mother. He's not happy about that, of course."

"I can see why he wouldn't be. It's like they're treating him differently because he's only their half brother."

"That's exactly how he sees it. But I see it from both sides. They didn't want him to feel bad."

"But here she is anyway. His mother has come back from the dead."

"So it would seem." Mom's forehead wrinkles. "The timing is interesting, don't you think?"

"I suppose so."

Mom squeezes my hand. "Ava, this is why you need to be very cautious. Wendy is back now for a reason. She reached out to you for a reason."

"That's my point, Mom. I want to know *why*."

"Even if she does level with you, the reason may not be good. Like I said, you could end up in a dark place."

"That's not me, Mom. I'm not a dark person."

"I know you're not. Stay as you are. Stay my sweet and talented Ava. My Ava who has always marched to the beat of her own drummer."

I force a smile as I sniffle. "I'm not going anywhere."

I leave the kitchen then. I've had about as much of this conversation as I can take.

I miss Brendan. I love him so much, but he's right about one thing. I need to put this thing with my grandmother to bed before I can give my all to our relationship.

I walk back to the room where my grandmother is staying. I open the door. My father sits in a chair next to her. Neither Jemima nor Dr. Parks is in the room.

"She's asleep," Dad says.

I draw in a breath, gather strength. "All right. Then I'm waking her up."

CHAPTER NINETEEN

Brendan

Ten minutes later, I set up a meeting at Lauren's house with Dad, Ruby, and me.

After calling to tell Ruby what time to meet us there, I take a look at the documents I found in the floorboards by opening my copy of *The Adventures of Tom Sawyer*.

I'm still not sure why the Steels have a lien on everything we own. Dale and Donny did promise to get rid of the lien on the bar, and I trust they'll get it done.

I regard the birth certificate for William Elijah Steel, with no mother listed. Only the father, George Steel, father of Bradford Steel. Unreal.

What no longer seems unreal, of course, is the deed transferring all the Steel property to Ryan Steel.

This was Wendy Madigan's ace in the hole. A chance to get the Steel property given to her son only.

She can never know this deed still exists.

Not that Ryan would allow his siblings to go without anything. I can't imagine he would ever do that.

I walk out of the bar, leaving Johnny and Laney to get ready for the day. I walk the few blocks to my parents' house in the residential area. Dad is already outside waiting for me.

"What did you tell Mom?" I ask.

He shrugs. "Same thing I told her when we went for the blood tests. That I had some errands to run. She didn't ask a lot of questions. I'm always running errands, fixing stuff up around the house now that I'm retired."

"Good. Better not to invite a lot of questions."

"So Ruby's meeting us there?"

"Yeah."

The drive into Barrel Oaks takes a mere fifteen minutes, and Ruby Steel is already there in her car, waiting outside Lauren Wingdam's home.

She's dressed in jeans and a leather blazer, her brown hair pulled back in a high ponytail.

"Brendan, Sean," she says.

"Ruby." Dad clears his throat.

"You all ready?" I ask.

Ruby nods. "Yeah, Brendan. Thanks for putting this together."

"Does Ryan know you're here?" Dad asks.

"No, but I don't plan to keep this from him. He and Ava are busy with Wendy at the moment."

Of course they are.

We walk to the door and ring the doorbell.

Jack answers. "Hello, Brendan, Sean."

"Hi, Jack," I say. "This is Ruby Steel, Ava's mother. Ryan's wife."

"Nice to meet you, Ruby," Jack says. "Come on in, all of you. Mom arranged for Margaret to serve some tea."

"You didn't have to go to any trouble," Ruby says.

"It's no trouble. Besides, Mom likes to take tea in the afternoon." Jack leads us into the same living room where Dad and I met him and Lauren only days ago.

"How is your mom doing?" I ask.

"She's as perplexed as the rest of us about the DNA results."

"I can assure you," Ruby says, "that Tucker Madden is the best in the business. He and I have worked together for over thirty years."

"He sure was quick," Dad says.

"He was," Jack says. "The guy my physician referred me to will take a few more days."

"I'm sure you'll find that the results are the same," Ruby says. "And if you don't, then something's wrong on the other end. I trust Tucker implicitly."

"You guys go ahead and sit down," Jack says. "I'll get my mom."

Margaret comes in and serves our tea while Jack returns with Lauren.

Dad and I stand.

"Lauren," I say, "thank you for agreeing to see us. This is Ruby Steel. She's Ryan's wife."

Lauren shakes Ruby's hand. "It's good to meet you. I guess you're my sister-in-law."

"So it would seem. It's nice to meet you, too." Ruby stares at Lauren. "You have your mother's eyes, but I see the resemblance to Ryan."

Lauren takes a seat, stirs a tiny bit of sugar into her tea, and takes a sip. "What can I do to help all of you?"

"I was wondering if I might be able to have a look around your house," Ruby says.

Lauren holds back a gasp. "Whatever for?"

"Please don't take the request the wrong way." Ruby smiles. "I'm just looking for anything out of the ordinary.

Anything that might clue us in to what's going on here. What your mother has put into motion. And the relationship between Jack and the Murphys."

"I understand your curiosity, Mrs. Steel."

"Please, call me Ruby." She widens her smile. "We're sisters-in-law, after all."

"Very well, Ruby, but I can assure you that you won't find anything here in this house. My mother and I are currently . . . estranged."

Ruby nods. "I understand, and believe me, I don't blame you for being estranged from her. Right now, your mother is in my home, staying in one of our guest rooms."

Lauren's eyes widen. "What's she doing there?"

"My husband and my daughter have a lot of questions for her, and Ryan felt he could keep a better eye on her at home."

Lauren lifts her cup of tea but doesn't take a sip. "I'm not sure I see his point."

"To be honest, I'm not sure I do either, Lauren. But she *is* his mother. As well as yours."

"I don't want to see her."

"I'm not here to pressure you into doing that."

Lauren places her cup back on her saucer, forcefully enough that a few drops fly out. "But you *are* here to pressure me into letting you look around my house."

"No pressure," Ruby says. "But I would like the chance. I promise you I won't disturb anything, but my husband, and especially my daughter, are seeking answers, and they won't rest until they find them. I'd like to help them if I can."

"I have nothing to hide," Lauren says with a sigh.

"We know that," I say. "But Ruby—and my father and I—have a vested interest in finding out more about what your *mother's* been hiding all these years. The DNA results show that Jack and my father share paternal grandparents. It doesn't seem possible, but DNA doesn't lie. Jack can't have come from my father's sister, and we know he didn't come from my grandfather, or he'd be a sibling. My grandfather only had one brother."

"My uncle Sean," Dad says. "Unless there's another brother we never knew about, but it would have to be a full brother, not a half brother."

"My father has always been convinced that the Steel family had something to do with his uncle's death by lethal overdose sixty years ago. We haven't been able to find anything linking the Steels to his death, but he did die at Brad Steel's wedding, and he never did drugs, according to his brother and sister. Yet many drugs were found in his toxicology report."

"And you think my mother had something to do with your uncle's death," Lauren says.

"I always thought the Steels were behind it," Dad says, "but now that I know about your mother and her involvement with the Steels . . . "

"You won't find anything here," Lauren says abruptly.

"If I know your mother," Ruby says, "she probably has hidden things in plain sight. If you would just let me have a look around. You can certainly accompany me or have Jack accompany me."

"It's not that I don't trust you, Ruby," Lauren says. "It's not that at all. It's just . . . I'd really like to distance myself from my mother."

"Don't you want to meet your brother?" Ruby asks.

Lauren picks up her teacup once more. "Does he want to meet me? He never knew I existed."

"Yes, he does. Right now he's concerned about our daughter. Your mother reached out to her, and she's obsessing on why that is. Why didn't she reach out to Ryan himself, or to our other daughter? Why Ava?"

"I'd like to know that as well," I say.

"Who knows why my mother does anything?" Lauren takes a sip of tea.

"Has she told you anything about your father? Brad Steel's half brother?"

"No. Not much. I didn't even know who he was until fairly recently."

"And you never met him?"

Lauren shakes her head.

"We found a copy of his birth certificate," I say. "Under the floorboards of my apartment above the bar. The bar my dad bought from Jeremy Madigan, Wendy's uncle."

"And you think maybe Wendy hid some documents up there?"

I frown. "How else could they have gotten there? Unless Jeremy himself put them there. He's long gone, so we can't ask him."

"Just let me have a look around," Ruby says. "I'll try not to be long."

Lauren sighs. "That's fine. Go ahead."

Jack rises. "I'll go with her, Mom."

Lauren nods, and then I rise as well.

"Do you mind if we tag along?" I ask, gesturing to Dad.

"Not at all," Jack says.

Ruby, Dad, and I follow Jack out of the living room.

"Where do you want to start?" Jack asks.

Ruby glances around the home. It's a large ranch house,

not unlike the one Ruby lives in, though not as sprawling. The layout is similar, though. "Do you have a basement or an attic?" she asks.

"No attic," Jack says. "Just some crawl space. We do have a basement that's partially finished."

"Let's start there, in the part that's not finished," Ruby says.

"You got it." The door to the basement is off the kitchen, and we go down a long flight of stairs into a carpeted rec room with a big-screen TV and a pool table.

"You play pool?" I ask.

"Yeah, I love it."

"How come you never come into the bar in Snow Creek? The Steels play pool there all the time."

"Just never thought about heading over to the next town," Jack says. "Once we get all this behind us, sure, I'd love to come hang out at your bar. I mean... I *am* your uncle and all." He lets out a sound that I'm not sure is a laugh or a scoff. Perhaps a combination of both.

Jack leads us to the part of the basement that is unfinished, and Ruby scouts it out like the professional that she is, pulling back layers of fiberglass and then rubbing her hands together. "Yes, I should've worn gloves."

"I can get you a pair."

"Too late now. So far the walls are clean." She looks around. "Do you have any electrical outlets down here? Other than the wiring going to these lights?" She points at the fluorescent lighting on the ceiling.

"Not sure there is, actually," Jack says. "I never thought much about it."

Ruby scouts it out, looking everywhere, until we find

a pile of cardboard boxes in a secluded alcove behind the furnace and water heater. Jack and I help Ruby pull them all down. They're full of books, papers, toys. Junk mostly, until we get to the last one. Ruby pulls it away, and a plug pops out of an electric socket that was hidden by the pile of boxes.

"Bingo," she says. "Here's something you don't see every day." She opens up the cardboard box, and inside is what looks like a college dorm minifridge.

Jack frowns. "A refrigerator?"

"This isn't a refrigerator," Ruby says. "It's a freezer." She starts to pull it out of the box, but I take it from her, even though it's not that heavy. The cord hangs out from a hole in the cardboard. I hastily plug it back into the socket.

"What do you think is in here?" Ruby asks.

"Clueless," I say.

Ruby opens it.

Vials.

Small vials.

"What the hell is all that?" Jack asks.

"This," Ruby says, pulling out a vial and reading the name on it, "appears to be your father, Jack."

She hands the vial to me. Written in a black sharpie is *Sean Murphy*, and the date?

Over half a century ago.

Dad grabs the vial from me. "Let me see that." He drops his jaw.

"It can't be," I say.

"You've always said Sean Murphy is a pretty common Irish name," Jack says.

Dad is still staring at the vial, saying nothing. His eyes are wide and his jaw rigid.

"I have, and it is." I squint to read the small print on the vial. "But the date checks out. I think somehow she got my great-uncle's sperm."

Ruby pulls out some more vials from the refrigerator.

And then she gasps.

Nearly drops the vial.

"What is it?"

She doesn't say anything, simply hands it to me.

I drop my jaw.

Bradford Steel.

CHAPTER TWENTY

Ava

"Wake up," I say.

My grandmother doesn't move.

"For Christ's sake," I mutter. "Wake up, old woman."

Nothing.

I know what I must do.

I nudge her again, this time more gently. "Grandmother? Wake up. Please."

Her eyes flutter open.

So manipulative. So manipulative to get what she wants.

"Grandmother," I say, "please tell me. Why did you reach out to me?"

"Isn't that obvious, Ava?"

"Not to me it isn't."

"Well, you're my granddaughter, first and foremost."

"So is Gina."

She smiles. "Yes, but I knew you would understand me."

"How? How do you think I could understand everything you've done?"

"Because, Ava, you are your own person. Just as I am."

She can't possibly be saying that we're similar. "What the hell does that mean?"

"For God's sake, Wendy," Dad says. "Stop this. Just stop

doing this to her. She's an innocent young woman."

"Dad . . ."

"She's manipulating you, Ava. Can't you see it? All those years ago, she tried to do the same to me."

"You're my son, Ryan," Wendy says. "I will always love you, and I will always protect you. No matter how horribly you speak to me."

"Right." Dad lets out a sarcastic laugh. "You were trying to protect me that day when you were ready to put a bullet through me."

"We would be together. You, me, and your father."

"What about Lauren? What about my sister?"

"I love Lauren."

"Then why didn't you want to take her with us on that horrific path of death?"

"I had already made plans for Lauren at that time."

"What plans?"

A sly smile curves onto Wendy's lips. "You see, Ryan, I didn't think your father would actually die that day."

"He didn't," Dad says, "and neither did you."

"He would have," she says. "If you had died, your father would've died. I made sure of it."

"So you shot him in the chest instead of the head for a reason."

"Yes, I did."

"How can the two of you just sit here and talk about this?" I nearly scream. "Shooting people like it's some freaking normal thing. Tell me why you shot Uncle Talon. Tell me that, Grandmother."

She says nothing.

Which says a lot to me.

She doesn't deny it.

"I didn't actually pull that trigger," she finally says.

"I know that, but does that matter?" I say. "You certainly aren't denying having anything to do with it."

"The Steels need to go down," she says. "All the Steels, except for you, Ryan."

"That's still what this is about, isn't it?" Dad says. "You're still so obsessed with Bradford Steel that you want to take out all his children with Daphne. And of course you had to start with Talon. Talon is the one you truly hate more than any of us."

I have to force myself to stay seated, not to rise and shake this old woman. "Why would you hate Uncle Talon?"

"Because Talon cemented everything," Dad says. "It was easy to think Joe was just an accident, and that's why my father married Daphne. But once Talon came along..." He shakes his head. "You are made of ice, Wendy. Pure ice."

Wendy's eyes flutter closed, and she wrinkles her nose before reopening them. "How can you say that? I love you, Ryan. I would do anything for you."

"Right. Anything, including allowing my brother to be taken as a child, tortured, abused, violated in the worst way. And then, after he's happy, after he finds the love of his life, starts a wonderful life with a family of four children, two of whom he saved from the same horrible fate, then you try to take it away from him again."

"He's a military hero," I say. "He's been through so much, Grandmother. Why? Why would you do that?"

She reaches toward me with her wrinkled hand. "For you, my beautiful granddaughter. I do it all for you. Your grandfather was the love of my life. And I was the love of his."

Dad groans. "That's not true, Wendy. We all know it."

"So you, my sweet granddaughter, are the first granddaughter from our love."

"That can't be the only reason you reached out to me," I say.

"Because you're a woman, like I am."

"What about Lauren?" Dad asks.

"Unfortunately, Lauren feels the same way about me as you do, Ryan. Neither of my children seems to understand my love for them. What I've done for them."

"This is such garbage," Dad says.

I bite my lip, twist my lip ring. "There's something about what you said, Grandmother."

"And what's that?"

"You specified grand*daughter* when you spoke of me."

"You *are* my granddaughter."

"Yes, but you said *first* granddaughter."

"And again . . . you *are* my first granddaughter."

I lock gazes with Wendy's blue eyes, so like my own it's almost creepy. "Why would you say grand*daughter*? Why not say grandchild? I could've just as easily been a boy."

"But you aren't." She flutters her eyes closed.

I look at Dad, gesture for him to leave the room with me.

"What is it?" he says once we're outside the room.

"Do you see how she didn't answer me?"

"No."

"You've said she has a brilliant mind, Dad, and I believe you. But she's old, and she's been in a medically induced coma for months. Her mind isn't as sharp as she thinks it is. She made a misstep."

"What misstep?"

"She specifically said grand*daughter* instead of grandchild."

"And you think that means . . . "

"I think, Dad, that it means I'm *not* her first grandchild from your father. Only her first grand*daughter*."

"You mean . . . But Jack comes from my father's half brother."

"Yes, but knowing how Wendy's mind works, she only considers progeny from her liaison with your father to count."

"Are you saying . . . " He shakes his head. "Yes. Damn it. I should have seen this. I should have known."

I nod. "I'm beginning to think your father's so-called half brother may not exist at all."

CHAPTER TWENTY-ONE

Brendan

Ruby pulls more vials out of the small freezer.

"Tom Simpson," she says. "Larry Wade." Then she gulps. "Theodore Matthias."

"Who are they?" I ask.

"Wendy's minions," she says dryly.

Dad is still holding the vial of Sean Murphy and staring at it.

"You know, this is great and all," I say, "but storing sperm in a house?"

Ruby rubs her forehead. "Oh, the sperm isn't good. If it even *is* sperm. It's probably just some kind of decoy. For sperm to remain viable, it needs to be processed in a special lab in liquid nitrogen storage tanks."

"What about those mail-in sperm-freezing kits?" Dad finally says.

I drop my jaw, staring at him. "Mail-in sperm-freezing kits?"

"I read about them somewhere," he says.

"Yeah, some companies do that," Ruby says. "They send you a kit, which allows you to collect the"—she clears her throat—"*specimen* in the privacy of your own home and then mail it in for processing, and the company stores it for you in cryo-tanks."

"I see." Dad reddens a little.

"So," I say, "first of all, we need to find out if this is indeed sperm, which I doubt it is. If Wendy Madigan is as smart as you all seem to think she is, she knows very well that you can't store sperm at home. Not without specialized equipment, which I do not see here. This is a simple freezer."

"How can we find out?" Jack asks.

Ruby pulls out the rest of the samples. "I can contact Tucker, and he can thaw these and look at them. See if there's actual sperm there. But I can already tell you there isn't."

"Why would she keep fake sperm?" Jack shakes his head.

"For the same reason she does everything," Ruby says. "Manipulation. My guess is . . . This is so screwed up."

"What's your guess?" Jack asks.

"My guess is she *does* have sperm, and this is her way of letting us find out. And my guess is she has Sean Murphy's sperm"—she gestures to Jack—"and that he *is* your father."

Jack shakes his head. "But I'm thirty-one. He died sixty years ago."

"Not all sperm survives the freezing process," Ruby says. "But the sperm that dies usually does so within forty-eight hours of freezing. Sperm can be stored for as long as fifty years without additional deterioration beyond that caused by the original freezing process."

"You're saying . . . " My father shakes his head, rakes his fingers through his graying hair. "You're saying that my uncle, who died at Brad Steel's wedding, is actually the father of Jack here?"

"That's what this would suggest. Your DNA indicates that you share paternal grandparents. Which means your fathers are full-blooded brothers. So unless your father had another full brother that we don't know about, which I doubt..."

"I'll be dipped in shit," Dad says. "All this time... Here it was under my nose. Our connection to the Steels and my uncle."

"How the hell did she get your uncle's sperm?" I ask. "He was dead."

"I'm not sure you want to hear this," Ruby says, "but it *is* possible to extract sperm from a dying man or a recently dead body."

"God," Dad says. "What did she do? Stick a needle in my uncle's balls?"

"To put it crudely," Ruby says. "Depending on who did the extraction. You can also do it through a testicular biopsy or complete removal of the testicles."

"So she fucking castrated him?" Dad yells.

"Look, Sean," Ruby says. "None of us knows how she got the sperm. For all we know, he could've jacked off into a cup some time before he collapsed at Brad Steel's wedding. With Wendy Madigan, anything is possible."

I gulp down nausea. "I suppose it would've been easier for her to convince him to jack off in a cup than for her to sneak into the hospital and extract sperm from his comatose body."

"Exactly," Ruby says.

"And apparently she got the same thing from Brad Steel."

"Actually..." She grabs her phone out of the back pocket of her jeans. "I need to talk to Ryan."

"You need to talk to *us*, Ruby," Dad says. "I've waited this long to figure out what the hell happened to my uncle. I want to know all your secrets now."

"My father, Theodore Matthias, is one of these men. And I think..." Color drains from Ruby's face. "I think they may have submitted their sperm knowingly."

"What the hell makes you think that?"

"Sixty years ago, this was a new technology. And knowing Wendy Madigan, she wanted to get in on it. You see, the future lawmakers club was all about money, about profit. About all of them getting rich. And this was something new. In fact… I'd bet they gave their samples while they were still in high school."

"Nope, that doesn't fly," Dad says. "My uncle didn't know them in high school. He and Brad met in college."

"Right," Ruby says. "Which was right after high school. And Brad Steel was still funding the future lawmakers club at that time."

"God, so he talked Uncle Sean into…" I shake my head.

"I said it's only a theory. But I'm a detective. I know how the criminal mind works. And, unfortunately, I know Wendy Madigan."

I pull my phone out, do a quick search.

"The timing doesn't quite add up. This source says that sperm freezing dates back to eighteenth-century Italy."

"Sure," Ruby says. "Everything starts way before it actually starts."

I check a new source. "All right, the first sperm banks began as early as nineteen sixty-four… So maybe the timing does add up."

"Exactly," Ruby says. "Those were only the *first* sperm banks, when it wasn't common." She shakes her head. "I'll be fucking damned."

"At least my uncle lives on," Dad says. "Through you, Jack."

"Why would my grandmother use your uncle's sperm to fertilize my mother?" Jack shakes his head. "It doesn't make sense to me."

"It doesn't make sense to me either," Ruby says. "There's something I'm not seeing here."

"I'm just glad you're here, son," Dad says to Jack. "I mean, I guess you're my cousin, not my nephew. But with you being the same age as Brendan here, well, it feels like I got part of my uncle back in a new nephew."

"Why are you so interested in what happened to your uncle?" Ruby says. "You must've been just a kid when he died."

"I was," Dad says. "But I was named after him, and he and I had a kind of special relationship."

Ruby simply nods. "I don't know that there's any point in searching anymore. I doubt that your grandmother has a cryogenic facility hidden somewhere in this house. Which means..."

"She *wanted* us to find this," I say. "It's a plant."

"Bingo," Ruby says. "And we need to figure out *why*."

CHAPTER TWENTY-TWO

Ava

"Do you think I could be right?" I ask Dad. "Why would she make up a half brother?"

"I wish I could tell you why my mother does what she does," Dad says. "But I can't, and I'm damned glad of that. If my mind worked the way hers did, I'd be pretty worried."

"And that's why you're worried about me."

Dad nods. "Ava, she's not a good person. If there is such a thing as pure evil in the world, my mother personifies it. I understand that you want to know why she reached out to you. But I'm concerned. You tend to see the good in everything, Ava. That's something wonderful about you. But don't try to find the good in your grandmother. It doesn't exist."

I swallow. "I'm hearing you. I know you think that I'm not, but I *am* hearing you, Dad."

He pulls me into a hug. "I'm glad. Because Ava, you and your sister mean everything to your mother and me. Don't let her into your head. I get it. It's difficult. She can be very... persuasive. Very charismatic."

"Until she admits some of the horrific acts she's done."

"Exactly." Dad kisses the top of my head and then lets me go. "I don't know about you, but I need a break from Wendy."

"Sure. You want me to make you some lunch?"

"Michaela can make our lunch. It will just be you and me today."

"Where's Mom?"

"She said she had some errands to run."

I nod. "Where's her head in all of this?"

"The same as mine. It brings back a lot of sour history for us, but she's okay. Your mother is the strongest woman I know."

"Yeah, she is strong." I cross my arms. "She's so different from me."

Dad cups my cheek. "Never doubt your strength, Ava. You *are* as strong as your mother, just in a different way. No one expected you and your sister to be carbon copies of your mother or of me."

"I know that." I regard my father's handsome face, his dark hair, his milk-chocolate brown eyes. "But Gina looks exactly like you. And I always thought I had Mom's eyes, until ... "

"They are a lot like Wendy's," he says. "That doesn't have to mean anything."

"Was she beautiful?"

"She was. In a totally different way from Daphne. But from the photos I've seen, yes, Wendy was very beautiful. She would have to have been to catch my father's eye."

We head to the kitchen, where Michaela is already working on lunch.

"Hey," Michaela says. "I figured you two would be out for lunch pretty soon. How do Cuban sandwiches sound?"

"Sounds great to me," Dad says. "Ava?"

I nod. "Anything you make will be perfection, Michaela."

"Thank you, Miss Ava."

I've told Michaela time and again to simply call me Ava, but all the household help in my family uses the formal honorifics. Dad says it's the way it was when he was a kid, and it just sounds right to him. Apparently his brothers and sister feel the same way.

If I ever have a house and family of my own, and enough money to afford household help, they will simply call me Ava.

I sigh.

I fear my chance for a house and family of my own ended when Brendan and I . . .

What did we do, exactly? Are we on a break? Are we split for good?

I don't know, and right now I need to compartmentalize. I'm not good at compartmentalizing, but I need to get good at it. I must figure out this whole Wendy Madigan thing and what it has to do with me.

Is Dad right? Is William Elijah Steel an illusion?

Dad and I take seats at the table, and Michaela brings us glasses of ice water.

"Would you like to have anything else to drink?" she asks.

Dad shakes his head. "I promised Dale I'd go over to the winery this afternoon and taste some of the barrels. But Ava, I don't want to leave you here alone."

"Mom will probably be back soon," I say.

"Probably, but I want you to promise me something."

"What?"

"Promise me that you will *not* go in that room and you will *not* try to talk to your grandmother without me present."

"Dad, I can handle an old woman."

"Ava, I have the utmost confidence in you, but Wendy Madigan is not simply an old woman. She's your grandmother, and she's a criminal. Please. Humor me."

I resist rolling my eyes. "All right, Dad. I promise. I have to go back into town this afternoon anyway and meet with the contractor for the bakery."

"Good. Can I assume I'll see you back here tomorrow?"

"Absolutely. First thing in the morning."

Michaela brings us our lunch, and I inhale the savory aroma of the cheese, ham, and toasty bread of the Cuban sandwich. I pick up half, take a bite, and then wince as the hot cheese burns the roof of my mouth. I take a sip of water.

Again, I've singed the skin off the roof of my mouth. I do it every time with a Cuban or grilled cheese sandwich because I can't wait to get to the melted deliciousness.

It's something I put up with.

Even though I know it hurts.

Kind of a metaphor for my life right now.

CHAPTER TWENTY-THREE

Brendan

Back at my place, I stare at the documents recovered from my floorboards.

The Steels. It all comes back to the Steels.

If I were a secret cryo facility, where would I be?

And why...

Why would Wendy Madigan want my great-uncle's sperm? Why would she use it to fertilize her daughter?

It's not like the Murphys have money like the Steels. What would be the point?

What am I missing?

I have no doubt that Ruby could use her detective skills and figure this out, but her loyalty will always be to the Steel family. To her husband and her daughters. I don't fault her for that.

Hell, my loyalty is to her daughter.

But I also have loyalty to my father. And now... Jack. And as much as I've tried to get my father to give up on his quest over the years, now I understand more than ever. I want to know what happened to my great-uncle, what it has to do with the Steels and with Wendy Madigan, and why he fathered a son twenty years after his death.

Is there a reason?

Or is Wendy Madigan just batshit crazy?

My guess is that it's a little of both.

I pick up my phone and call the city administration building.

"Snow Creek admin. May I help you?"

"Donny Steel, please."

"Just a minute. I'll see if he's in. May I ask who's calling?"

"This is Brendan Murphy."

"Hold on."

Pause.

"Mr. Steel will be with you in a minute."

Pause.

"Hey, Brendan."

"Hey. I'm sitting here looking at these documents. I want to make sure that you remove the lien from my property as you promised."

"Right. I've been working on that."

"Any problems?"

"Only one, but it's a big one."

"I should've known. What is it?"

"Well ... the lien isn't technically held by my family. It's held by something called the Steel Trust, which of course Dale and I assumed was one of our family's assets. But ... I can't seem to find any record of it."

"For God's sake."

"Believe me, Brendan, I want to resolve this as much as you do. Our family does have trusts, but nothing specially called the Steel Trust. This Steel Trust has a lot of transactions with something called the Fleming Corporation, which Brock came across recently. But no one knows what either of those entities are. Seems my grandfather died with a lot of secrets."

"Wendy Madigan is still alive," I say. "She probably knows a lot of those secrets."

"Probably. But Uncle Ryan has asked that we all leave her alone."

"Bullshit."

"She's his mother," Donny says.

"I get that. She's also Lauren Wingdam's mother. I'm going to get to the bottom of this."

I end the call quickly, and then I go downstairs and hop into my truck. I'm paying Wendy Madigan a visit.

★ ★ ★

I pull into the Steels' driveway. Hmm... Ava's truck isn't here. It wasn't behind the bakery when I left. Is it possible we drove past each other without noticing?

Probably not.

I knock on the door.

The housekeeper, Michaela, answers. "Mr. Murphy, what can I do for you?"

"I'm here to see your houseguest."

"I'm afraid you just missed Ava. She's not here."

"I'm not talking about Ava, Michaela. I'm here to see Wendy Madigan."

"Oh, I see." Michaela shifts her gaze around. "You'll have to talk to Mr. Steel about that."

"Talk to Mr. Steel about what?" Ryan approaches from the kitchen.

I step inside the house. "Good afternoon, Ryan. I need to speak to your mother."

"Whatever for?"

"I'm sure your wife clued you in."

"My wife? Ruby went on errands today, and she hasn't returned."

"Did she happen to tell you what those errands were?"

"No."

"She was with my father and me. We were at your sister's home doing a search."

Ryan's eyebrows rise. "A search?"

"Yes, and I think you'll be interested in what we found."

Ryan blinks. "I am. Come on in."

I follow Ryan into the kitchen.

"Have a seat. I just need to text Dale and tell him I'll be late for our meeting at the winery. Have you eaten?"

"No. Not since breakfast."

"Michaela, can you make Brendan a Cuban sandwich?"

"No, thank you."

"Have it your way. Now tell me, what exactly were you doing with my wife this morning?"

I quickly spill the details of what we found.

Ryan's eyebrows rise several times, but he doesn't gasp or show any other indication of surprise.

"You don't seem overly shocked," I say.

"I learned a long time ago never to be shocked where my mother is concerned. I was surprised enough, and freaked out, as you know, when she turned out to be alive. Shocked enough that I ended up at the hospital. That's over. I won't allow her to affect me physically again."

"For the life of me," I say, "I can't figure out why she impregnated her daughter with my great-uncle's sperm, but our DNA results indicate that's the case."

"These sperm samples you found in Lauren's basement, I

assume that's what you want to ask her about?"

"Ruby explained that they may not even be sperm, and if they are, they certainly aren't viable because they weren't frozen correctly. What Ruby thinks, and I agree, is that they're decoys. We were *meant* to find them. And that somewhere, she has sperm from your father, my great-uncle, and Ruby's father as well."

"I see . . ."

"Where's Ava, by the way?"

"She went home. Said she had to meet one of the contractors for the remodeling of the bakery."

"It's just as well that she's not here. I want some answers from your mother, Ryan. And I don't want Ava involved."

"I'm afraid Ava is already involved," Ryan says. "My mother has made sure of that, and I'm not sure why. But we have a theory."

"You and Ruby with your theories. What's the newest?"

"Ava and I think there may be a reason why there's no mother listed on that birth certificate for William Elijah Steel."

"Oh?"

"Yes. We're not sure he ever existed. He may be Wendy's invention."

"Oh God . . ."

"And now . . . Now that you've mentioned the fact that Wendy may have my father's sperm somewhere . . ."

"My God. You think Lauren may be the daughter of *your* father?"

Ryan draws in a breath, rubs his forehead. "Yes. I believe she may be my full sister."

"And if that's the case, Pat Lamone . . ."

"Is a full-blooded Steel. Yes."

"Did you ever have a DNA test done with Pat?"

"No. We didn't care. Three generations down from a half-sibling wouldn't be conclusive. But I think it may be time to have Pat submit his DNA. Lauren too."

"Here's a question, though," I say. "Lauren is younger than you."

"Yes, by a couple of years, as I understand it."

"Do you think *you're* the product of artificial insemination?"

Ryan shakes his head. "No. My father admitted to sleeping with Wendy. But only once."

"If she had his sperm, why didn't she just inseminate herself? Why sleep with him?"

"Because of her obsession," Ryan says. "She thought they were soul mates. She never could accept that he chose Daphne over her."

The door clicks open, and Ruby arrives.

"Oh, Brendan. What are you doing here?"

"I have a question for you, Ruby," Ryan says. "Where the hell have you been?"

Ruby sighs. "I wasn't going to keep any of this from you, Ryan. But I had to check things out. I went to see Tucker."

"The lab tech," I say.

"Right. I assume Brendan has already told you what we found today."

"Yes, and I have a theory of my own. I think Lauren Wingdam may be my full sister. I don't think William Elijah Steel ever existed."

"Why do you say that?"

"Ava figured it out, actually, and I know my mother. I know how her mind works . . . at least sort of. She referred to

Ava as her first granddaughter from my father."

"Ava *is* her first granddaughter."

"Yes, but she specifically said grand*daughter*. Not grand*child*."

"Because she's *not* her first grandchild. Jack is."

"Exactly. Think about how my mother's mind works. She specified that Ava was the first granddaughter from Brad Steel. Jack, though he is technically her grandson, didn't come from Brad Steel. At least, we thought he didn't."

"So you're saying…"

"I'm saying she wouldn't have specified grand*daughter* unless Jack *also* came from Bradford Steel."

"That's a little out there, Ryan," Ruby says.

I'm glad Ruby said it, because I agree with her.

Ryan holds up a hand. "But it makes perfect sense with regard to my mother and her obsession with my father. I mean, why is there no mother on William Steel's birth certificate? Everyone knows who the mother is. That's where the baby comes from."

"If you think Wendy forged the birth certificate," I say, "why didn't she just forge the name of a mother?"

"My grandfather was a lot of things," Ryan says thoughtfully. "I don't know a lot about him, only the few things my father told me. He tended to take a blind eye to ethics, which is why my father taught my brothers and me to be ethical. Even though he himself turned out to break his own rules. My grandfather wasn't very nice to his wife, Mazie Bradford Steel. Mazie was in an accident after Dad was born, and she couldn't bear George any more children."

"All the more reason why he may have looked elsewhere to have another child," I say.

Ryan shakes his head. "I don't think so. He may well have had affairs, but I feel that my father was his only child. Otherwise, why wouldn't he have made arrangements for another? Another child of his body?"

"I don't know," I say. "I didn't know the man."

"I didn't know him either. But I *did* know my grandmother. And if George Steel had had another child, I'm almost certain he would've rubbed her nose in it."

"So you think William Elijah Steel is Wendy's invention?" I say.

"That's my working theory," Ryan says. "But I need to talk to my brother."

"Talon?" I ask.

Ryan shakes his head. "No. Jonah. He's the only one who knew that our grandfather had a half brother. He didn't tell us, and I never quite understood why. Now I really want to know. Joe may know something else that he hasn't told us."

"Don't keep Ava in the dark about this," I say. "Whatever you talk to your brother about, please let her in."

"I have every intention of taking Ava with me," Ryan says. "My mother wants her involved. For what reason, I have no idea. But I won't leave her out. She knows everything now anyway."

"I agree," Ruby says. "And I'll be going with you to talk to Joe as well. Melanie is my best friend."

"All right," I say. "Now . . . I need to talk to Wendy."

"She doesn't know who you are," Ryan says.

"She reached out to Ava. And she reached out to my family. She knows."

"I agree," Ruby says. "She kept your great-uncle's sperm for some reason. My theory on that is that the future lawmakers

156

all those years ago might've seen some money in cryotherapy and sperm freezing."

Ryan nods.

"It was fairly new at that time. That would make sense. But of course, there was much more money in human trafficking." Ruby shakes her head. "It's just all too much."

"Come on." Ryan rises. "Let's go, Brendan. Time for you to meet my mother."

CHAPTER TWENTY-FOUR

Ava

The contractor canceled, so I find myself pacing around my apartment, thinking.

My gaze falls on my tarot deck.

The wheel of fortune card.

What is my destiny?

Does it lie with Brendan? In my bakery? With my family?

Or is there even such a thing as destiny?

Perhaps I make my *own* destiny.

In which case... What the fuck does the card tell me then?

The fact that all three cards are in the major arcana is in itself odd. Those cards tend to show up when something is pulling a person toward something.

I can't deny that I feel pulled toward Wendy Madigan.

It frightens my father. This whole thing has frightened him, but not because he's frightened of his mother.

He's frightened about what this may mean for his family.

The gold bracelets from my grandmother clink against my wrist.

And I feel very strongly...

I feel very strongly that they have some kind of significance.

I take the bracelets off, set them each in front of the tarot spread that still sits on my table.

Three cards. Three bracelets.

Three golden rings.

Rings symbolize commitment. Eternity.

Then I pull out my grandfather's future lawmakers ring.

Gold, like my bracelets.

I pick up my bracelets one by one, look at them.

On the inside, something is etched. Probably 14k or 10k for gold. Mom did say they were real gold, though not worth much. They're lightweight, so that's probably what she meant.

I run my fingers on the inside of them, and I feel . . .

I feel something else etched on the inside.

I take a look, but whatever it is isn't visible to my naked eye. I need a magnifier of some sort. Maybe a jeweler's loupe, but I don't have one.

We don't have a jewelry shop here in town, but Lucy at the antique shop probably has a loupe.

I leave the apartment and head to the antique shop.

"Ava!" Lucy looks up from a magazine. "Such a slow day today. It's good to see you."

"Hi, Lucy."

"Are you looking for anything special?"

"I actually was wondering if you had a jeweler's loupe I could borrow," I say.

"Sure." She pulls a loupe out of the drawer and hands it to me.

"Thanks, Lucy."

First I take my grandfather's ring out, take a look at the ridiculous symbol that Wendy Madigan created. Creative as well as evil. A painter, she said. Taking credit for Gina's artwork.

Then I see the GPS coordinates etched inside along with my grandfather's name. Bradford Steel.

Time to take a look at the bracelets. I grab one, view the etchings.

Turns out they're just scratches. Nothing.

Then the next one.

The same. Simple scratches.

The third one then.

And I nearly drop the bracelet.

Clear as day, there are initials.

WM.

This doesn't make any sense. These came from my mother's mother, not Wendy Madigan.

Must be some bizarre coincidence.

Yet I don't think it's a coincidence at all.

I place the loupe back on the counter. "Thank you, Lucy."

"Sure, Ava. Anytime. I sure miss your croissants in the morning."

"We'll be back open soon." I leave without saying goodbye and walk across the street to the tattoo shop.

"Hi, Kiki. Does Cy have any open appointments today?"

"He's free right now."

"Good. Book me."

Cyrus comes out front. "Ava? I thought I heard your voice."

"Kiki says you're available."

"I am."

"Remember that design you created for me? Ink me. Now."

"Are you sure, Ava? Last Friday you seemed to really want to think about it."

"I have. I want the tattoo, Cyrus."

"All right. You decided on the triquetra in black with the yellow lightning bolt cutting through it, right?"

"That's the one."

"All right, Ava. Come on back."

I follow Cyrus back to his studio, where a seat resembling a dental chair beckons.

He flattens it out. "You said you wanted it on your hip, right?"

"Yes."

"Right hip or left hip?"

"I don't care. Pick one."

He shakes his head. "That isn't how this works, Ava. You need to know where you want the image, and yes, right or left matters."

"It doesn't matter to me."

"It matters to me." He cocks his head, twisting his lips. "I don't think it's the best idea for you to get the tattoo today."

"I'll pay you double."

This time he laughs, shaking his head. "Who are you, and what have you done with Ava Steel?"

"What's that supposed to mean?"

"I might expect to hear those words from Donny. Or Brock. Maybe even your sister. But from you?" Cyrus shakes his head. "You have never been one to throw Steel money around."

"It's not Steel money. I have my own damned money, Cy."

"All right, Ava. You don't have to pay double, but you are going to have to choose which hip you want your tattoo on."

I look down. I'm wearing baggy jeans. Which hip is more meaningful? Hell, I don't know.

"I'm right-handed," I say, "so let's put it on my right hip."

"Good enough." He shuffles some papers. "I just need you to sign a few things."

"Sign a few things?"

"Yeah. That you're going to pay for the tattoo. You do know how much tattoos cost, don't you?"

"Honestly, I don't have a clue."

"My tats start at five hundred," he says.

I drop my jaw. "Dollars?"

"Five hundred potatoes, Ava." He scoffs jovially. "Of course dollars."

He's trying to be funny, but I don't see the humor. I'm putting all my savings into the remodel of the bakery, and I don't have five hundred dollars lying around.

"Can I make payments?" I ask.

"I don't have a payment plan," Cyrus says, "but you can put it on a credit card and make your own payments."

I pull out my Visa. "Sure, that's what I'll do."

Cyrus smirks. "You're something, Ava."

"Why is that?"

"Because everyone knows you have a healthy trust fund. You could easily take five hundred dollars out. Hell, you could easily take five grand out, but you don't do it."

I shrug. "That's not who I am."

"I know that. You know what I'm going to do?"

"What's that."

"I'm going to give you a discount."

I shake my head. "You don't have to do that, Cy. I was just a little taken aback by the prices. I didn't realize tattooing was so expensive."

"It's expensive if you want it done right," he says. "And I do it right. You've seen my work."

"Indeed I have."

I've seen it on Brendan, and Cy's work is phenomenal. Plus, of course, I've seen the pictures in his books. But none of them holds a candle to Brendan's sea warrior.

"I don't want any special treatment, Cy."

"I know that," he says. "Which is why I don't have any trouble giving you a deal. Four hundred for the tattoo that you want, Ava."

I shouldn't take money out of Cy's pocket. He's a simple working man, trying to make a living in Snow Creek, and I have a ton of money at my disposal. Just because I choose not to use it is no reason for Cy to take a hit.

"I'm paying full price." I set my credit card down. "I won't hear another word about it."

He chuckles. "Full price it is, then."

He waves to Kiki and hands her my credit card. "Take a seat. You're going to have to unbuckle your jeans and move them down about halfway, about where a low bikini would hit."

My cheeks warm for a moment, but Cy goes about his business. He's probably seen a lot more than just a client's bikini line.

I follow his instructions, unbuttoning my jeans and moving them down to where he needs them, focusing on my right hip.

"I've got to warn you, Ava. This won't be pleasant."

"I can take it."

The whir of his tattoo gun begins, and I close my eyes.

I don't even jolt when the needle hits my skin.

The pain is good. Good in a strange way.

As if it's what I deserve.

CHAPTER TWENTY-FIVE

Brendan

At first glance, Ava's grandmother looks completely harmless. She's an old woman. An old woman whose eyes are closed and who's hooked up to a heart monitor and pulse ox machine.

A nurse in light-blue scrubs sits with her.

"How is she, Jemima?" Ryan asks.

"She's fine, Mr. Steel. No changes." She glances at me.

"I'm Brendan."

"Brendan is Ava's friend," Ryan says. "He wants to talk to Wendy."

It doesn't escape my notice that Ryan refers to her as Wendy and not as his mother.

"I'll give you some privacy." Jemima rises and leaves the room. "Oh, by the way, Dr. Parks has a family event tonight, but she'll be back first thing in the morning."

Ryan nods. "Very well, then."

The nurse leaves the room, closing the door behind her.

"Can she hear me?"

"She hears what she wants to hear."

Wendy's eyelids flutter then.

I see what he means.

"Wendy," Ryan says, "Brendan Murphy is here. He's Ava's . . . friend."

Ryan hesitates a bit. Has Ava told him we had an argument? I don't know. I'll work things out with Ava later. For now, I need to find out what this woman knows about my great-uncle.

"Good afternoon, Ms. Madigan," I say.

No response, but she still flutters her eyes.

"Wendy," Ryan says, "Brendan's here to talk about your grandson, Jack. Apparently they're cousins."

Wendy smiles then, and her eyes flutter open. "So you found out my secret."

"Not really," I say. "It's nice to meet you, though."

She looks at me, her eyes moving without her head moving. "You look a lot like your father. But you're a dead ringer for your great-uncle."

"Am I?"

I know the truth of her words. I've seen pictures of Sean Murphy. I'm older now than he was when he died, but I do look quite a bit like him, except he wore his hair short, of course.

"Ms. Madigan—"

"Please, call me Wendy."

"All right. Wendy. My father, Sean's nephew, has tried very hard to unravel the mystery behind his death at Brad Steel's wedding."

"That *was* a shame, wasn't it?"

"Yes. My grandfather was Sean's older brother. My father's named after him."

"Yes, I'm well aware of who your father is, Brendan. Now tell me about you and my Ava."

Her Ava? I look to Ryan, who simply shakes his head, clearly resisting an eye roll.

"Ava and I are . . . good friends."

"Good friends? Or are you lovers?"

Her word takes me aback. What kind of grandmother uses that kind of language when talking about her granddaughter?

"Good friends," I say. "Perhaps something more, but that's not what I came here to talk to you about."

"That's what *I* want to talk about."

"Listen," I say, "Jack and I were at your daughter's house, and we found the freezer that you hid in her basement."

Wendy's lips move slightly, but she says nothing.

"We're taking the vials in for lab testing," I say, "but we figure they're probably decoys, Wendy."

"Oh, they're not decoys."

"Whether they are or not is of no consequence. If they *are* frozen sperm, they're not viable. They weren't frozen correctly."

"Oh, they're viable."

I look to Ryan again, and he shakes his head again. The woman is clearly delusional.

"What I want to know"—I grit my teeth—"is why you saved my great-uncle's sperm?"

"And why I used it to impregnate my daughter?" she says.

I stop my jaw from dropping. "Yes. I'd like to know why."

A smile cracks her lips. "Your great-uncle was a prime specimen. Like I said, you look just like him. Don't you think it's a good thing to keep prime lines going?"

"Okay . . . "

What is wrong with this woman? I have no idea what she's getting at.

"I can only tell you this, Brendan," she says. "Ava is the key."

"The key to what?" I ask.

"The key to everything." Then her eyes flutter shut.

Ava? I look again to Ryan, who shrugs. Then he gestures me quietly to leave the room.

Once we're outside the door, he takes me aside. "She seems to think there's something about Ava."

"Ava *is* your child, isn't she?"

"What the *hell* kind of question is that?"

"I mean, she doesn't look like you, not the way Gina does."

"No. She looks like her mother. I trust Ruby. I watched Ava come out of Ruby, and I know Ruby was only with me. She got pregnant with Ava soon after our marriage. Besides, I know my mother. Ava wouldn't be the *key* to anything if she didn't come from me."

"What the hell does your mother mean? The key?"

"You got me."

"Ava is different," I say. "She always has been."

"She has been, but how could Wendy have even known that?"

"Well, you thought Wendy was dead, but she wasn't. She changed her identity. Who's to say she wasn't watching Ava all this time?"

"You know as well as I do that we have excellent security."

"Yes. Excellent security. So excellent that Brittany Sheraton got a message to Donny by putting something in his medicine cabinet in his room."

"That was—"

But I keep speaking. "So excellent that a human trafficking cartel was operating on your property without your knowledge, and someone left that information for you."

He clenches his fists. "You're treading on thin ice, Brendan. Brittany Sheraton left the information. And Doc."

"Are you sure about that?"

Ryan runs both his hands through his hair and sighs. "I'm not sure about anything anymore, Brendan."

"Me neither." I sigh. "We need to figure it out. We need to figure it out for Ava."

"I agree with you. My mother seems to have some kind of hold over her. I'm not sure how or why, but it has to end."

"She's an old woman. She can't live forever, can she?"

"You heard the nurse. She's in good health. She could easily live another decade. Besides . . . " He grits his teeth. "The Steels are a lot of things, but we're not murderers."

I nod.

"What happened with you and Ava?"

"Nothing we won't work out. She and I both have different things to focus on right now. I'm helping my father figure out this whole thing with the original Sean Murphy, and she wants to find out why your mother reached out to her."

"Those two things don't necessarily have to be at cross-purposes," Ryan says.

I regard him. He's being serious. I certainly do see the connection. "All right. I'll reach out to Ava. I hope we can work things out, Ryan. I'm in love with her."

Ryan offers a worn smile. "I know you are, son. And she couldn't do any better than you."

Ruby walks toward us quickly then. "Good, you're no longer in there. I need to talk to you about something."

"What's that, babe?" Ryan asks.

"Something that just occurred to me. Something that may be related. I can't believe I didn't see it before."

CHAPTER TWENTY-SIX

Ava

My tattoo is covered in a clear plastic bandage so I can see the beauty of it.

I feel strengthened by it, more like myself than I have in a while.

By inking my skin, I found myself. I gained strength.

The bracelets still clink on my right wrist, and now I wonder... Where did they truly come from?

Perhaps Grandmother Didi bought them at an antique place. Perhaps they weren't hers to begin with, so they have someone else's initials. After all, WM aren't necessarily odd initials. QX would be odd. But not WM.

I head back into the antique shop where Lucy is still sitting.

"Hey, Ava, twice in one day?"

"Yeah. Could you have a look at these bracelets?" I pull them off my wrist and hand them to her. "Are they vintage?"

Lucy takes the loupe, which is still sitting there on the counter where I left it, and puts it to her eye to examine the bracelets.

"I'd say these are about thirty to fifty years old. Nothing antique."

"I see."

That doesn't really help me at all since both my grandmothers are around the same age. Either could've gotten them around the same time.

"Is there anything on them that could tell you where they were made? A marking or anything?"

"No, I don't see any kind of jeweler's marking." She holds up the third bracelet. "Other than this WM. I don't know of any jeweler that uses that particular marking. Not from when these were made, anyway."

"All right. That's interesting." I take the bracelets and put them back on my wrist. "Thanks again, Lucy."

"Anytime. See you around, Ava."

I head back to my place, making a stop at the pharmacy where I pick up a tube of ointment that Cyrus recommended for caring for my tattoo as it heals.

As I'm leaving, I run into Brock.

I so don't need to deal with him right now.

"Ava," he says. "What's this about the bakery closing down?"

"I'm allowed to take some time off, Brock."

"Yeah." He cocks his head to the side. "Of course you are. Except that you don't."

I brush past him and outside the pharmacy. "See you later."

But he follows me, of course. I knew he would. No one brushes off Brock Steel.

"What are you doing down here on a weekday anyway?" I ask.

"Just some paperwork for Rory's holiday concert. You'll be there, right?"

"Yes, of course. I wouldn't miss it."

"Good, because we have a special guest coming."

"Oh? Who?"

"We're keeping it under wraps. But believe me, you don't want to miss it."

Normally I would press Brock for details, but my mind is elsewhere right now.

"You want to stop in the bar for a drink?"

"No, thank you." I don't want to see Brendan, and Brendan will be at the bar.

"If it makes a difference, Brendan's not there."

I pop my eyes open. "What?"

"Yeah, apparently he's taking a few days off. Doing something with his dad. He's got Johnny and Laney working double shifts, and he brought in temps."

"Why would he take time off during the same time I'm taking time off?"

"Hell if I know. It's weirder that you don't know. Can I tempt you with a libation now?"

"Yeah, sure." I grab Brock's arm. "Let's go have that drink."

It's early yet, just after four, so the bar isn't overly busy. I order a mineral water while Brock has a bourbon.

"Where's Rory?"

"She's back at the cinema, working with Jesse on the sound and lighting for the concert."

"Boy, I guess that's only a week away, isn't it?"

"Yeah, I had to pull some strings. Jenny at the cinema wanted to start her holiday film fest on that day, but I talked her out of it."

"Using your usual charm."

"If you say so, cuz."

"I'm wondering..." I fiddle with my bracelets. "What

haven't you told me about the stuff happening on our property?"

Brock shifts his gaze to the wooden bar. "I've told you pretty much everything. I mean, you know *everything* now, right?"

"I know about my father. About his biological mother. About Pat Lamone. About ... everything."

"Lamone's an ass."

"I agree with you, but I found out something about his birth that's kind of sad."

"What's that?"

"He's the product of rape. Lauren Wingdam was raped by three men and left pregnant."

Brock widens his eyes. "Wow. I guess that explains why she couldn't keep him."

"Right. But what it doesn't explain is why the couple who adopted him changed their name and his."

"More to figure out." Brock sighs. "I swear to God, growing up, I had no idea we had this many skeletons in our closet."

"Neither did I. All our parents were determined to give us idyllic childhoods."

Brock takes a sip of bourbon. "Tell you what, Ava. I'm taking some time off myself this week, helping Rory and Jesse get ready for the concert. Let me help you."

I take a sip of my mineral water. "With what?"

"With all the shit that's going down. Rory doesn't need me underfoot, and I—"

"I want to talk to your father," I say.

"Why?"

"I just do."

"Good enough." Brock pulls out his phone, sends a quick text.

"I just told him we'll be there tonight. After dinner."

"Good. I can't eat anyway."

"I can. Rory and I are heading over to Lorenzo's with Jesse, and you're coming along."

"I don't—"

"You need a break. Rory knows what's going on, but Jesse's still in the dark, so we won't be talking about any of this at dinner."

"Brock," I say, "that sounds like a freaking dream come true."

CHAPTER TWENTY-SEVEN

Brendan

Ruby walks toward us quickly then. "Good, you're no longer in there. I need to talk to you about something."

"What's that, babe?" Ryan asks.

"Something that just occurred to me. Something that may be related. I can't believe I didn't see it before."

My phone buzzes.

It's Dad.

"I've got news. Come home right away."

I want to stay and listen to what Ruby found out, but I need to go.

"When are you going to talk to Joe?" I ask.

"Tonight, if possible," Ryan says.

"All right, I've got to go. My dad needs me. But would you please call me? Let me know what's going on?"

"Yeah, of course."

I have no idea if Ryan is telling me the truth, but Dad's voice sounded desperate. I hop in my car and head back to town.

★ ★ ★

"What is it?" I say, walking into my house. "Where's Mom?"

"It's bridge night. I'm just as glad she's not here, because look..." He hands a paper to me.

"What's this?" I scan the document.

"A demand letter. From the Steel Trust. Demanding we pay our lien now or they're going to foreclose on our property." Dad shakes his head.

I blink several times, reading the words. "I don't understand. I don't understand at all. I just talked to Donny about this. He doesn't even know what the Steel Trust is."

"This law firm sure seems to know." Dad gestures to the law firm logo at the top of the stationery. "And who the hell is the Fleming Corporation?"

"Let me call Donny. He'll know what's going on."

"No, Brendan. Do *not* bring a Steel into this."

"Donny's a friend, and he's the city attorney for Snow Creek."

Dad shakes his head vehemently. "I won't have you bring them into this."

"But he can help. Dad, I was just talking to—"

"No, Brendan."

That's Dad's final word on the matter. He's using *that* voice. I won't push him further, but I will talk to Donny once Dad and I figure this out.

I scan the document again. The address is a law firm in Denver.

"I guess we could go talk to these people," I say.

"For the life of me," Dad says, "I look back and I don't know why I bought that damned bar subject to that lien. The realtor at the time said it was nothing. That nothing would ever come of it. And for forty damned years, nothing did. Until now."

"I'll figure this out, Dad."

"We need a lawyer."

"We'll have to go to the city, then. There aren't any law firms here in Snow Creek."

"Yeah, you're right. I wouldn't even know who to call."

"I can ask Don—" I stop. Better not mention Donny Steel again. "Dad, don't worry about this. Nothing will come of it. Nothing has happened for forty years, and nothing will come of it now."

"I'm glad your mother wasn't here when I opened this. I don't need her worrying about it."

"Don't you think," I say, "that this is coming at a very strange time? I mean, just when we find out that your uncle had a kid? Over twenty years after his death?"

"Yes, the timing has occurred to me." Dad shoves his fingers through his hair. "I need a fucking drink."

"I could use one myself."

Dad heads to the kitchen, pulls out a bottle of rye whiskey, and pours two glasses.

Rye is what Dad drinks when he's worried about something. It's grainy, acidic, and damn, it tastes good.

"Have you eaten?"

"I fend for myself on bridge night."

"Let's go out. We can go to Lorenzo's or something."

"I can't go out, Brendan. I'm not fit to be around other people right now."

"All right. I'll order something from Lorenzo's and pick it up."

He shoves his hands through his hair again. "Yeah. That's fine. Get a pizza. Everything. No anchovies."

"Good enough." I pull out my phone, order the pizza from Lorenzo's, and then head over.

And as soon as I get there, who do I see?

Ava, sitting at a table with Brock and Rory and Jesse Pike. For God's sake . . .

"Hey, Brendan!" Brock motions me over.

"Hey, Brock. Ava, Rory, Jesse."

Ava meets my gaze for a moment but then looks away.

I can't blame her.

"You want to join us?" From Brock.

"No, thank you. I'm just picking up a pizza for my dad and me. It's Mom's bridge night."

"I can't believe you're taking time off," Brock says.

"Yeah, we've got some family matters going on. That's what Dad and I are discussing tonight."

Ava looks down at her plate, stares at a piece of bread that she just dipped in olive oil.

"What have you guys been up to?" I ask.

"We were working on the holiday concert that Rory and Jesse are doing," Brock says.

"It's going to rock," Jesse says. "I hope you're planning to be there."

"Oh, yeah, I wouldn't miss it. Mom and Dad are coming too."

"They like rock and roll?"

"They like your band, Jess," I say. "But they're also looking forward to hearing Rory's operatic numbers."

"It'll be my last time singing some of those," Rory says. "Time to definitely hang up that hat and then get ready for the tour."

"I know. So amazing that you guys are going on tour with Emerald Phoenix."

Rory's eyes shine.

"You seem excited."

"Wouldn't you be? Emerald Phoenix?"

"Yeah. I'm a big fan," I say.

Then Rory bursts into a huge smile.

"Oh, for God's sake," Brock says. "Just tell him, Rory."

"All right, but you're sworn to secrecy. Both of you." She looks at Ava.

"My lips are sealed," Ava says, still not looking at me.

"Sit down for a minute, Brendan. This is a secret."

I take the seat next to Ava and intentionally nudge my thigh against hers.

"Emerald Phoenix is going to be at the concert," Rory says quietly. "It's a secret, so don't tell anyone else."

"Seriously?" Ava says, a little too loudly.

"Yeah. They're only going to do a couple of numbers. And we're not allowed to advertise it that way or people will be coming from all over the state to see the concert, and the venue just isn't big enough for that."

"Yeah, I get it," I say.

"Brendan," Lisa yells from the front. "Your pizza's ready."

I rise. "Good luck getting ready, and that's wonderful news. I can't wait to see the concert."

I don't look at Ava as I walk to the front, grab my pizza, and go.

CHAPTER TWENTY-EIGHT

Ava

"Trouble in paradise?" Jesse drawls.

"I'm sure I don't know what you're talking about." I take a bite of my olive oil–soaked bread.

"No biggie, cuz," Brock says. "You can do better than Brendan Murphy."

"Hey," I say.

He elbows my ribs. "I knew that would get you. Brendan's a great guy, I'm kidding."

"We'll work it out," I say. "We've just both got a lot going on right now in our personal lives."

"Anything we can help with?" Rory asks.

Brock shoots her a look.

"I mean, I understand if it's personal."

I take a drink of water. "Yeah, it's personal. Like I said, we'll work it out."

And now can we please stop talking about it?

Lisa comes by with our orders.

"Where are Nora and Sadie tonight?" Brock asks.

"They both had some party they wanted to go to. I could only get one of the shifts covered, so I'm pulling double duty tonight. Anything else I can get you four?"

"I'm good." I inhale. Lisa's robust marinara sauce always

smells great, even when I'm not feeling hungry.

"Good enough. Anyone need a refill on drinks?"

Brock, Rory, and Jesse are sharing a bottle of Chianti.

"Actually," I say to Lisa, "bring me a wineglass. I think I'll have some of that."

"Then we're going to need another bottle," Brock says.

★ ★ ★

Later, I drive back to my parents' house on the ranch. I packed a bag, and I'll be spending the night in my old room.

What I really want to do is see Brendan. I miss him. I want to show him my tattoo.

But for some reason, I feel like I need to talk to my grandmother.

Mom and Dad are nowhere to be found when I get there, so after dropping off my bag in my room, I head to my grandmother's room, disregarding my promise to my father that I wouldn't see her without him present.

I'm a big girl. I can take care of myself.

The night nurse is there, checking her vitals. My grandmother's awake, and she looks at me and smiles.

"I was hoping you'd come tonight, Ava."

I pull my bracelets off my wrist. "Grandmother, I need you to tell me about these bracelets."

"So your mother finally gave them to you."

"She did. After she told me about . . ."

Wendy nods. "Yes, about what a horrible person I am."

I say nothing for a moment. Then, "Mom told me they came from my Grandmother Didi. That Didi gave them to her because I was an old soul."

"You *are* an old soul, Ava. Who do you think told Grandma Didi that?"

"You?"

"I'm the one who led your father to your grandmother," Wendy says. "Ruby's father told her that Didi was dead, but she wasn't. Your father loved your mother so much, so I allowed him to find Didi and give Ruby the gift of her mother."

"You? This whole time?"

"You already know I didn't die that day, don't you?"

"How can someone..." I shake my head. "Help me understand, Grandmother."

"I think what you want to know is, how can I do both horrendous things and wonderful things?"

"Yes."

"Nothing is black-and-white in this life, Ava. Surely you know that. Being the old soul that you are."

I nod. She's right. I do know that.

"So did these bracelets ever belong to Grandma Didi?"

"Oh, they did. They were a gift from me."

"But Didi... She lived with us."

"She did. For several years. But those bracelets came from me. She knew me as a friend."

"How would Mom and Dad not have known that?"

"I knew your grandmother long before you were born, Ava. From the time your mother was just a child."

"Of course. Because you knew my grandfather, Theo Matthias. And my mother."

"Yes. I couldn't have chosen a better woman for my son than your mother."

"Did you—"

She shakes her head. "No, I had nothing to do with them

getting together. That happened all on its own."

"But my mother . . ."

"Yes. She tried to kill me. I didn't die, of course, but when she tried, she proved, beyond a shadow of a doubt, how much she loves my son."

"Tell me about my grandfather. Theodore Matthias."

"Theo was brilliant," Wendy says. "I hated putting an end to his life."

"Then why did you?"

"His time had come. He had come full circle. He had grown to love his daughter again, and I knew he wouldn't be any good to the organization at that point. Besides, Tom and Larry were both gone already."

As much as I want to keep talking about this, find out more about what my grandmother knows, we're getting off the subject at hand.

"Grandmother, the bracelets . . ."

"You're a smart girl, Ava. You saw the etching, didn't you?"

"Yes. The WM."

"I doubt Didi ever noticed. But once you were born, and I told her they were meant for you, I knew you would notice the initials someday."

"How did you know that?"

"I've known since the day you were born, Ava. You're the key."

"What's that supposed to mean?"

"You want to know why I reached out to you. Why you, and not your sister. Or your father." Wendy closes her eyes, sighs, opens them again. "Your father has no love for me. As much as I yearn for his love, I'll never have it. And your sister . . . Even though she and I share artistic talent, she is your father's daughter through and through. But you, Ava. You're not just your father's daughter. You're also *my* granddaughter."

"Grandmother, you're not making any sense."

"Think about it, Ava. Think about it. Think about who you are, and you'll see that I'm making sense."

"I am my father's daughter."

"You are."

"But so is Gina."

"She is. Biologically, you are as much your father's daughter as I am his mother. So is Gina."

"And I don't understand—"

But then I *do* understand.

What the cards have been trying to tell me this whole time.

Who I am isn't *changing* so much as it is *emerging*.

"I think I've always known, Ava, that you were more mine than Ryan ever was. More than Lauren, more than Jack, more than Gina. I was there the day you were born."

I gasp.

"I was. I was in the delivery room."

"But how—"

"Simple enough. Colored contact lenses. A surgical mask. Disguised as an intern, simply observing."

"Does Dad know?"

"No, and I have no intention of telling him or your mother. When you were born, Ava, I felt something. Something I didn't even feel when your father was wrestled from my body. You, Ava, are my true progeny. Heir to everything that I am."

"I don't want to be like you, Grandmother."

"But you are, Ava, and I'm afraid there's nothing you can do about that."

I curl my hands into fists, and without saying goodbye or good night, I leave the room, slamming the door.

She's wrong about me.

I'm nothing like her.

And I will prove it.

CHAPTER TWENTY-NINE

Brendan

Dad and I reach the city attorney's office the next morning before Donny. In fact, before the office is even open.

Finally, a security guard unlocks the door. "Sean, Brendan. What are you doing here so early?"

"We need to see Donny."

"Good timing. Callie and he are just arriving now."

Callie and Donny enter through the door.

Dad shoves the paper in front of Donny's face. "You want to explain this, Steel?"

Donny takes the paper. "Sean, I haven't had any coffee yet this morning."

"Do I look like I care? What the fuck is this?"

Donny glances down at the paper, scans it, and then looks at me. "Brendan, I don't understand this."

"Neither do I," I say, "because you just told me the other day that you don't know what the Steel Trust is. That your family has no record of it."

"I don't. But whoever sent this document seems to know." Donny looks to my father. "I told Brendan I would take care of this, and I will. I don't know anything about this letter. I need to talk to my father and my uncles, but I can tell you now, none of them know what the Steel Trust is either."

"I want to get to the bottom of this, Steel," Dad says.

"No more than I do, Sean." He lifts the paper. "May I make a copy of this?"

"Sure. But I can tell you right now, I don't have the money to pay off this lien."

"Don't you worry about that."

"And I'm not taking your money either," Dad says.

"Did I offer?" Donny continues to examine the paper. "We'll get to the bottom of this. I promise you."

"How can you?" I ask. "You work for the city. The city's your client. Not the Steel Trust, and certainly not the Murphys."

"I didn't say you were my client. This is a family matter, and I'm part of the Steel family."

He marches toward the staircase, Callie following, and then instructs an intern to make a copy of the document while Dad and I wait.

"Did you need anything else?" Donny asks.

"Just your assurance that you'll call as soon as you find anything out."

"You have that," Donny says. "You've always had that."

I haven't told my father about the Steels paying for my apartment. He definitely would not take that well.

Some way or another, I will repay them all.

But before I can even think about that, I have to figure out how to pay the damned lien on the bar.

And no, I will not take more money from Donny Steel to do it.

"Let's go, Dad," I say.

"Yeah. I guess our business is done here." Dad takes the paper from Donny, nearly ripping it from his hands. "You haven't heard the last of this."

"I'm sure I haven't," Donny says. "I can assure you my family has no interest in your property."

"I'd say your family has a huge interest in my property." Dad points to the paper.

"You know what I mean. No interest in taking your property from you. Whatever the Steel Trust is, I will find it."

"You see that you do." Dad turns and heads out the door.

"It's not you so much he's angry at," I say.

"I'd say he's very angry with me. And frankly, I don't blame him."

I shake my head. "No, it's not you. It's the Steels as an entity. He's convinced you guys had something to do with his great-uncle's death, and now with Wendy Madigan back in the picture, and this long-lost cousin we found, it's a lot to take."

"It is a lot to take," Donny says, "but isn't your father glad that his uncle has a son? His uncle may be gone, but his progeny lives on."

"His progeny lives on because of the Steels."

"Don't forget, Brendan. Wendy Madigan is *not* a Steel."

"She considers herself one, Donny."

"That may be true, but her reality isn't *actual* reality."

"No, it sure isn't." I shake my head. "I sure as hell don't like this pull she's got over Ava right now."

"Ava's strong. She'll be all right."

"She is strong," I say, "and yes, in the long run, she *will* be all right. But something's tugging at her. Something that's keeping her away from me. And that's not what I'm most concerned about. What I'm most concerned about is *her*. Her sense of self. It's being threatened, and it's being threatened by her newfound grandmother."

"Yeah. I've talked to Brock about that. He's worried too. But like I said, she's strong."

"I wish I knew how to help her."

"And I wish I had some advice to give you, but you know my cousin as well as I do. She doesn't accept help."

"Yeah, I understand that."

"Thanks for rubbing some salt in that wound," Donny says.

"Hey, you can take my words at face value, or you can read into them."

"What I did was try to right a wrong. But unfortunately, I may have made things worse. Because now, if there *was* anything else hidden in that apartment, we don't know what it is."

"I know," I say, "and Donny, I don't blame you. You were trying to protect your family, and I'm doing the same thing. Do I agree with your methods? Hell, no. You obviously didn't agree with them either. But unfortunately, that one night I was gone gave whoever burglarized my place the chance to take anything else that was there. And I wouldn't be surprised . . . "

"Neither would I. Information about this Steel Trust."

"You got it. And maybe information about my great-uncle."

Donny nods. "We'll figure it out, Brendan. Dale, Brock, and I are committed. Uncle Joe and my father are committed. Uncle Ryan as well. In fact, I think he's more committed than the rest of us all combined because he knows exactly what kind of havoc his mother can wreak. And he knows that as long as she's alive, the rest of us aren't safe."

"Ava's not safe?"

He shakes his head. "Ryan and Ava. Gina. Probably even Ruby. All very safe. But you see, Wendy Madigan has an ulterior motive, and it's becoming pretty clear."

"Right. That deed transfer."

"Exactly. There is one way that her son and *only* her son will inherit all the Steel property, and it doesn't have anything to do with that deed, which was probably signed under duress."

A shudder runs through me. "I may be angry with you, Don, but I sure as hell don't wish anything bad on you or any of your family."

"I appreciate that, and I know it. But the only way..."

"The only way that happens...is if the rest of you are dead and buried. Leaving no heirs."

CHAPTER THIRTY

Ava

I'm back at my place, still staring at the cards on the table, when my phone buzzes.

It's Brendan.

"Hey," I say into the phone.

"Hey yourself. I just wanted to check in. See how you're doing."

"Oh, Brendan... I think I've made a terrible mistake."

"You haven't made any mistake, Ava."

"But I have... I've been trying to see something in my grandmother that's not there."

"That's not a mistake, Ava. That's just being human."

"Where are you?"

"I'm just leaving the city attorney's office. I had to see Donny."

"Is everything okay?"

"What a loaded question." He chuckles softly in an unhumorous way. "You feel like getting some breakfast?"

"Not particularly. Why don't you come over to my place, and I'll make you some eggs? You know I don't ever have bacon."

"Too bad I can't have one of your almond croissants," he says, "but the bakery's closed."

"I have some in the freezer. I'll put one in the oven for you. Come on over, Brendan. I miss you."

"I miss you too, baby. I'll be there in a sec."

I head to my bedroom and look in the mirror. My face is a mess. My eyes are swollen, and my nose is red. I cried last night, and I'm not even sure why. Some of it was because of Brendan because I thought I had destroyed what we had. But I haven't. I can hear it in his voice. But a lot of it wasn't Brendan. It was just me. Just Ava. I let my grandmother mess with my head. And I let the cards mess with my head. I doubted myself. I doubted who I am.

But no more.

I'm nothing like my grandmother, and I am *not* her progeny. Not in the way she means.

She still, even in her old age, has a brilliant mind, a manipulative mind.

And I almost let it happen.

But I won't.

I absolutely will *not*.

I was right about the cards. I'm not changing. I'm emerging. And the realization of who my grandmother truly is proves that.

Brendan has seen me at my worst, and this won't matter to him. I quickly pull on some baggy jeans and a tank top with no bra. I leave my feet bare.

I head back out to the kitchen, not even glancing at the cards on the table, and I pull out an almond croissant from the freezer. Then I pull out another. I'll join Brendan. I need to eat. I make him some eggs, pour him a glass of orange juice, and brew a pot of coffee.

And something occurs to me.

I feel more like myself in this moment than I have in the last couple of weeks.

Making breakfast for the man I love.

Instead of trying to figure all this other stuff out.

Sometimes a cigar is just a cigar.

Sometimes a crazy person is just a crazy person.

And sometimes I am just me—a person who's constantly growing. Life is a journey.

Ava Steel. I may not be descended from Daphne Steel, but I am who I always was. The daughter of Ryan and Ruby, and though I'm the granddaughter of Wendy Madigan, that does not have to change my life.

And I will not let it.

I'm emerging as Ava Steel—a woman who knows her true genetic background but who will not let herself be defined by it.

My phone buzzes with a text. It's Brendan.

I'm here at the door.

I go down, let him in, and then I melt into his arms.

He embraces me, his warmth a welcome respite.

"You okay?" he says.

"Now that you're here, I will be."

I lead him back up the staircase to my apartment where I've already set his place at the table.

I pour him a cup of coffee and set it down next to his plate.

He takes a seat. "Thank you."

I sit down next to him, in front of the plate where my lone croissant sits.

Brendan brings a forkful of scrambled eggs to his mouth, chews, swallows.

I just stare at him.

"I'm sorry," I finally say.

"I'm sorry too, baby. We're both going through a lot right now, but we're going to be okay."

I nod. "Thank you for that. I need it."

"I need it too." He puts down his fork, picks up his croissant, and takes a bite. The dough flakes, and light crumbs scatter to his plate.

"What did you need to see Donny about?"

"The Steel Trust has called its lien on the property."

"I don't understand."

"Nobody else seems to either, baby. Donny and your uncles don't even know what the Steel Trust is."

"Who got in contact with you?"

"Some law firm in Denver."

"How much?" I ask.

"More than I've got."

More than he's got. I've got the world. I don't want to touch my trust fund, but if I can help Brendan...

"I can handle that."

"You?"

"I have a trust fund. I've been able to access it since I turned twenty-one. I just haven't. That amount is a drop in the bucket for me, Brendan. I'd like to take care of this for you if you'll let me."

His lips curve downward into an angry frown. "Didn't we just have this discussion, Ava? About your family paying my insurance claim? I don't take charity."

"This wouldn't be charity, Brendan. This would be a gift. A gift from me to the man I love."

His features soften then. "You're so generous, baby. But I

can't take your money."

"What if..."

"What if *what*?"

"What if... What if we got married? Then it wouldn't be my money. It would be *our* money."

He drops his fork, and it clatters against the ceramic of his plate. "What?"

"For God's sake, Brendan, don't make me repeat it."

"Ava, the man is supposed to propose marriage."

"Says who?"

Brendan smiles then. A great big one that splits his face. "You, Ava Steel, would break with every tradition in the free world, wouldn't you?"

"When it's a stupid tradition that makes no sense, then yes, sir, I would."

"You're very sweet, Ava. But paying off a debt is no reason to get married. We've talked about this. I all but proposed already, and you turned me down."

I look down at my plate. He's right, of course. I clear my throat. "I didn't turn you down because I don't love you. In fact, I *do* want to marry you. I just want to get through all my family stuff first."

"You're not through that yet, Ava. I'll repeat myself. Paying a debt is not a good reason to get married."

I meet his gaze. "Being in love is."

"Yeah, I reckon it is."

I laugh. "That's the first time I've ever heard you say the word *reckon*."

"I may be a townie, but I suppose there's a little bit of cowboy in me." He snorts. "That's a lie. I think that *is* the first time I've used that word."

"Let me level with you, Brendan."

"I sure wish you would."

"I didn't think I was ready for marriage. Not for a long time. But now?" I gaze at his handsome face, his fair skin, his marble jawline, his full lips. And that fabulous red mane of his. "You're the one. I don't think I've ever doubted that. And even though I originally thought we'd wait a few years, I really do want to get married to you. And no, not just so I can pay off your debts."

"Good, because Ava, I'm not going to let you pay that debt."

"Once we're married, it becomes *my* debt."

He shakes his head, chuckling. "Then I reject your proposal."

I shouldn't be surprised. And I shouldn't let my heart break. But it does, just a bit, because I do want to be married to Brendan. I really, really do.

"Tell you what," he says. "Why don't we get engaged, Ava? I'll get you a nice ring."

"How can you—" I close my mouth.

I was about ready to ask how he can afford to get me a ring when he's in debt up to his eyeballs, but then I thought better of it.

"All right, Brendan. But I don't need a ring."

"Well, you'll get one. It just so happens that my mother has my grandmother's engagement ring, and since she has no daughters, she told me when I found the woman I want to marry, I should give it to her. And I found her, Ava. I found you."

Warmth spreads through me, like a giant hug. "Oh, Brendan."

He rises then, pulls my chair away from the table, and then swoops me up over his shoulder as if I'm nothing more than a sack of potatoes.

A moment later, I'm naked, in my bed, Brendan on top of me, kissing me deeply.

Until I gasp at a sharp pain.

"You okay, baby?"

"Yeah, it's just my hip . . ."

He pulls away, looks down at the transparent covering on top of my new tattoo.

"Wow. A triquetra split with a lightning bolt. There's got to be a story there."

"I just got it. That's why it still has the bandage. And yes, there's a story."

"Did it hurt too badly?"

"It hurt like a mother, but it was good pain. Pain I needed."

"I see."

"Do you?" I sigh. "I'm not sure I did until this very moment. All this time I've been thinking I was being challenged for who I was, but I believe my grandmother was trying to manipulate me into thinking I'm something I'm not. This tattoo reminds me that there will always be challenges to my balance, but if I'm secure in who I am, they won't matter. I know who I am, Brendan."

"You're Ava. Sweet, simple Ava."

"Simple?" I chuckle.

He traces my lower lip with his finger. "I mean that in a good way. You know who you are. You always have, and nothing changes that. Not your newfound knowledge of your genetic makeup, and not the fact that your grandmother reached out to you."

"I know, and now I have this tattoo to remind me that sometimes life will throw me curveballs, but that doesn't have to change anything."

"Ava..." His lips come down on mine in a gentle but passionate kiss.

We kiss for a while, his hard dick pushing against my belly, until he stops, looks down at me, pushes my pink hair out of my face.

"I love you so much. I can't wait until you're my wife."

"I can't wait either, Brendan. But you know, we're going to have to figure something out about the bar and the bakery. If we ever want to see each other, that is."

"I know. I think we're both going to have to learn to delegate," he says.

"I never thought I'd want to, Brendan. But if it means spending time with you, I will gladly learn to delegate."

His lips come down on mine again, and he thrusts his cock inside me.

And we make slow sweet love, for a long, long time.

CHAPTER THIRTY-ONE

Brendan

Later that evening, Ava and I head to the ranch to meet Ryan and Ruby at Jonah and Melanie Steel's house. It's after dinner because no one wants to mess with small talk.

"I don't know much about our grandfather," Jonah says. "But from what I *do* know, I wouldn't put it past him to father a bastard child, so it never occurred to me to think it might not be true."

"But this is all just a theory," Ruby says. "What we need is for Ryan and Lauren Wingdam to get DNA tested. That will tell us if they're full or half siblings. Tucker is the best at DNA analysis. He's quick too, and he owes me many favors."

"I need to talk to Wendy," Ava says.

"Sweetie . . . " From Ruby.

"No, Mom, she feels some kind of connection with me. I let it get to me, partially because I feel it too, but now I see that she was trying to manipulate me."

"She's good at that," Ryan says dryly.

"I think I can get her to level with me. If I play my cards right."

"Ava, she'll hold nothing back," Ryan says. "She'll pull out every trick in her book to manipulate you."

"I know that, Daddy. But still, I've got to try. If anyone's going to get information out of her, it's got to be me. She feels like I'm her"—air quotes—"*progeny*, which I don't understand. You're her progeny, Gina's her progeny. Lauren and Jack too. Even Pat Lamone. But for some reason she chose me." Ava jingles the bracelets on her wrist. "Do you remember Grandma Didi having these when you were little?"

"Yeah, I do," Ruby says.

"Are you sure? Think hard, Mom."

"Ava, I—"

"Wendy told me they were hers. That she gave them to Grandma Didi and made her promise to make you give them to me one day."

"She's lying, of course," Ryan says. "Truth, to Wendy Madigan, is all relative."

"Her initials are inside one of the bracelets." Ava removes them from her wrist. "It's hard to see without magnification, but WM is engraved in one of these."

Ruby takes the bracelets Ava hands her, runs her fingers over the gold bands. "I . . . I think she had them. I'm sure she had them. Times were tight for us when I was little, and I remember her saying she'd never sell them."

"Are you sure?" Ava asks.

"It was a long time ago, Ava. For years I thought my mother was dead." She hands the bracelets back to Ava. "I don't know. They could be different bracelets than the ones she had. It's not like I memorized them. But she did have bracelets, and if Wendy switched them out—"

"Then she got to Didi while she was still alive," Ryan says. "We all thought she was dead, so it never would have occurred to us . . . Jesus fuck."

"She was in the delivery room when I was born," Ava continues.

Every eyebrow in the room goes sky high, including my own.

"That's what she says, anyway. She disguised herself in scrubs, a surgical mask, and colored contact lenses. She would have looked like an intern."

"She's lying," Ryan says. "It's what she does."

"I don't think she's lying," Ava says. "You all thought she was dead, so you wouldn't have noticed an intern observing. They're everywhere at teaching hospitals."

"She was in her early sixties at that time," Ryan says.

"But would you have noticed her age if her face were half covered by a mask?" Ava asks.

"Ava," Ruby says, "she's lying to you."

"She's not, Mom. It's okay that you think she is, but she's not. Trust me. She *is* trying to manipulate me, but I won't fall for it. I'm stronger than she is, and that's something she hasn't considered."

"So you think she somehow exchanged Didi's bracelets for those." Ruby gestures to Ava's wrists. "My mother wouldn't fall for that."

"Wouldn't she?" Ava shakes her head. "Wendy's very charismatic. I know everything she's done, everything she's put this family through. And still . . . her charisma affected me until I realized what she was doing and shielded myself from it." Ava absently sets her hand on her hip—the same hip that was recently tattooed.

That's her shield. For Ava, symbolism is important. That's why she loves the tarot.

And that's what this tattoo is. A symbol of her shield against Wendy Madigan. Against anything that tries to disrupt her balance.

"But sweetheart..." Ruby continues.

"Trust me," Ava says. "Wendy could have easily slipped a decoy to Didi. Or borrowed the bracelets and given them back with her initials inscribed."

Ryan shakes his head. "You do get my mother, Ava. I should have given you more credit."

"That's my point, I guess," Ava says. "I believe that if anyone can get through to Wendy, it will be me. I can get the information we need. The information about William Elijah Steel, if he even ever existed. The information about why she kept sperm samples."

"But the Steel Trust..." I interject.

"We'll get to the bottom of that too," Jonah says. "In the meantime, don't worry about that lien that's come due."

I frown. "I can't help but worry about it. I don't need a blemish on the title to our property. I'm sure everyone else in town will feel the same."

"There will be no blemishes," Joe says, "if I have to pay those damned things myself."

I draw in a deep breath to keep from reacting. I manage to keep my mouth shut.

"Ava," Melanie says, "you've been through so much in the past couple of weeks. Are you sure you're up for this?"

"I have to be, Aunt Mel. I'm the only one who can do this."

"I can do it," Ryan says.

Ava grabs Ryan's arm. "Daddy, no. Not as long as you won't call her Mother. And if you start calling her Mother now, she'll see right through that. I've been calling her Grandmother this whole time, partially because I felt it, but partially also to manipulate her. She has a soft spot for that."

Ryan nods. "You're right. All right, Ava. If you think you can do it. But I want to be with you."

"But Daddy, can't you see? You *can't* be with me. She loves you. You're her son and she loves you, but she doesn't trust you the way she trusts me."

"She's right, babe." Ruby pats Ryan's arm.

"I want to go with you," I say.

"You can't, Brendan," Ava says. "This is all me. It's what she's waiting for, and I have to pretend to play along."

"I suppose you're right." I sigh. "When will this end?"

Joe's phone buzzes, and he pulls it out of his pocket. "It's Donny." He puts it to his ear. "Hey, Don."

Pause.

"Jesus. Seriously?"

Pause.

"I'm on it." Joe ends the call. "Apparently Donny got some more visitors at the office today. More people in town who got letters from a law firm saying the Steel Trust is closing on their liens. Not just business owners either. Residential property owners."

"Those people can't afford that," Ava says.

"I know that, Ava," Joe says. "Ryan, we need to get Talon, Bryce, and Marjorie and have a meeting. Tonight if possible."

Ryan nods. "I'll text Talon and Bryce."

"In the meantime," Ava says. "I'm going to talk to my grandmother."

"Baby . . ." I begin.

"I'll be okay, Brendan. I promise."

★ ★ ★

I drive home alone, leaving Ava at her uncle's without a car to get home. That's no biggie. The Steels have plenty of cars.

It's early still, so I stop at my parents' home. Dad is still awake, watching TV.

"Brendan, what are you doing here?"

"I came by to pick something up." I walk into the living room. "By the way, I talked to some of the Steels. Evidently others have gotten letters like ours."

"I know that. I've been fielding calls all day about it. We're going to have a city meeting tomorrow."

"A city meeting?"

"Yeah, son. The Steels are basically foreclosing on the town."

"But it's not the Steels, Dad. You heard Donny. They don't even know what the Steel Trust is."

"I don't see how that matters, Brendan. We're going to fight it. Tooth and nail."

I rake my fingers through my hair. "Dad . . . "

"I expect you to be at that meeting tomorrow, Brendan."

"Did you forget I—" I shake my head. I was about to say I have to work, except I took the week off. "Fine, I'll be there." I stalk out of the family room, walk upstairs, careful not to wake my mother, and sneak into my old room. My grandmother's engagement ring is in my top dresser drawer in a velvet box. It's an old-fashioned setting, an emerald cut diamond surrounded by four baguettes. I planned on taking it to a jeweler to have it reset in a more contemporary style, but as I gaze at it, I see that it fits Ava. Eclectic Ava. She'll love it just as it is.

I slide it onto my pinky and then leave the back way, neglecting to say goodbye to my father.

I understand where he's coming from. But I don't believe the Steel family is behind the Steel Trust. At least not the Steel family I know. The trust could be old. These liens could have been put in place before any of the current Steels were born. In fact, they probably were.

Ava is the key to this mystery. She has to get the information out of Wendy Madigan before the woman up and croaks.

For good this time.

CHAPTER THIRTY-TWO

Ava

"You're the key to my legacy," Wendy says.

"I appreciate your confidence in me, Grandmother."

The lie is bitter on my tongue, but it's a sweet bitter. I will do what I must to get the answers I seek in order to end this, once and for all.

"I knew it was you. I knew it was you the day you were born."

"Then will you be honest with me?"

"Once I know that you plan to use the truth to fulfill my legacy."

"I've accepted that fate, Grandmother. I've accepted my destiny. I saw it in the tarot cards. I will do whatever you ask of me."

"What does your father say?"

"He says you're trying to manipulate me."

"And you believe that, Ava?"

"I did at first." I take off my bracelets, caress them gently, and then hold them up so my grandmother can see them. "But it was these bracelets that changed my mind. Somehow you knew they were meant for me. Plus, the cards, the numbers . . . It's all been leading me to you, Grandmother."

Wendy's eyes flutter closed, and a look of pure serenity graces her wrinkled face.

"Finally . . ." she says on a sigh. "Finally I can go in peace."

Oh, hell no. She's not going in peace yet. Not before she gives me all the information I need.

"Grandmother, are you all right?"

Her eyes flutter open then. "Oh, yes, child. I'm just fine. I'm not going anywhere. Not yet, anyway."

"Thank goodness. Just when I was getting to know you."

"I've left many things for you, Ava. Some of them you'll find here in your own house."

"Here?"

"Yes. Left here by your grandmother. At my request."

Anger fills me. I don't try to suppress it, but it's imperative that I at least hide it.

This woman manipulated Didi for God knows how many years. Didi, who I was close to. Didi, who had a damned shitty life until she moved in with us, according to my mother.

"Just tell me where they are, Grandmother. I will find them all."

"Not yet, Ava. First of all, there are a few things you need to know."

"Yes?"

"Your father will soon find out that Lauren is his full-blooded sister."

"I see."

"But, Ava . . . There's a reason why you are my true progeny rather than Lauren's son."

"Why?"

"Because Ryan was made the natural way. Through Brad's and my love. Lauren came a few years later, through artificial insemination."

"Why didn't you tell Brad he had another child?"

"He wouldn't have believed me."

"Did he know you had access to his sperm?"

"No." She shakes her head, trembling a bit. "All the future lawmakers chose to immortalize ourselves, including me. The technology was fairly new at that time, so we were interested. I had my eggs extracted and frozen as well. A year later, when Brad met Sean Murphy, he told him about the process. Sean decided he wanted to take part as well."

"So that was his decision?"

"Sean's? Yes, it was. No one coerced him into it." She pauses, breathing in deeply. "What your grandfather and the others didn't know is that I retained access to their donations. I retained access to everything the club did. To everything, Ava. *Everything.*"

"You mean . . ."

"All their funds, earned through both legal and illegal means. Every cent, Ava. I retained access."

"I see. And why did you choose Sean Murphy for your daughter?"

"I certainly wasn't going to impregnate her with her father's sperm. And the others weren't even slightly worthy of my daughter."

I nod. Since three of the others were rapists and child molesters, I see her point, though she's the pot calling the kettle black. Big time. I clamp my lips shut, determined not to call her out on her hypocrisy.

"I've set it all in motion for you, Ava. You will continue my legacy and find your destiny."

"My God . . ."

"What?"

"The future lawmakers club. The one in Snow Creek.

That's how this all started, with that club."

Wendy shakes her head. "I didn't go to Snow Creek High School. I went to a private prep school in Grand Junction."

"So the club..."

"If there's a future lawmakers club here in Snow Creek, it's not related to anything I've done."

"It's not? Are you sure?"

She narrows her gaze a bit, frowning. "Do you doubt that I'm being honest with you?"

Now isn't the time to piss her off, but... "Why would they use the same name? Ten years ago, the club talked about sticking it to the man."

"I can assure you I was never involved in sticking it to the government or any other authority, Ava. The club in Snow Creek is not related to any of my business."

Good enough. I'll be able to tell Brendan and Donny they don't need to bother with the club notes from Darrell Hutchins. I begrudgingly take her hand. Her skin is dry.

"Of course. I was just confused by the name of the club."

At least that's one less thing to be concerned about. I can tell Brendan and Donny that the club is on the up-and-up. Or at least not related to Wendy and her motives.

"I do have things in motion, though."

"How can you? You've been hospitalized, sedated at your own request, for the past... I don't even know how long."

"I had to go underground."

"Then why not actually go underground? Why sedate yourself? Who would agree to that, anyway?"

"It's easy to find people to agree to do just about anything when you wave enough cash in front of them."

Of course. I should have known. My own family waves

cash around. This is why I'll never do that. I don't want to be anything like this woman.

"What do you have in motion?" I ask. "What was in motion while you were hospitalized?"

"I have people all over who see to my interests. In Grand Junction, but mostly in Denver."

My mind flies to the letter Brendan and his father received. It came from a law firm in Denver.

I work hard, keeping my facial features noncommittal.

"Grandmother, I want to do what you ask. I want to find my destiny. But there are certain things I can't do."

"I understand, Ava. It's difficult at first. It was difficult for me, too. But these things have to get done, and you're the only one who can carry out my wishes."

"I don't know why you need me, Grandmother. The nurse says you're in excellent health. You may live another ten years."

"I may, but it's not likely. I've already lived more lives than a cat. Will you do what I ask of you?"

Fulfill her legacy? Of killing? Of human trafficking? Of drug smuggling? Of God knows what else?

Not only no, but hell no. If I were Rory Pike, a trained actress, I could easily convince my grandmother otherwise. But I'm not an actress. I'm simply me.

But I can do it. I can do it because I have to do it.

I take her hand. Again hold it in my own. She has pretty nails, shaped like mine. And though her hand is wrinkled, I see that it bears a strong resemblance to my own.

"I'll do what I have to do, Grandmother. I will find my destiny."

"I know you will, Ava. Now, listen closely. Here's the first thing you need to do."

CHAPTER THIRTY-THREE

Brendan

My family's small house is filled to the brim at ten the next morning. Mom ordered coffee and pastries from Rita's café, and Rita delivered them herself, as she's attending the meeting.

If Ava's bakery were open, would Mom have ordered from there? Probably not, because the town is coming together to plot against the Steel family.

Ava may be her own woman, but she is still a Steel. That's how everyone standing in my living room sees it.

Ava spent the night at her parents' house, and we talked after her conversation with her grandmother. She's holding her own, even though it's very difficult. She has to maintain her act, or her grandmother will see right through her.

People are mingling, talking, drinking coffee, and eating cinnamon buns.

Until my dad clangs a spoon on his coffee mug.

"Hey, everyone," Dad says. "I wish we had more seating, but feel free to take a seat on the floor if you need to take a load off."

"Let's get to it, Sean," Cyrus, the tattoo artist, says.

"Good enough, Cy," Dad says. "We're here because we all got letters saying we had to pay off liens on our respective properties held by the Steel Trust."

"Mr. Murphy," Carmelita Mayer says, "I can't afford to pay off this lien. I'm still holding a mortgage on my property, and you know I'm widowed."

I take a look at Mrs. Mayer. She's a lovely older woman with graying black hair. She makes delicious empanadas, and . . . Pat Lamone rents a room from her.

Pat Lamone isn't present, of course. He doesn't own property in this town.

"I know, Mrs. Mayer," Dad says. "To varying degrees, we're all in the same boat as you, and I'm sure sorry."

"What if we start a pool?" someone says. "Maybe we can help those with the most to lose pay off the liens."

"That's a nice idea," Dad says, "but it won't work long-term, and we all know it."

"I've got family in Denver who can help me," someone else says, "but I'm one of the lucky ones."

"Now wait a minute." I walk to the front and stand next to Dad. "Donny Steel, who as you all know is our city attorney, doesn't know what the Steel Trust *is*. Neither do his father and uncles. They are not the Steels that we have beef with. We have the issue with whoever is behind the Steel Trust."

"Who the hell else would be behind something called the Steel Trust?" Hardy Solomon, the sheriff, asks.

"Steel could refer to anything," I say. "It may even refer to the Steel family that we know. That doesn't mean the Steels created the trust or even know about it, which they don't."

"I'm not paying," Hardy says.

"I agree." I nod. "I don't think any of us should pay a damned cent until we find out *who* it is we're paying."

"That's the ticket," someone yells. "We don't pay them a damned thing. Let's send those Steel fuckers into the poorhouse!"

I can't help an eye roll. I'm not sure who made that comment, but if they think not paying off these liens can send the Steels anywhere near the poorhouse, they're delusional.

"That's not my point," I say. "Right now, we don't know who we're sending money to."

"So you think the Steel family has nothing to do with something called the Steel Trust," Rudy Kline, our mechanic, says.

I meet his gaze. "I know it, Rudy. I've talked to Donny Steel."

"He's probably lying to you."

"No, he's not. Most of you know that I'm dating Ava Steel."

"None of us blame Ava for this," Rita from the café says. "She's not like the rest of the Steels."

"No, she's not," I agree, "but that's not my point, Rita. Most of you know the Steels. Most of you know they're good people."

Murmurs of *yes* flow through the room, though there are a few who aren't buying it.

"I agree with Benji," someone says from the back. "Let's take the Steels down."

My dad speaks up then. "Porter, we don't have the resources to take the Steels down. But I agree with my son."

"Your son is in bed with a Steel, Sean!" Porter Holland, the grocer, yells.

"That's enough." I advance toward Porter in the back.

My father pulls me back. "Brendan, now is not the time."

I gaze at my father, my fists clenched. "Did you just hear what he said?"

Dad lets go of me. "I did, and you're out of line, Porter. My son trusts Donny Steel, and I trust my son. I don't think the Steels know about this trust."

"We were all idiots to purchase our property with the liens in place," someone says.

"No, we weren't idiots," Dad says. "We were told by our realtors at the time that the liens were inconsequential. And for the last fifty-odd years, they have been."

"The realtors were probably in bed with the Steels," someone says.

I say nothing. I've thought of this myself. Ever since Donny told me that the Steel family doesn't know what this trust is or does, I figured it had to start with a Steel somewhere—just not any of the Steels we know. The citizens of Snow Creek aren't morons. They wouldn't have purchased property subject to a lien unless a realtor or lawyer convinced them it was inconsequential.

"We can't go back in time to question those realtors or any of the deceased Steels," I say. "All we can do is deal with the *now* of the situation. We have to be proactive. My father and I aren't going to pay these liens."

"You can just get your damned girlfriend to pay for you." Porter sneers.

This time I don't let Dad hold me back. I push through the crowd, and I grab Porter by the collar, throwing him against the wall. "You say one more word about my relationship with Ava, and I'm going to take you out."

"Hey, Brendan, I didn't mean nothing."

"Son . . ." My father's voice makes its way through the din. I let go of Porter.

"What, no apology?" Porter says.

God, this man has a lot of nerve. I'm way bigger and way younger than he is, and I could push him into the next week with a flick of my fist. "No. No apology." I turn, walk back to the front of the room, and join my father.

"We're all in this together," Dad says. "So we need to act as one."

Porter scoffs from the back.

"And Porter," Dad says, "if you're not with the rest of us, I invite you to leave."

Porter looks to Benji. "I'm not with them. Are you?"

"Yeah, I am," Benji finally relents. "None of us has the resources to fight the Steels on his own. We need to stick together, Port."

I'm hoping Porter will walk out, but he shoves his hands into the pockets of his work pants and finally nods. "All right."

"That means," I say, "no more talk about Ava, Donny, or any of them. The Steels of my generation are good, solid people. Remember, all of this started before any of them were born."

Murmurs of general agreement, but Porter and Benji still don't look convinced.

The two of them won't go against the crowd, though. They're not strong enough. They're a couple of old geezers who are set in their ways, and they like to think they know everything. They may remember Brad Steel for all I know. But they'll fall in line. My father will see to that. He commands a lot of respect in this town, and he'll keep them from going off half-cocked.

"All right," Dad says. "Now that we're all in agreement, please enjoy the pastries that Rita brought over, and have another cup of coffee."

"Wait a minute, Sean," Cyrus says. "How are we supposed to respond to these letters?"

"I thought about that," Dad says, "and I think we need

to hire an attorney in the city to respond on our behalf. We'll operate as a group from now on."

"Who's going to pay the attorney?" Porter asks.

"We're all going to chip in," Dad says. "However much you can. Brendan and I can each throw in a thousand bucks. What can you throw in?"

"I'm good for a couple of pennies."

"For Christ's sake, Port," someone says from the peanut gallery. "Put me down for five hundred, Sean."

"Perfect, perfect."

"I just don't have anything," Mrs. Mayer says.

"Carmelita, that's okay."

She pulls a five-dollar bill out of her purse. "This is what I've got left from this month's groceries. You can have that."

Dad holds up a hand. "No, you keep that. We've got you covered."

"If she ain't paying—"

"Shut up, Port."

"If you guys all trust me," Dad says, "make your checks out to me. Or put in cash. We've got a basket up front here. Put your donation in there. Keep track of what you paid, because whatever we don't use will be returned based on what you put in."

More murmurs of agreement, and people come forward and throw cash and checks into the basket.

"Who's going to find this attorney?" someone asks.

"Brendan and I will take care of that. Now have some more coffee and enjoy Rita's pastries."

CHAPTER THIRTY-FOUR

Ava

Driving to the city by myself wasn't in my plans, but it's where I need to go. My grandmother gave me the address of a bar and a storage facility on the outskirts of Grand Junction. She trusts me to go there to finish whatever she has set in motion.

But of course I have an ulterior motive.

I'm going to save my family.

I drive to the dive bar that's open at ten in the morning and walk in.

"I'm supposed to ask for Mike," I say to the bartender, an older man with graying hair and striking dark-brown eyes.

He meets my gaze, a rag in his hand. "Yeah? Who sent you?"

"Sabrina Smith."

No facial reaction as he turns. "Good enough."

"Are you Mike?"

He looks over his shoulder. "Does it matter?"

"I suppose not."

He heads to the back for a moment and then returns with a manila envelope. "Here you go, miss."

"Thank you."

"How is she?" the man asks.

"How's who?" Then I leave the bar, not waiting for his response.

Inside the manila envelope is a key to storage unit 528 at the facility.

So I drive. It takes about twenty minutes to hit the other side of Grand Junction, the industrial area.

U-Stor-It.

Cute.

Not.

I drive in. No one appears to be on duty, but why would they be? It's an old facility. I pull into a parking spot and then walk through the rows of units until I find 528. It's a larger unit with a garage door instead of a regular door. My God, what does she have in here? I inhale. All I smell is dust and gravel. No dead bodies... Still, I'm expecting to find the worst.

I breathe in deeply, grasp the key between my fingers, and turn it into the lock.

Then I open the garage door. It's heavy, and it takes quite a heave for me to get it moving. Who knows the last time it was even opened?

I expect something horrid. Evil. Satanic.

I sure don't expect what I see.

One lone box sitting in the corner.

A cardboard box, about the size for holding ten reams of paper.

I sit down on the cold concrete floor and open the box.

More manila file folders inside.

One is marked *Western Slope Family Planning Clinic.* Inside are several papers, instructions on how to get to the clinic and who to ask for.

The second one is marked *The Fleming Corporation.* Inside are leases, deeds of trust, and other things.

The third one...

Steel Trust.

I'll be damned.

My family *doesn't* own the town of Snow Creek.

Wendy Madigan does.

I pull the documents out. I'm no lawyer, but I'm capable of reading the first page of a trust.

Then I drop my jaw.

Because the beneficiary of the Steel Trust is none other than...

Ava Lee Steel.

My heart drops into my stomach.

All for me. The trust is administered by some law firm in Denver.

I don't bother looking at the rest of the papers. I shove the lid back on the box, carry it to my car, and start driving.

To Denver.

CHAPTER THIRTY-FIVE

Brendan

"Where did you get the name of this law firm?" Dad asks in the car, after everyone has left our house.

"Donny Steel."

"Are you kidding me, Brendan? You got the name of a lawyer from the Steels?"

"Who did you want me to ask, Dad? He's the only lawyer I know. He and Jade, and she's his mother."

A silver truck whizzes by us.

I do a double take, nearly running off the road.

Dad grabs the steering wheel, maneuvering the car into the right lane. "What the hell are you doing, Brendan?"

"Dad, that was Ava's truck."

Dad glances behind him. "How do you know that?"

"Because I've never seen another pickup truck that color, Dad. Who the hell else has a silver truck?" I can't help but smile. "A silver sedan, sure, or an SUV, but a silver pickup?"

"A lot of people. You're imagining things."

I shake my head. "I'm not imagining things. That *is* Ava's truck. What is she doing here in the city?"

"Why don't you call her and ask her?" He holds up his hand. "Scratch that. Don't talk on the phone while you're driving."

"Screw that." I grab my cell phone out of my pocket, keeping my eye trained on the road in front of me. "Siri, call Ava Steel."

It rings several times before it goes to voicemail.

"Ava? It's me. I'm not sure, but I think I just saw your truck on the road to Grand Junction. Dad and I are on our way to talk to an attorney. Where are you? I'm worried about you. Call me, please. I love you." I end the call and toss the phone into the cupholder.

Dad eyes the phone. "So she didn't answer."

"Nope. Which means it probably *was* her. She's very careful about talking on the phone while driving."

"Surely she would've picked up when she saw it was you."

"Only if she looked."

Something gnaws in my stomach. I don't like the feeling. I feel like Ava's walking into something...or *driving* into something...

What was she doing in Grand Junction today?

"How much longer until we get there?" Dad asks. "I could go for a bite. I love Rita's pastries, but they don't keep you full for long."

"We'll have time to grab a quick lunch before the meeting," I say. "Not that I can eat."

"For God's sake, Brendan. Ava's fine. That wasn't her truck."

Except it *was* her truck. I won't be able to convince my father of that, but I know it was.

She was going awfully fast.

★ ★ ★

"Misters Murphy." A tall man in a gray pinstripe suit holds out his hand. "I'm Linus Brown. Yes, my parents had a sense of humor. Nice to meet you both."

"Call me Brendan," I say.

"Very well, Brendan. Why don't you and your father come on back? I set up one of our small conference rooms for us to talk."

We follow Mr. Brown to a large conference room where two other individuals are already sitting—a young woman with blond hair and a dark-haired man wearing a navy-blue suit.

"I'd like you to meet my associate, Mary Finnegan, and my paralegal, George Stearns."

We shake hands all around, and then Dad and I sit across the table.

"I did some research into the Steel Trust," Mr. Brown says, "and unfortunately I can't find a lot of information. Trusts aren't required to be registered or recorded anywhere, so we have only limited information available. These are old liens, some of which predate the mortgages on the properties, which is unusual in itself, as most mortgage companies won't write loans on encumbered properties."

Dad nods. "The whole thing stinks. This can't possibly be legal."

"I assure you it's legal. It's just unusual. But we're getting ahead of ourselves." Mr. Brown shuffles some papers. "The first thing we'll do is send a letter to this law firm to let them know that all of you who received letters are declining to pay the liens at this time. We can hold them off for a couple of weeks with some legal jargon. That will give us more time to look into this trust with more specificity. We can also put our investigators on it if you'd like."

"If the Steel investigators haven't been able to find anything, I doubt that yours will," I say.

"So you believe the Steel family has nothing to do with this trust?" the paralegal asks.

"I do," I say. "Which is why I asked Donny Steel to recommend a lawyer."

"Don's a good man," Mr. Brown says. "He and I went to law school together. I never understood why he gave up that cushy partnership track in Denver to be the city attorney for Snow Creek."

"As a favor to his mother," I say.

"Yeah, that's what he tells me. I guess when you're born rich, it doesn't matter if you make any money in your chosen career."

I'm not sure what to say to that, so I simply nod.

"Mary and I have drawn up a letter." Mr. Brown slides a paper toward us.

We glance over it.

"This is just a standard language letter, telling the law firm that you're refusing to make payment at this time until we find out more about the trust. We're throwing around some legal terms to give us the few weeks we need."

"Looks fine to me," I say. "But tell me this. Can this trust force foreclosure?"

"A mortgage lien will usually take priority over all other liens, so if they do end up forcing foreclosure, the mortgage companies will get first dibs on any moneys from the property." Mr. Brown shakes his head. "Like I said, this is highly irregular. The letter will hold them off for a few weeks, and even if they force the issue, foreclosure is a long process. You'll all have ninety days to surrender the properties."

Dad pulls out his checkbook. "This is fucked up."

"I agree," Mr. Brown says.

"I'm ready to write a check for your services, Mr. Brown."

"There's no need," Mr. Brown says. "My fees are taken care of."

"By whom?" I ask, already knowing the answer.

"Donny Steel."

"That's ridiculous," Dad says. "We took up a collection from the citizens of Snow Creek. They're willing to pay to get this taken care of."

"Apparently Donny's also willing to pay. He says his family feels terrible about all of this."

"Well, they should," Dad says. "But we don't want their tainted money."

"With all due respect, sir," Mr. Brown says, "the Steel moneys are not tainted."

"Maybe you and I have a different definition of tainted." Dad swiftly writes out a check and hands it to Mr. Brown. "Here's a retainer. That should cover this letter that you wrote and the next several hours. Let me know when you need more." Dad stands. "Brendan, let's go."

I smile apologetically at Mr. Brown. "We'll be in touch."

"But, Mr. Murphy . . . "

Dad has already left the conference room, and he's walking down the hall toward the exit sign. We plow through the reception area, and he hits the elevator button.

"Some nerve," Dad says.

I'm not sure what to say. A big part of me agrees with my father. The Steels had some nerve paying for my place to be reconstructed as well. Dad doesn't even know about that, and if I mention it now, smoke is liable to come out of his ears and his head might pop clean off.

We get back in the car and head back to Snow Creek.

Dad doesn't say a word.

So I stay silent.

No reason to rock the boat.

I check my phone since Dad is driving this time. Ava still hasn't returned my call, so I try again, this time not leaving a message. Then I send her a text.

> *Hey, baby. Worried about you. Please get*
> *in touch with me.*

Just as I'm about to shove my phone back in my pocket, I get another text, and Dad's phone rings at the same time.

It's the other clinic, where we had our DNA test. They have our results.

"Dad?"

"What is it?"

"Turn the car back around. We're heading back to the city."

"What for?"

"The other clinic has our DNA test results."

Dad takes the next exit, turns around, and heads back. "Can't they give us the results over the phone?"

"Probably, but I want to see them on paper. Don't you?"

He nods. "Yeah."

A few minutes later, we're back in the city, and we pull up in front of the lab, exit the car, and walk in.

"We just got a text that our results are in," I say to the

receptionist.

"Of course. Your name, please?"

"Brendan Murphy. This is my father, Sean Murphy."

"Just a moment, please." She taps on her computer. "Yes, we do have the results. Did you want to discuss them with someone?"

"Just looking at the report is fine."

"All right. One moment please." She taps again, and then she goes to her printer, pulls off some papers, and hands them to us.

"May I see your IDs, please?"

"Yeah, sure." I pull out my wallet, extract my driver's license. Dad does the same.

"Good enough." She hands me the papers. "If you have any questions, let me know."

Dad and I leave the office and stand outside in the hallway. I glance through the results. There's a lot of garbled language about DNA sequences, but the result is the same.

Dad and Jack share paternal grandparents.

"Just as we thought," I say.

"Yep."

"We'll figure it out, Dad."

Except I'm not sure if we will. Sean Murphy is long dead, and whoever took his sperm? Damn... He could've just donated it himself. But then, how could Wendy have gotten access to it?

"Let's look on the bright side," I say. "You have a cousin. A cousin who could marry and have his own children. Your uncle's line will go on, even though he died."

"I suppose that should be some solace," Dad says. "But

you know what? It really isn't."

"I'm going to give Jack a call."

"Why? He probably got the same text we did."

"True." Before I shove my phone back in my pocket, I check to see if Ava has gotten back to me.

She hasn't.

CHAPTER THIRTY-SIX

Ava

It's three in the afternoon by the time I make it to downtown Denver. Ugh. I hate driving here. Parking is terrible. I find the building but have to park two blocks away.

Once inside the building, I take the elevator to the tenth floor, where the law firm of Wolfram and Burke is.

"May I help you?" a receptionist asks.

Her nameplate says Lola Smiley. Seriously.

"I need to see"—I glance at the document—"Frederick Jolley."

"Frederick Jolley?"

My God, did I stutter?

She wrinkles her brow. "He's one of our founding partners."

"Okay. So what? I need to see him."

"I'm afraid . . . he's dead, ma'am."

I shove the folder at her, showing her the paper. "This is your firm, isn't it?"

"Ma'am"—she scans the form as her eyes widen—"this is dated . . . twenty-four years ago. That's longer than I've been alive."

"All right, whatever. If Mr. Frederick Jolley isn't here, then I want to talk to somebody about this particular trust."

"Just a minute, ma'am." She gestures to the seating area. "Have a seat, and I'll try to find someone who can help you."

A coffeemaker sits in one corner along with coffee pods. Sugar cookies with what I assume is the Wolfram and Burke logo sit next to the coffeemaker. Why serve simple Oreos when you can have personalized cookies baked to order? Maybe I need to add those to my repertoire. I laugh out loud. Who would buy those in Snow Creek?

I take the folder and plunk myself down on the clearly expensive brocade couch. Magazines are fanned out on the coffee table in front of me.

I wait for what seems like an hour before someone comes to get me. He's an older gentleman, wearing a navy-blue suit and an oddly bright-red tie.

"Ma'am?"

"Yes?"

"My name is Duke Wolfram. I'm one of the senior partners here. I understand you have some questions about Mr. Jolley?"

"I do." I hold up a paper. "This is a trust, apparently. And you see what it says there? For the benefit of Ava Lee Steel?"

"Yes."

"I'm Ava Steel, and I don't know anything about this. And I don't know why it's called the Steel Trust when my family had nothing to do with putting it together."

"Come back with me to my office, Ms. Steel. Perhaps we can figure this out."

I follow Mr. Wolfram to an elaborate corner office. Picture windows line both exterior walls, and I can see all of downtown Denver and the Rocky Mountains in the distance.

The Rocky Mountains are in the west here. Where I live, they're in the east.

"Mr. Jolley was one of the founders of our firm," he says, "along with my father, Brick Wolfram, and Leonel Burke."

"Why wasn't his name in the firm's name?"

"Would you go to a law firm called Jolley and Burke?" He smiles.

I'm not in the mood for levity. "Look. My family is going through some major crap right now. People coming back from the dead, you know."

"I'm afraid I don't."

"I need to talk to this Mr. Jolley, so it would be helpful if he, like some of the members of my family, could come back from the dead."

Wolfram raises his eyebrows. "Uh . . . ma'am . . . "

I slam the papers down on his desk. "Please. This trust is tearing my family apart. It's tearing my town apart. You've got to give me something."

"If you let me look at your documents, ma'am, perhaps I can shed some light on it. We may have a record somewhere."

"Good. I want to see all the records."

"I'm afraid that's not possible. Attorney-client privilege."

I pick up the paper, pointing to my name. "My name is right there. I'm the beneficiary of this trust."

"That may be true, Ms. Steel, but you're not my client. You're not the firm's client. The firm's client is whoever created this trust."

I heave out a sigh, rub my hand over my face. "Please. Just please help me."

"I'm going to try, Ms. Steel." He turns to his computer and types. "All right. This is interesting."

"What is?"

"Again, attorney-client privilege. I can't tell you. All I can

229

tell you is that this file has been active recently."

I stand then. "Please. Please just tell me. Who's behind this trust? Is it my grandmother? Wendy Madigan?"

"This is all I can tell you, Ms. Steel. I think maybe you need to talk to your grandmother."

"I *have* been talking to her, Mr. Wolfram. She speaks in . . . riddles."

"I really do wish I could help you."

I rise. "Fine, then. I'll figure it all out for myself. Like I always do."

As I leave his office, I listen intently. Mr. Wolfram picks up his phone. "Dion, get the hell in here. Now."

As much as I'd like to stay and eavesdrop, a woman with pink hair standing outside a senior partner's office will stand out like a sore thumb.

I head back to the reception area, walk back past Ms. Smiley, and grab one of the cookies. I'm not hungry, but I feel like I have to get something for my trouble. I take a bite. The cookie is so dry I can barely get it down my throat. Who the hell baked these and charged up the wazoo for them?

Once I'm outside the office, waiting for the elevator, my phone dings with a text. It's Brendan. In fact, there are several texts from him, along with two missed calls. My phone was buried in my purse as I was driving the four hours to Denver. I didn't hear any of it.

I don't want to talk, so I send him a quick text.

I'm sorry to worry you. I'm fine.

He texts back immediately.

Where are you?

In Denver.

In Denver? What are you doing in Denver?

Nothing. I'm on my way back now.

Drive safe. We need to talk when you get back.

All right. I should be home by about eight o'clock. Meet me at my place.

I'll be there.

★ ★ ★

Brendan is waiting in the alley when I pull up.

"So that *was* your truck I saw today, wasn't it?"

I scrunch my forehead. "What do you mean?"

"I was driving into Grand Junction with my dad, and I saw your truck barreling out of town."

I give a small smile, even though I'm not feeling it. "Yeah, that was probably me."

He caresses my cheek. "You shouldn't drive like that, Ava. It's not safe."

"I got there and back, didn't I?"

"Yeah, you did, and I'm damned glad. But please, you've got to be more careful."

The cardboard box from storage is sitting on the passenger

seat. I grab it and exit the truck.

Brendan takes it from me. "Let me get that for you."

"It's okay. It's not that heavy."

"I'll do it anyway."

He carries the box to the back door of the bakery, and I unlock the door. We walk in and go straight up to my apartment. He sets the box on the kitchen table, where my tarot cards are still spread.

Brendan places his hand on the box. "What is this anyway?"

"The key to everything," I say on a sigh. "At least according to my grandmother."

"What?"

"I'm the key, Brendan." I shake my head. "I never wanted to be any damned key, but apparently I am." I jingle my bracelets. "And these? They didn't come from Grandma Didi after all. They came from Grandma Wendy." I twist my face into a scowl.

"Ava, I've had a long couple of days. I've missed you so much." He grabs my hand. "And I wish I knew what you were talking about, but I don't."

I let out a breath. "It's a long story, Brendan. Believe me, I wish I knew what I was talking about too, but I really don't."

"Can I look in the box?"

"You and I promised we wouldn't keep any more secrets from each other. So yeah, go ahead and look inside."

He takes the lid off the box, pulls out the first file folder, which of course is the one from Wolfram and Burke, since it was the last one I threw back in after my ill-fated meeting today.

"Shit…"

"What?" I ask.

"This is the law firm that..."

He pulls a folded letter out of his pocket. "Take a look at this."

My eyes widen of their own accord. It's signed by an attorney named Dion Hays of Wolfram and Burke. "He said the file was active lately."

"Who said?"

"Duke Wolfram. That's where I was today, Brendan. I was in Denver, paying a visit to Mr. Wolfram."

"Whatever for?"

"I found the Steel Trust." I pull out another file folder. "Look at the beneficiary."

Brendan's jaw drops. "What the hell is this, Ava?"

"Are you accusing me of something?"

"Of course not. But that's your name. It freaked me out."

"I know." I run my hand over my forehead. It's sticky with sweat. "This is all fucked up, and it's got me pulling my hair out."

He strokes my hair. "Don't do that, sweetheart. But you're going to have to tell me what you know."

"I know nothing." I riffle through the box's contents. "I've never seen any of this before."

"Neither has Donny," Brendan says. "He says his family doesn't know what the Steel Trust is."

"And you think I do? The only ones who do are those people at the law firm, and they wouldn't talk to me. Something about attorney-client privilege."

"But your name is on this document."

"Right, but I'm not the client."

"Then who the hell is?"

I sigh. "Brendan, if I knew, I'd tell you."

He pulls the band from his ponytail and then threads his fingers through his hair until he looks like a wild man. A wild beast.

A wild and sexy beast.

But I can't be getting turned on now. Too much else going on.

"This is nuts," he says.

"You think?"

"Ava, what are you telling me, exactly?"

"My grandmother. She told me to go to some dive bar in Grand Junction and ask for Mike. When I did that, I got a key to a storage unit. A big storage unit, one with a garage door instead of a regular door, so I was expecting to find... You know. Not good stuff. But this box was all that was there."

He shuffles through the folders. "Western Slope Family Planning Clinic?"

"Yeah. I meant to go there today, but once I saw my name, I kind of cracked. So I drove to Denver. Demanded answers. Got none."

"This is it," Brendan says.

"This is what?"

"This must be where she's storing her sperm samples."

I drop my jaw then. "Sperm samples?"

"Your mother hasn't told you?"

I shake my head. "Uh... no. I've been busy with Wendy, and... Jeez."

"It's a long story," Brendan says. "I'll fill you in, but we need to go to that clinic."

"I will. Tomorrow."

"And I'll be going with you."

I frown. "Wait a minute ... "

"What?"

"You said you saw me hightailing it out of Grand Junction. What were *you* doing there today?"

"Seeing an attorney."

"About that letter you got?"

"About the letters we *all* got, Ava. Everyone in Snow Creek whose property contains a lien held by the Steel Trust— and that's almost all of us—got the same letter. They're calling the liens. Hell, we don't even know what the liens are for, or how much. They're calling them due as soon as they send documentation on the amounts."

"They haven't done that yet?"

"Nope."

I frown. "That's strange. Why wouldn't they tell you the amount?"

"According to our attorney, this whole situation is highly unusual. Most mortgage companies wouldn't write loans on properties with any encumbrances, no matter how insignificant."

"I may be the beneficiary of this trust, Brendan. But I swear to God, I have nothing to do with any of this."

"Easy, baby." He cups my cheek. "I believe you. And I believed Donny when he told me your family doesn't know what this trust is."

"Thank you."

"You don't have to thank me. I know you and your family are good people. But I have to warn you ... "

"About what?"

"Not everyone in town feels the same as I do. My dad and I had a meeting at the house yesterday with everybody who got these letters. Some of them are out for blood."

"My blood?"

"Your family's blood. Listen, Ava, we can't let anyone know that your name is on this as the beneficiary."

"But I didn't have anything to do with it."

"I know that. We need to go to Donny. Go to your father. Figure out what to do about all of this."

I shake my head. "No, not yet."

Brendan narrows his gaze. "Are you kidding me? Why not?"

"Because I'm trying to get this information out of my grandmother. I don't have everything yet, and if she knows I'm going to other people behind her back, she'll stop talking."

Brendan sighs. "Ava . . ."

I clutch his forearm. "You've got to trust me on this, Brendan. For some reason, my grandmother has decided she and I are connected in some weird way. I don't know why, and I don't know how, but she seems to trust me."

"And you don't think you're in any danger from her?"

"She's an old woman."

He twists his lips. "An old woman who probably orchestrated the shooting of your uncle. His poisoning too. An old woman who likely orchestrated all that horrid stuff taking place on your family's property."

I pause a moment, thinking. "It's starting to make sense now," I say more to myself than to Brendan.

"What do you mean?"

I absently place my hand over my heart. "She said I was

the key. I don't know why she chose me, Brendan. I don't know why, but I need to find out. For my own peace of mind. For my family's safety. And for you. So that you and I can have a life together, free from Wendy Madigan's madness."

CHAPTER THIRTY-SEVEN

Brendan

While Ava talks to Wendy, I sit in the kitchen with Ryan and Ruby, showing them copies of some of the relevant documents that Ava and I made this morning before heading to the ranch.

Ryan stares at the trust for the benefit of his daughter. "Jesus Christ."

"I took the liberty of asking Jade about trusts," Ruby says. "This appears to be a simple revocable trust. The trustor, the creator of the trust, being the Fleming Corporation, the trustee being the law firm, Wolfram and Burke, and the beneficiary being Ava. However, Ava's only been in existence for twenty-four years, and this trust has been in existence a lot longer, which means, someone changed the beneficiary, which only the trustor should be able to do."

"I guess we find the Fleming Corporation," I say.

"Joe and Brock found some files concerning the Fleming Corporation when they were on Doc Sheraton's property," Ryan says.

"Apparently it's been around for a while," Ruby says.

"When we first came across it twenty-five years ago," Ryan says, "we thought it was a dummy corporation put together by Larry Wade, Theo Matthias, and Tom Simpson. Now, it seems to be much more."

"I imagine it was probably the brainchild of Wendy Madigan," I say.

Ruby nods. "That's what we think as well. She probably *is* the Fleming Corporation, which would make her the trustor. She changed the beneficiary when Ava was born."

"Why Ava?" I ask. "She told me she thinks that Wendy feels the two of them share some kind of connection."

"I don't know," Ruby says. "Somehow, Wendy got to my mother while she was alive. My mother never mentioned it."

"She probably threatened her," Ryan says.

"I don't think so," Ruby says. "If my mother felt threatened, she would've come to us. No. What Wendy did was much more sinister. I believe she befriended my mother and somehow got her to keep their friendship a secret. I'm sure she probably used a fake name. Perhaps Dyane Wingdam, which was what she was going by at that point, or maybe even Sabrina Smith. But I don't think she threatened my mother."

"Your mother's been gone for a while," Ryan says. "There's certainly no way to corroborate anything."

"Unless . . . " I say.

"Unless what?" Ryan asks.

I look to Ryan and then back to Ruby. "Unless your mother's not actually dead. People in your family have a tendency not to stay dead."

"Believe me," Ruby says, "I've thought of that. My mother's gone. I was with her when she passed, and I stayed with her body. After Ryan's father turned out to be alive twice, I learned to do that with everyone in our family who passed."

I rise from the table and pace across the tile kitchen floor. "I don't like Ava in there alone with her."

"Neither do I," Ryan agrees.

Ruby sighs. "We've talked about this, both of you. This is what she feels she needs to do. We have to trust Ava."

Ruby is right, of course. I do trust Ava.

But I don't trust Wendy Madigan.

"It's my mother I don't trust," Ryan says, voicing my thought.

"None of us do, but the nurse is right outside, and Wendy's bedridden."

I pull out the paper with the name of the family-planning clinic on it. "It's possible that she's storing the actual sperm samples here."

"We can destroy those," Ryan says. "If we can get our hands on them."

"Do we want to destroy them?" Ruby says. "I mean, it's a question of ethics at this point. Bioethics."

Ryan shakes his head. "It's fine to destroy them. If they were fertilized embryos, there would be a question. We'd have to look to science, philosophy, theology—and that would be a nightmare, trying to figure out the best thing to do. But they're not. If they're just sperm, it's no different from jacking off."

"True," I agree. "But they're from dead people. People who maybe wanted their specimens preserved."

"I agree with Brendan. I don't think we can ethically destroy them." Ruby taps on her cheek. "Plus, I'm afraid of what we may find. What if we *do* find frozen embryos? I wouldn't put it past Wendy to have frozen her own eggs and fertilized them with Brad's sperm. For all we know, that's how Lauren came about."

"We don't know," Ryan says. "We still don't know if William Steel was a figment of Wendy's imagination. The only way we'll know that for sure is if Lauren agrees to a DNA test."

"I can have Jack ask her. She adores her son, and she would do anything for him." I text Jack quickly.

"And what now?" Ryan asks.

"We wait," Ruby says. "We trust Ava, and we wait."

Ryan rises. "I can't wait. Come on, Brendan. You and I are going to visit this family-planning clinic."

"Okay. That's fine with me. I hate sitting around anyway."

Ruby nods. "I'll stay here with Ava. You two be careful."

"We will be."

★ ★ ★

A little over forty-five minutes later, Ryan and I—in one of Ryan's luxury cars—pull into the parking lot for Western Slope Family Planning. We take the papers that Ava and I copied, and we go inside.

"Good morning," the receptionist says. "How can I help you today?"

"We represent the Fleming Corporation, and we'd like to have a look at these samples." Ryan shoves the paper in front of the receptionist.

She glances at it, furrows her brow. "I'm not sure what you're talking about here."

An attractive woman walks by, smiling.

"Davey, do you have any idea what this is about?" the receptionist asks her.

Davey takes the paper from her, scans it, and furrows her brow as well. "I sure don't. Is there something we can help you with, gentlemen?"

"We have reason to believe that sperm samples are being stored here," Ryan says, "and we'd like to have a look."

"I'm afraid I don't have any authority to let you look at anything," Davey says, "but let me get our manager."

"Thank you," I say. "We'd appreciate that."

"You gentlemen have a seat." The receptionist nods to the waiting area.

"I think we'd prefer to stand if it's all right with you." Ryan raises his eyebrows.

I see what he's doing. He's a Steel, after all, and Steels aren't used to being told what to do. The Steels always put forth a strong front, and staying on their feet displays that.

I'm going to stay standing with him because we need to figure this out.

A few moments later, an older gentleman appears. "Hello, I'm Dr. Sloan Franklin. Can I help you?"

"Are you the manager of this clinic?" Ryan asks.

"I am, and you are?"

"Ryan Steel." He holds out his hand. "This is Brendan Murphy."

I take the doctor's hand as well.

Ryan hands Dr. Franklin one of the papers. "We have reason to believe that some old sperm samples are being stored here, some of which may belong to my father, Bradford Steel. We'd like to see them. Now."

"We don't store sperm samples here."

"This is a family-planning clinic."

"It is. But all our samples are stored at a cryotherapy lab."

"Could you tell us where that is?"

Dr. Sloan frowns. "I don't normally divulge that information."

"You know what?" I say. "You're lying." I whisk past him down the hallway and start opening doors.

"Sir!" Davey runs after me. "There are patients in some of those rooms."

"Fine. I will stop bothering your patients, and I will stop bothering you, when you tell me where your samples are stored."

Dr. Franklin has followed us, and Davey looks at him, pleading.

"It's okay, Davey," he says. "Go back to your office."

Davey nods and walks back, disappearing behind another door.

I approach Dr. Franklin. "So you *do* store samples here. You lied to us."

"Mr. Steel," he says to Ryan, "why don't you and your friend here come back to my office? I think we all need to talk."

"Yes, I think we do too," Ryan says, "but first, you're going to show us where you store your samples."

"I'm only doing this because you're a member of the Steel family," the doctor says to Ryan. Then he turns to me. "And I don't know who the hell you are."

"I'm soon to be a Steel in-law," I say.

We follow the doctor to the end of the hallway and enter an office. The doctor takes a seat behind his desk and gestures for us to sit in the chairs facing him.

Ryan remains standing.

I remain standing.

I peruse his credentials hanging on the wall and framed in dark cherry. BA and MD from the University of Colorado.

"We use the most up-to-date cryofreezing technology there is," Dr. Franklin says. "As you can see, space is minimal here at the clinic, so I was not lying when I said we do not store our specimens here."

I nod. "We'd appreciate it if we could have a look anyway."

"There's nothing to see here."

"Then we need the address of your lab. We have reason to believe you have sperm samples from fifty years ago stored somewhere."

"I told you, we—"

But Ryan reddens. He stalks behind Dr. Franklin's desk, pulls him up by his collar, and forces him against the wall. "Your clinic's name is on our sheet of paper. Someone is storing *something* somewhere. I want to know what it is and where it is. I want to know now. Or I swear to God, no one will *ever* find your body."

I stop my jaw from dropping.

Has he gone completely mad?

"Ryan . . . "

Ryan turns to me, his face twisted and nearly unrecognizable. "Brendan, I'm sick to death of this. My mother has come back into our lives and is trying to take my daughter away from me. I won't have it. I want to find the truth." He turns back to the doctor. "You tell me now. I've got a Glock strapped to my ankle, and I know how to use it. My brother Joe taught me how to shoot. He never misses, and neither do I."

The doctor's eyes widen, and I see that they're not brown as I originally thought but a brownish green. A very frightened brownish green.

"Everything here is on the up-and-up," he says. "We're paid. We're paid for storage services."

"I'm sure you are. I don't have any desire to hurt you, Doctor, and I won't if you show me what I came to see."

"What makes you think I won't call the police?"

Ryan slowly loosens his grip on the doctor. "Because I

think you know better than to mess with my family. You can have me arrested, thrown in jail, and I'll be out in less than twenty-four hours with all charges dropped."

Whether Ryan is telling the truth I have no idea. But the Steels have been known to be able to buy their way out of anything.

"All right, all right. Just let me go." Franklin's eyes shift toward the door.

That's my cue. I go to the door and block it. "You're not going anywhere, Doctor."

"Fine. What's the name again? Of the corporation?"

Ryan finally unclenches his fists around Franklin's collar. "The Fleming Corporation."

The doctor walks to a file cabinet. He opens it and pulls out a folder from the back. "Here's the information." He opens the folder, pauses. "And yes, we have the specimens."

Ryan takes the folder while I still stand by the door.

"We're going to need a copy of all this," Ryan says.

"There's no copy machine in here."

"No worries." Ryan pulls out his phone and begins taking pictures of all the documents while I'm still standing against the door.

"Ryan . . ."

"They're here, Brendan. Samples from my father, from your great-uncle, from Tom, Theo, and Larry, along with others. Rodney Cates. Ennis Ainsley. Damn."

"Who's that?"

"He was the first Steel winemaker. He taught me everything I know."

"The name does sound familiar."

"Brock and Rory went to visit him in London." Ryan looks

back at the file. "Frozen eggs, too. Wendy's."

"Are there any frozen embryos?" I ask.

"No. Doesn't look that way." Ryan sighs. "Thank God."

"That would've been a pretty advanced technology back then," I say. "In vitro fertilization was a thing, but freezing embryos for later use? That was pretty new."

"It's actually been part of our technology for longer than you think," Dr. Franklin says.

Ryan glances at the doctor, his eyes narrowed. "Is there anything you're not showing me? Are there any frozen embryos that we don't know about?"

"No. This storage is just for sperm and ova."

I take a slow step toward Dr. Franklin. "And where are these sperm and ova?"

"It looks like they're in one of our units at the lab where we rent space."

"What would it take to destroy them?" Ryan asks.

Dr. Franklin raises an eyebrow. "You sure you want to do that?"

Ryan rubs his chin. "This stuff is over a half century old. It can't possibly be viable."

"It is reaching its limits," the doctor agrees. "But I'm afraid there's nothing I can do about it unless the person who contracted our services asks."

"We represent the Fleming Corporation," Ryan says.

"You represent the Steel family," Dr. Franklin says. "I'm not buying."

Ryan stares him down. "Are you sure about that?"

"Listen," Dr. Franklin says. "This is all before my time. Whoever contracted the clinic to store these samples paid for their storage indefinitely. They're not hurting anything where they are, and they're probably no longer viable anyway. You have the documents. You have the address where they're stored. The cryo facility can't release them unless we ask for them, which we won't. We'd never use such old specimens."

"And why, exactly, should we trust you?" Ryan asks.

Dr. Franklin shakes his head, sighing. "I don't know. You have to decide that for yourself."

"Christ." Ryan rakes his fingers through his hair. "I'm damned tired of history repeating itself. Damned tired of people coming back from the dead."

Dr. Franklin's eyes go wide. "Coming back from the dead?"

"It's a long story," I say. "Ryan, are we done here?"

"For now. But we'll be back."

My phone buzzes. It's Jack. I walk out of Dr. Franklin's office to take the call.

"Hey," I say, still walking until I'm outside the clinic.

"Yeah, just got your message. You want my mom to have a DNA test?"

"It's a hunch, but we think her father may be Brad Steel."

"We've had the same hunch over the years."

"Have you?"

"Well, *I* have. She's always been convinced that she didn't belong to Brad Steel, or her mother would've treated her better."

"I can see your concern. Ruby's been in touch with Tucker Madden. If your mother could get over there, he can do the test and get it done quickly like he did for us."

"Yeah, okay."

I inhale. "I have some more news for you, Jack."

"What's that?"

"Ryan Steel and I found your father."

No reply.

"His sperm, that is. You truly *are* the son of Sean Murphy, and you and my father are cousins. I'm not sure why Wendy chose him to father her grandchild, and we may never get a straight answer out of her about that, but if anyone can, it's Ava."

More silence.

"You still there?" I ask after a few seconds.

"Yeah. Damn."

"I know, man. Listen, Ryan and I are on our way back to the ranch. Ava is there now. Let me know as soon as you can get your mother up there for the test."

"Maybe this afternoon. Thanks. I'll be in touch."

I end the call.

Ryan looks at me. "You gave him a lot of information."

"I did," I say. "But he's my cousin. Wendy Madigan made him my cousin. I'm not sure why, but I'd like to find out."

Ryan sighs, shaking his head. "I gave up trying to figure out my mother long ago. If Lauren is my full sister—if she's Brad Steel's daughter—I have to share the fortune with her."

"That deed we found," I say, "transferring everything to you. I'm wondering if that was signed before Lauren was even born."

"It could've been," he says. "Or perhaps not. You have to think like my mother. Even if Lauren is Brad Steel's daughter, she was probably conceived through artificial insemination. In my mother's mind, that means Lauren doesn't mean as much as I do, since I came from her actually having sex with my father."

I frown. "Why would that matter?"

"To a normal person, it wouldn't. Wendy Madigan is about as far from a normal person as you can get. She was obsessed with my father. She felt they were soul mates, life mates, whatever. I mean, she was willing to kill him and herself so they could be together forever. She never accepted the fact that he chose Daphne over her. My father admitted to the sex that resulted in me. She trapped him into it, and I'm sure he probably refused to do it again."

"But if she had your father's sperm all those years, why didn't she inseminate herself before?"

"My mother—I mean, Daphne—was pregnant with Joe before they got married. And then Talon came along three years later. Wendy was busy finishing school, becoming an investigative journalist. And doing God knows what else with her secret organizations. The timing makes perfect sense when you think of it from Wendy's point of view."

"Ryan, none of this will ever make perfect sense to me."

"Yeah, it's kind of scary that it makes sense to me. But only because I've grown to understand her. Which freaks me out more than a little."

"I hate Ava being in there alone with her."

"I'm not a fan of it either," Ryan says. "But I know my daughter. And I think you know her too, Ryan. She's her own person, and she feels she needs to do this. So we need to let her do this. Remember, she's smart. She *will* ask for help if she needs it."

"I hope you're right."

CHAPTER THIRTY-EIGHT

Ava

"Grandmother, I want to be honest with you about something."

"What is that, my dear?"

"I'm in love with a man. I'm in love with Brendan Murphy."

Wendy's eyes close. Her skin of her eyelids has a translucent look.

"Yes, I see," she says. "I believe he's the great-nephew of Sean Murphy, who was a friend of your grandfather's."

"Yes. What happened to the original Sean Murphy, Grandmother?"

Wendy opens her eyes. "It was a shame. It was a needless death."

My pulse races, but I work to appear calm. "What do you mean? A needless death?"

"He was very important to Brad, and Patricia Watson was very important to Daphne."

"Brendan swears that his great-uncle didn't do drugs. That someone must've drugged him."

"Ava," she says, turning to look into my eyes, "sometimes the innocent get caught in the middle of a battle for a person's soul."

"What is that supposed to mean?"

"It means..." She sighs. "It means that there are casualties in every war."

"War?" My heart thrums against my sternum. "I'm not sure I follow, Grandmother."

"Know only this. When you were born, I realized the purpose of everything I'd put into motion. It was for you, Ava."

"Please, I'm trying to understand."

Wendy sneers. "Brad and I should have been together. I was his true love. Daphne... She was a siren. She stole my man out from under me, trapped him, and she had to pay."

"But..."

"Oh, Ava. I didn't have to do much to make Daphne pay. I took her best friend. I took Brad's best friend. But Daphne... Her own mental illness was her cross to bear."

My skin chills. Did my grandmother just admit to being behind the death of Sean Murphy? All this time, and Brendan and his father may have their answer.

"I think Brad always knew," Wendy says. "He couldn't prove it, but he knew."

"Knew what?"

"He knew... that I... that Sean..."

My grandmother sucks in a breath.

Sirens on her equipment start blaring.

Jemima and Dr. Parks race into the bedroom.

"Miss," Jemima says, "you need to get out of here. Right now!"

I back up from the bed, but I have no intention of leaving.

"Damn it!" She was in excellent health.

"Jemima, get the crash cart!" Dr. Parks checks Wendy's neck. "A faint pulse."

"No! You can't let her die." Tears erupt in my eyes. "I need her! I don't have all the answers!"

"Get out of here, now!"

But I don't leave. I watch as Jemima takes over with CPR while Dr. Parks readies the paddles.

"Come on, come on!" Jemima pants.

"Charging to two hundred," Parks says.

Jemima moves Wendy's gown out of the way, and Dr. Parks places the paddles on my grandmother's chest.

Bam!

The electricity flows into my grandmother.

"I've lost her pulse, Doctor," Jemima says.

"Damn it, old woman." Dr. Parks places the paddles on Wendy's chest once more.

Bam!

Then again.

Bam!

And again.

Bam!

"Come on," I say through gritted teeth. "If you care anything about me at all, Grandmother, do. Not. Die."

Bam!

And then—

Just a line.

A beeping line.

Dr. Parks pulls away. "I'm sorry. She's gone."

★ ★ ★

I'm not sad exactly.

I don't really know what to feel.

I didn't love this woman, my grandmother. I did feel a connection to her. A bizarre connection, and now that life has left her body, the connection has . . .

It's still there, but there's no doubt in my mind that Wendy Madigan is gone.

For good this time.

"Are you going to be okay, sweetheart?" my mother asks, rubbing my shoulders.

"Yeah, of course I will be." I sniffle. "But I didn't get all the answers, Mom."

"I'll tell you one answer we *will* get. I had the nurse draw some blood from Wendy, and I have it in my hands. I saw it come out of her body, and I saw the nurse hand the tube to me. No sleight-of-hand, no nothing. It is Wendy Madigan's blood, and I'm going to get a DNA test. We're going to make sure that it is your father's mother who died today. Then we'll get an autopsy."

"Oh, God . . . " I run down the hall toward Wendy's room.

Mom follows me. "What, Ava?"

"Don't you see? It could all be a trick again. She could—"

Mom grabs my hand right before I enter the room.

"Honey, I thought of all that. Jemima hasn't left the room, and when she does, either you, your father, or I will be there. No one is going to leave that body until it is safely at the crematorium."

"Okay. But can Jemima be trusted?"

"Yes. Your father and your uncles vetted her very carefully. Along with Dr. Parks."

"Are you sure? Because Dr. Parks assured us Wendy was in perfect health."

"Yes, and we'll have an autopsy done to make sure Wendy didn't end her own life, but she was an old woman, Ava. An old woman who kept herself comatose. That was not easy on her body. She may have just died. It was her time."

"Have you told Dad?"

"I texted him. He's on his way home."

A few moments later, Dad and Brendan return.

I run into Brendan's arms.

"I'm sorry, baby," he says.

"I didn't get all the answers, Brendan. I need more answers."

"We may be able to get them," Dad says. "Now that Wendy's dead, truly dead, any contingency mechanism she had in place will engage. There will probably be more information. It wouldn't surprise me if she knew she were about to go, and that's why she started calling in those liens."

"But the nurse said she was in good health." I shake my head. "And her name isn't anywhere on that trust."

"I know, baby. We'll figure it all out."

"Brendan?"

"Yes?"

I stare into his eyes. I don't want to tell him, but he deserves the truth. "You can put one thing to bed. You and your father. She admitted to me that she orchestrated your great-uncle's death. His and Patty Watson's."

He hugs me to him. "At least that will give my father some peace."

"Do you want to call Jack and Lauren?" I ask.

"Yeah. I will. By the way, Jack and Lauren have agreed to a DNA test for Lauren. To find out if . . . "

Dad nods. "If she's my full-blooded sister. Yes, I know." He walks out of the kitchen, Mom following.

"If she is . . . " Brendan says.

"If she is, then I have an aunt. And she will be very rich, I'm sure."

"I suppose your family will have to decide how to handle that."

"We'll cross that bridge when we come to it," I say. "In the meantime, Brendan, I have to stay here. Someone has to be with my grandmother's body at all times until we see it get cremated."

"I understand, baby. After everything you've been through, with her coming back to life once before, but don't you think that, given her age, that's unlikely this time?"

"I've learned not to go with the odds when it comes to my family, Brendan."

"All right." He brushes his lips over mine. "I need to get home. I have a lot to tell my father."

CHAPTER THIRTY-NINE

Brendan

Mom and Dad listen intently as I tell them what Ava told me.

"But all we have is her word?" Dad finally says.

"Oh, Sean," Mom says. "She was an old woman, and now she's dead. Those were her last words. Can't you accept that? Accept that maybe she knew she was not long for this world, and she was letting go of something that's been eating you alive for so long?"

Dad looks to the floor. "But I always wanted proof. Not just the word of some crazy woman."

"That *is* your proof, Dad," I say. "From what I understand from Ava and her father, Wendy Madigan was brilliant. I'm sure you could've searched forever, especially given how long ago it was, and you never would've found the proof. Hearing it from her mouth is as good as you're going to get."

"Brendan's right," Mom says. "This is the proof you've been looking for. From Wendy Madigan herself."

"But we don't know *how* she did it. How she got the poison, how—"

"That's enough, Sean." Mom's voice is harsh. "I put up with this quest of yours for decades now. This is the best you're going to get. It's over now. I won't have it brought up again."

"What about the Steel Trust?" Dad asks.

"You just let the attorneys deal with that, Sean."

Dad scoffs. "While they're being paid off by Donny Steel? I don't think so."

"What? What do you mean they're being paid off by Donny Steel?" Mom asks.

"Your son here went to Donny Steel for a recommendation for an attorney in the city."

"Well, Donny Steel *is* an attorney."

"But it's the *Steel* Trust—"

"Enough." Mom sets her hands on her hips. "I think we've established that the Steel family doesn't even know what that trust is."

"*I* haven't established that," Dad says.

Mom walks to Dad, cups both his cheeks, looks directly into his eyes. "I mean it, Sean. This is over now. Your uncle has been dead for over fifty years. Let it go. Let it fucking go."

I nearly fall backward. My mother never curses. She means business.

Dad is as surprised as I am. He actually takes a step backward. "Lori?"

"It's over. We will take care of this lien business. That's what our attorneys are for. And yes, I agree *we* should pay them. Not the Steel family."

"I agree with that as well," I say. "I'll talk to Donny."

"You do that," Dad says. "I expect that firm to cash the check I wrote. The citizens of this good city will take care of our own mess."

I inch toward the door. "I have to get home. Can I leave here and trust that you two won't be at each other's throats?"

"If your father promises to let this go."

"Someone should pay," he says.

"Yes. Wendy Madigan should've paid sixty years ago when she did it. And everyone else who helped her should've paid. But they're all dead now, Sean, so they're paying in hell."

Dad doesn't look convinced, but he finally sighs. Then, "I love you, Lori."

"I love you too."

That's my cue to leave. "And I love you both. Dad, I'll be in touch after I talk to Donny."

Dad simply nods, and I leave.

CHAPTER FORTY

Ava

I stayed home until the county coroner came and pronounced my grandmother dead. We kept the body there until Mom's lab tech confirmed the blood we took from the body indeed came from my father's mother.

Dad talked to Lauren, Wendy's actual next of kin on paper, and she wouldn't sign off on an autopsy.

"She said she didn't care if her mother was dead from natural or unnatural means," Dad relayed to us. "I could have overridden her wishes, but I chose not to."

We all understood. Later, the mortuary came, took the body, and Dad went with them, keeping his eye on the body the whole time, watching as they took her into the crematorium, and because he paid them extra, he was allowed to watch the body go up in flames.

No ceremony.

None of us wanted one.

Now we have to wait to see if Dad's hunch is right—if Wendy's daughter Lauren is his true sister.

Three more days until I open the bakery back up for business.

The noise of construction hasn't bothered me much, but I've also spent several nights at my parents' house.

Tonight, though, knowing Wendy Madigan is gone for good, I plan to sleep well. And I want to be in my own bed.

Before I do that, it's time to draw a card.

Just one card, so I take my deck, replace the three cards that I still haven't put away, shuffle it once, twice, three times, and hold it to my heart.

I infuse it with my warmth, my energy, my soul.

Already I know what it's going to be before I draw it.

And there it is.

Death.

A skeleton riding a horse and wielding a sickle.

Dying people—from the highest elite to the lowest peasant—surround death.

I drew the card upright.

And already I know what it means.

It doesn't signify Wendy's death or my own. Or anyone's, for that matter.

It simply means ... the end.

The end of the mystery. The end of the story. No, I didn't get all the answers I sought, but I got a lot of them, and I understand myself better.

My grandmother is gone, and that's the best thing for my family. Especially for my father.

It's time to move on.

If Lauren turns out to be his full-blooded sister, we'll deal with that then.

And the Steel Trust.

I have my own ideas about how to deal with that fallout.

I'll be talking to the attorney Wolfram soon.

My phone rings.

A Denver area code, and not a number that I recognize.

"Hello?" I say.

"Hello, Ms. Steel. This is Duke Wolfram from Wolfram and Burke in Denver."

"Funny, I was just thinking about you guys. What can I do for you?"

"I think maybe it's what *I* can do for *you*, Ms. Steel. An envelope came to our office this morning. It was hand-delivered, but no one saw who dropped it off. Inside is the last will and testament of Wendy Madigan. And you are her sole beneficiary."

"What?"

"Yes. It appears to be legal. The will was signed about a year ago."

"Before she went into a coma."

A pause. "When was Wendy Madigan in a coma?"

"It was self-induced. Or something. None of us got any concrete answers."

"Apparently, Wendy Madigan was the sole principal of the Fleming Corporation, which is the trustor for the Steel Trust."

"So this all means ... "

"What this means, Ms. Steel, is that you're a very rich woman. As the beneficiary of the trust, and as the beneficiary to Ms. Madigan's sizable estate, you're now worth about thirty-five million dollars."

"Wait, wait, wait ... " My heart nearly stops. "I don't need her money. I don't *want* her money."

"That's certainly your prerogative, but you're entitled to it. Can you come into my office tomorrow?"

"Yeah, yeah. I want to bring my dad with me. And my boyfriend."

"You can bring whomever you need to bring," he says.

"Can you be here by ten o'clock?"

"Can we make it one in the afternoon? It's a four-hour drive."

"Yes, of course. One o'clock it is. See you tomorrow, Ms. Steel."

"Yeah. Tomorrow." I end the call.

And I stare again at the card in front of me.

Death.

The end.

But the end of one thing always signifies the beginning of another.

I didn't get all the answers I wanted, but apparently I got a bunch of money. That plus my trust fund? God only knows how much I'm worth.

I don't want Wendy Madigan's dirty money, but I know exactly what I'll do with it.

CHAPTER FORTY-ONE

Brendan

I sit with Ava and Ryan in a conference room at the Denver law firm of Wolfram and Burke.

"So, Ms. Steel," Duke Wolfram says, "we have some papers you need to sign. Then we'll get this will probated, and you can get your money."

"I told you I don't want it."

"Well, it's yours. You'll need to decide what you want to do with it, then."

"I've already decided," Ava says. "How much will it cost to pay off all the liens that the Steel Trust holds on all the property in Snow Creek?"

"That's a sizable chunk, Ms. Steel."

"I don't care. Tell me how much."

"Close to fifty million dollars, but—"

"Good enough. I want to use the money that I inherited from my grandmother, Wendy Madigan, to pay off those liens."

"But you don't have to do that. Wendy Madigan was the sole principal of the Fleming Corporation, so upon her death, all ownership in that entity passed to you, Ms. Steel."

"I'm not sure what you're getting at."

"The Fleming Corporation holds the liens on the properties in Snow Creek," Wolfram continues. "As Ms.

Madigan's sole heir, you, for all intents and purposes, *are* the Fleming Corporation, so you can release the liens."

Ryan shakes his head. "I'll be damned..."

"Do you think Wendy thought about this?" I ask.

"Hell if I know," Ryan says. "She was brilliant, but she was old." He runs his hand over his face. "My God, she was willing to bankrupt our town for my daughter. This is crazy even for her."

"Is it?" I ask. "At least this is only money. She hurt people. She *killed* people."

Ryan shakes his head. "I'm not comparing the two. What I mean is that the amount of this trust—these liens—is nothing compared to what Ava is entitled to as a Steel heir. It's like a drop in the bucket. I don't understand why..."

Ava pats her father's hand. "It's better that you don't understand, Dad." She turns to Wolfram. "Does the trust have any assets other than the liens?"

"Most of it was tied up in the liens," Wolfram says, "but there is some cash value. About two million dollars."

"What happens with that money?" she asks.

Mr. Wolfram leans forward. "It's yours. The grantor, Ms. Madigan, through the Fleming Corporation, specified that upon her death, the beneficiary, you, may receive all trust assets without restriction."

Ava bites on her lip. "I think... It's not a lot of money, but I think I'd like to distribute it to the people of Snow Creek. To all the lienholders equally. For the emotional duress my grandmother put them through."

"That's generous of you, sweet pea." Ryan smiles.

Ava shakes her head. "Hardly. It's money I never knew I had, and as you said before, it's a drop in the bucket. In fact...

I want to give the rest of the inheritance to the people of Snow Creek as well. We'll form a committee. Figure out what the town needs. Wendy's money will do good, not evil."

"Are you sure about this, young lady?" Wolfram asks.

"I've never been more sure of anything in my life." She looks to me. "Except for when I told this man that I love him."

My cheeks warm, and Ryan glares at me.

But Ava smiles, squeezes my hand. "I understand now. I understand all of it. Everything the cards were trying to tell me, even everything my grandmother was trying to tell me. In a way? I owe her some gratitude."

Ryan rolls his eyes. "You don't owe that woman anything, Ava."

"I owe her my life, Dad, and so do you. You and I wouldn't be here but for her."

"I stopped thinking about that a long time ago," Ryan says.

"But don't you see? She wasn't a good person," Ava says. "I think we can all agree on that. And in the end, we didn't get all the answers we wanted, but Brendan, now you know who was behind your great-uncle's death. You can let that rest. Now we know why Patty Watson died. We can let that rest."

"We still don't know who shot my brother," Ryan says. "Though my mother did imply she was behind that. And we still don't know..."

"What, Dad?"

"A lot of things. Who was behind the crimes that were being committed on our property..." He rakes his fingers through his hair. "My mother was behind it, but she wasn't acting alone. And who that orange diamond ring belongs to... We don't know everything yet, Ava."

"If we're meant to know, we'll find out. But the point is

that Wendy Madigan is dead, and I'm going to see that her money does some good."

"It's very generous of you, Ava," I say, "but we need to make sure the money is clean."

Ava bites on her lip, fiddles with her lip ring. I try not to get turned on.

"That's a good point, Mr. Wolfram. How *do* I know this money is clean? My grandmother was involved in some criminal activities. A *lot* of criminal activities."

"We can look into that for you, trace the origins of the money."

"Yes, I'd like you to do that."

"However, if it's been laundered, we won't find the origins, and if we begin the investigation, it will stay in probate, which means it could be years before you get the money."

"Fine," she says. "Then I want to take the same amount of money out of my trust fund and give it to the town. Make up for the havoc my grandmother has caused."

"Ava . . . " I begin. "Are you sure?"

"Yes, I am, Brendan." She grabs my hand. "It's my money, and this is what I want to do. If it turns out my grandmother's money is clean, I'll repay my trust fund."

"And what if it's not?"

"Then I'll still probably have some money in my trust fund, right, Dad?"

"That will drain a lot of it, Ava," Ryan says. "But if Wendy's money is clean, you'll have something. You'll never be destitute, of course. Your trust fund isn't your only inheritance. But it's yours to live on now, before you inherit everything along with your sister and cousins."

"Since I haven't touched it yet, and I don't plan to, I'll be fine."

I squeeze her hand. "Ava, baby, you've got to be sure about this. You didn't create this mess. Your grandmother did."

"She did. None of it is my fault, Brendan. I know that. But I feel in my heart and my soul that I'm the one who needs to clean this up. There's a reason why I'm me. Why I am Ava. Why I haven't touched my trust fund up to this point. I was saving it. I was saving it for something like this. And in some way, perhaps my grandmother knew. Perhaps that's why she reached out to me."

"You're giving her way too much credit," Ryan says.

"Perhaps. But this feels right to me, Daddy. So right. I understand all of it now. I think we can all move on."

"Even without finding out who shot your uncle? And the other questions?"

"I feel certain that it will all be revealed in time," Ava says. "And I also feel certain that, now that Wendy is truly dead, the rest of these things are going to take care of themselves."

"I wish I shared your feelings," Ryan says. "Are you sure about this?"

"How many times do I have to say it, Daddy? I'm very sure. This makes sense to me. This is the end. The end of this portion of our lives. We're going to take care of all of this. We're going to give the good people of Snow Creek their property. If my grandmother's money turns out to be clean, I'll repay my trust fund, and I'll share it with Jack and maybe even Pat Lamone. They're her grandchildren too, and they deserve it."

I shake my head. "Ava, you're amazing."

"I'm not amazing, Brendan. I just know this is the right thing to do. My grandmother chose me to right her wrongs."

"That's not why she chose you, Ava," Ryan says.

"It's the way I choose to see it, Daddy. This will fix things in town."

"First, Ava, you don't have to share your trust fund with Jack and Pat. I've already started talking with your uncles and your aunt. If Lauren turns out to be a daughter of Brad Steel, we're going to set up funds for both of them. And as for the town, they may not want your money," Ryan says.

"Leave that to me," the attorney says. "We can do it anonymously. I'll contact all the property owners in town, let them know the liens have been released, and send them checks for their portions of the two million dollars. They'll never know it came from you."

"They'll assume it's from the Steels," I say, "but they won't have proof. These are special circumstances. It's because of Wendy Madigan's dealings with the Steel family that this all happened in the first place. She chose Ava. She chose Ava because she felt the two of them had some kind of connection, but she underestimated the size of Ava's big heart."

Ava squeezes my hand again. "Thank you for understanding, Brendan. And Daddy? Please understand too."

"I understand, darlin'. And I agree with Brendan. Your heart is bigger than most. If this is what you want to do, I will facilitate it. And Mr. Wolfram here will make sure the good people of Snow Creek accept your generous gift."

"What about your fees, sir?" Ava asks.

Mr. Wolfram nods. "We've been on retainer from the Fleming Corporation for years, decades even. Our fees have already been taken care of. Now that Wendy is gone, the Fleming Corporation basically no longer exists. All her assets will be transferred via the will to Ava."

"You send me a bill for anything that's not covered," Ava says. "We'll take care of it."

"You're an amazing young lady," Mr. Wolfram says. "And

you, sirs, are lucky to have such a fine daughter and girlfriend."

"I know," Ryan and I say in unison.

"I'll get the paperwork started. We will make this happen."

"We need to get on the road if we're going to be home for dinner," Ryan says.

"Yeah," I agree. "Sir." I shake Mr. Wolfram's hand. "Thank you for everything."

Ryan drives, and I sit in the front seat with him because of my long legs. All I can think, during the entire four-hour drive home, is how the one woman who was the culmination of all the evil and greed in the world could be only two generations removed from the most generous and wonderful person I've ever met.

CHAPTER FORTY-TWO

Ava

Once we're back, we find Mom sitting with—is that Dr. Sheraton, the veterinarian?

"Doc?" Dad narrows his gaze. "What the hell are you doing here in my house?"

"I've already been in touch with Jonah and Bryce," Doc says. "I came because that's what my instructions told me to do."

"What the fuck are you talking about?"

"Easy, Ry," my mom says. "He's not here to make trouble, are you, Doc?"

"No." Doc Sheraton shifts uneasily in his chair. "I'm here to answer some of your questions."

"So it's all related," Dad says. "You, Wendy, everything."

Doc looks at his hands clasped in his lap on top of a manila envelope. "I don't expect you to understand why I got involved."

Dad shakes his head. "I know exactly why you got involved. You were mad at Joe for not giving you the veterinarian position on staff at the ranch."

"That was my initial reason, yes. But it was pretty clear, once things escalated, that I had gotten in way over my head, and for all the wrong reasons."

"Yeah. I can't think of any right reasons to get into human trafficking."

Doc holds up his hands. "Hey, I didn't know what was going on, and I stand by that."

"Sell it to someone who believes you," Dad says.

But I walk forward. "My grandmother chose me to clean up her mess, Doc, so I want you to level with me."

"That's what I came here to do, Ava." He holds up the manila envelope. "It's all right here in this packet I received this morning at my office."

"Another contingency," I say. "Just like the one the law firm received upon Wendy's death."

"She always did dot her i's and cross her t's," Dad says. "That's how she kept my father in line. Why he never went to the authorities, why he never got Talon the help he needed as a boy." Dad clenches his hands into fists. "I'm not interested in apologies, Doc. I'm interested in seeing you behind bars."

"Hear him out, Ryan," Mom says.

Dad plunks down in the seat directly across from Doc Sheraton. I take a seat next to Mom.

"I'm not here to talk to you, Ryan. I'm here to talk to Ava."

Dad sneers at Doc. "Then why didn't you go to Ava's place?"

"I did, first. She wasn't there, so I came here."

"Well, when you're in my house, I'm going to listen to everything you have to say. So is Ruby."

Doc nods. "I don't have a problem with that. I'm sure Ava would tell you everything anyway." He sighs. "First of all, I'm going to need your assurances that you won't have my daughter arrested."

"I've talked to my brother, Doc," Dad says. "I'm well aware

of Brittany's involvement... Not just in the recent activities, but also in her mother's death."

My jaw nearly drops.

Clearly there's a lot I still don't know. A lot Brock hasn't told me.

"You'll have to start at the beginning, Doc," I say.

"It's a long, sad story," Doc says. "Brittany is not well, and ever since Brock and Joe visited my property in Wyoming, I've had her under the care of a psychiatrist. She's currently hospitalized."

"Where?" Dad asks.

"A facility in Denver. One of the best."

"Did she go voluntarily?"

"She did, but not until after I made it clear what would happen to her if she didn't."

"That she'd probably be arrested," Dad says.

"Yes."

"Did you work this out with Joe?"

"No. This was my decision." Doc pulls documents out of the envelope. "Though Joe knows. I told him as soon as this folder crossed my desk this morning."

"And what was his take?"

"He's deferring to you on everything, Ryan. Because you're Dyane Wingdam's—that's the name I knew her by—son."

"So everybody's going to know now," Dad says. "Just what I *never* wanted."

"Dad," I say, "it doesn't matter. You're still a Steel. And you may have a full-blooded sister, who is also a Steel. None of this matters anymore. We are who we are."

"Ava," Mom says, "your sister doesn't know any of this yet."

"She's strong. She'll be okay."

Mom doesn't look like she believes me, and I know from experience that it will be difficult for Gina. Hell, it was difficult for me. But Gina is strong. She will be okay.

"All right," Dad says. "Tell me. Tell me everything you know."

"I don't know a lot, but here is the information that I just got. There aren't any names, but it appears that this Fleming Corporation was behind the attempt on Talon's life."

"Shocking." Dad rolls his eyes.

"My daughter was a lot more involved than I would have preferred her to be. Her psychiatrist says she has a personality disorder that will be hard to treat. However, she's willing to do the work."

"None of us wants the nurse who tried to poison my brother to be charged," Dad says. "She did it under duress. Her daughter was threatened."

"Yes, I know. It's all here in these documents."

"Tell me," I say to Doc, "what does Brittany say about Pat Lamone?"

"They've been on-again, off-again for so long, but she hasn't said anything about him recently."

"He's responsible for some bad stuff when he was younger," I say. "He poisoned my cousin Diana, and he drugged Rory and Callie Pike and took compromising photos of them."

"Yes. Brittany told me. And she told me about her involvement in the same thing."

"Statutes of limitations have long passed," Dad says, "but we can't let Pat Lamone get away with this."

"I don't know that we have a choice," Mom says. "He's a Steel. And he's Lauren's son. And if Lauren turns out to be—"

"We'll cross that bridge when we come to it," Dad says, turning back to Doc. "What about this trafficking ring?"

"From what I can understand from all this," Doc says, "and you're welcome to look at it, everything is supposed to cease to exist upon Wendy's death."

"Yeah. But there are other people involved," Mom says. "Other people making a ton of money doing this. So my guess is . . . " She lets out a sigh.

"I agree with you, sweetie," Dad says. "The ring will rise again. All we can do is make sure they stay far away from our property and our family."

"Absolutely," Mom says.

"I'm willing to give you all of this information," Doc says. "Do with it what you will. If you want to have me arrested and charged, I will live with that. But I do hope you understand that I did not know about the illegal activities on your property. All I did was follow their instructions."

"I was only following orders." Dad shakes his head. "How many times have we heard that?"

"Like I said," Doc says. "I wish I'd never gotten involved in it. I spent a lot of time blaming your brother for it. I even told him that if he had given me the job, none of this would've happened. But I'm beyond that now. I can't blame anyone for my actions but myself. I can tell you I didn't know what was going on, that I was only following orders, which is the truth. But you will choose to believe what you choose to believe."

"Mom, Dad, Doc," I say. "You're right. The statute of limitations precludes our family from going after Pat Lamone for what he did to Diana. Rory and Callie also have no recourse for the same reason. I personally believe that our family has a chance here. We're good people, but not everyone believes that we are. That's not our fault. My grandmother started this a long time ago, and she's gone for good now. All those rumors that the Steels own this town were started by her. Her and her Steel Trust. We're going to take care of that fallout, and we're going to do it anonymously. I'd like to think this is a chance for all of us." I turn to look specifically at Doc Sheraton. "Doc, I don't condone anything you did. But I believe you. I believe you didn't know. Although Wendy didn't pull the trigger, we now know she was responsible for the attempt on my uncle's life. Just like she was responsible for—"

I have to stop. Gulp back some nausea.

Doc may not know what I'm talking about, but Mom and Dad do, and I don't want to go into any more detail.

"Uncle Talon was always the one she went after to punish my grandfather. Clearly that didn't change. Uncle Joe thought the attempt was meant for him, but knowing what I know about Wendy, I don't think that's true. I think Talon was the intended target, because if he weren't, why would someone have tried to finish the job in the hospital?"

Mom nods. "That's my thought as well."

"Wendy left her legacy to me," I continue, "and this is what my destiny is. To reverse it all as well as I can. I don't want to have Doc charged with anything. What I do want is to take down this ring for good. Do what you all thought you had done twenty-five years ago. And I want everyone who's gotten inadvertently caught in the cross fire to have a chance. Like Doc here. And even Brittany. She needs help, and she's getting it now. Let's give her a chance. We all deserve a chance." I sigh. "Even Pat Lamone. He's . . . Well, he's family now."

Mom smiles at me. "I always knew you were an amazing woman, Ava. My mother knew. Apparently your father's mother knew as well. But I don't think any of us could've imagined what a truly good soul you actually are."

"You and Dad were excellent examples for me," I say. "Grandma Didi as well. But I'll give credit where credit is due. Wendy Madigan really helped me see."

"For God's sake, Ava." Dad shakes his head.

"Don't take that the wrong way, Dad. She wasn't a *good* influence. But it was clear what she wanted. She wanted me to be her next incarnation. And for a few perilous moments, I wondered if that was my true destiny. But it's not. My destiny is to do what I can to reverse the havoc that she caused. There's so much I can't do. I can't give Uncle Talon back that time of his life he lost when he was ten. I can't change our genetic makeup, Daddy. I can't change what Pat Lamone did all those years ago, and I can't bring back his adoptive parents to find out why they changed his name and theirs, but I'd bet anything that Wendy had something to do with all that. Let's all start again. That's my purpose. To get the Steel family back its dignity. To forgive. To be grateful for everything we have—and we do have everything, Daddy."

"We don't have—"

"Stop. We have everything."

Dad sighs. "All right. Doc, I have to talk to my brothers. To Bryce and Marjorie. But if they all agree with Ava, we won't be seeking any charges against you."

"I wouldn't blame you if you did, Ryan." Doc closes the folder and slides it across the coffee table to Dad. "But I thank you. And Ava, I thank you too."

"All I ask in return," I say, "is that you be a good man, Doc. Take care of animals. Oh . . . and stop using electric shock collars on your guard dogs."

"I've given up the guard dog business," Doc says. "My dogs are up for adoption, and most of them have already found good homes."

"Good," I say. "But if you're good at it, guard dogs are necessary. Just stop using electric shock."

"It's all right, Ava. I'm no longer training dogs."

"Then I'd like to adopt one," I say.

"A Doberman or Rottweiler in your tiny apartment?" Mom says.

"Yeah, why not?"

"All right," Doc says. "I've got some one-year-olds and a litter of pups still."

"Great. I'll get Brendan, and we'll drive to your place in Wyoming to pick one. Sometime in the next three days, before I have to reopen the bakery."

"All right." Doc stands. "Ryan, Ruby, I appreciate your candor and your hospitality. And Ava"—he sighs—"I don't know what else there is to say."

"You said it all. Brendan and I will see you tomorrow or the next day in Wyoming if you'll be back by then."

"I'm heading back tonight. I've been in Denver, visiting Brittany, and I got back here yesterday, where I found the folder." He rises and slowly heads toward the front door.

Once Doc leaves, I kiss Mom and Dad goodbye, and I drive home.

Home.

Where Brendan is.

CHAPTER FORTY-THREE

Brendan

"Yeah, Jack?" I say into the phone.

"Bingo," he says. "Your hunch was right. Or Ryan's or whoever's it was. Turns out my mother is a full sibling to Ryan Steel."

Damn. I need to tell Ryan. "Jack, I think you're about to become a rich man."

"Mom and I are doing fine. We don't need any of the Steel money."

"Be that as it may, you're entitled to it. And I think Ryan will see it the same way. So will Joe, Talon, and Marjorie."

"This is all so unreal. My grandmother is gone, and my mother is a daughter of Brad Steel. I can't believe this."

"Believe it. It all makes an eerie kind of sense. I'll tell Ryan, and he'll call you. I'm sure he's going to want to meet you and your mom."

Jack is silent on the other end of the line.

"You okay?"

"Yeah, yeah. In the last week, I've found two cousins in you and your dad, and—"

"You have two more. My dad has a sister, Ciara, and a niece, Carmen."

"Jesus . . . Plus now I'm related to all the Steels."

"You always were. You knew that."

"Right, but Mom always said her mother said they'd never accept us. So we never reached out. We never wanted to."

"They would have always accepted you and Lauren, Jack. Wendy was the bad seed."

"Right. I know."

"So you want to meet them?"

"Sure. I do want to meet them. Ruby was nice enough, so I'm sure her husband is a good man."

"He's the best. After all, he made Ava. I can't wait for you to meet her too."

"All right. Get everyone together, and just let us know where."

"I think at your house, if you don't mind. You and your mom will feel more comfortable on your own turf."

"Makes sense," Jack says. "Mom is reeling about all of this."

"I'm sure she is. She'll get through it, and so will you. I'll be in touch."

CHAPTER FORTY-FOUR

Ava

Dad and I arrive, along with Brendan, at a beautiful ranch house in Barrel Oaks. Brendan knocks, and a nice-looking young man with auburn hair opens the door. I can't help it. I gape. He does look a lot like Brendan.

"Jack," Brendan says, shaking his hand. "I'd like you to meet your cousin Ava, my lovely fiancée, and your uncle, Ryan Steel."

Jack nods, gesturing for us to come in. "Please."

"Where's your mom?" Brendan asks.

"She's in the living room. This has all been a lot for her to process."

"For all of us," Brendan says.

Dad takes the lead, following Jack into the room where my aunt sits. She's pretty, and in a way, she looks like me. No pink hair, of course. But the blue eyes—the blue eyes that I always thought came from my mother.

She rises, smiling weakly.

"Hello," Dad says, holding out his hand. "I'm Ryan Steel."

"I'm Lauren Wingdam." Her hands shake as she hands Dad a paper.

He takes it. "Thank you. I've already seen this, as my wife is a good friend of the lab tech who ran the test. I know you're my sister. And I . . . I'm just so sorry that we didn't get to grow up together."

A small smile tugs on Lauren's lips. "Don't you worry about that."

"I do worry about it, Lauren. I'm going to talk to my brothers and my sister. We're going to cut you in on the Steel fortune. It's your birthright."

"But it's not."

"It is as much as it is mine. We're both illegitimate children of Brad Steel. If I deserve it, so do you."

"I don't think our mother saw it that way."

"No, she probably didn't. But Brendan tells me that you and your mother had a falling out."

"We've never been close." Lauren drops her gaze. "She never felt I was worthy. I always figured it was because I didn't come from the one love of her life, Brad Steel. Now, it turns out that I *do* come from him."

"Because you came from an artificial insemination," Dad says. "That's how our mother's mind worked. I came from the sex act itself, and I grew up in Brad Steel's house."

"In what world does that make sense?" Lauren asks.

"In our mother's world, unfortunately. She was a mess, Lauren, as I'm sure you know. And I, for one, am glad she's gone—for good, this time."

I approach from behind my father. "Hello."

"This is my daughter, Ava."

I hold out my hand. "It's nice to meet you," I say.

"It's nice to meet you too, Ava. Did you bring your mother?"

Dad shakes his head. "Ruby wanted to come, but she and I both agreed that we didn't want to overwhelm you, even though the two of you have already met. I have another daughter as well, Gina. She just finished her fall semester at Mesa, and she's still there, partying before the holidays."

Lauren simply nods.

Dad sighs. "I'm so sorry for everything you've been through. But I have to ask ... "

Lauren nods. "The thought has crossed my mind."

"What are you two talking about?" I ask.

"Later, Ava," Dad says.

"There is one thing we haven't found out yet," Ava says. "Where Daphne's orange diamond ring came from. What the initials LW mean."

"We may never know, sweetheart," Dad says. "But now that Wendy is gone, things should fall back into place."

Lauren takes a seat back on the couch.

Dad gestures to the place next to her. "May I?"

"Yes, of course." Lauren stares at Dad as if she's memorizing his face. "After all these years, I just can't believe it. I have a brother. A full-blooded brother."

"You mean you didn't know who your father was?"

"I was told he was an illegitimate son of George Steel," she says. "I just didn't know that *you* were the son of my mother."

"Yes," Dad says, "we've kept that under wraps over the years. But I also thought my mother was dead all those years. Now that I know she was alive, the news may have spread."

Lauren shakes her head. "It didn't. My mother kept quiet about it. Whatever her reasons were, we will never know."

"Her reasons," Dad says, "were probably for my protection. As far as the world knows, I'm a legitimate son of Brad and Daphne Steel. She didn't want anything to taint my inheritance."

"All this time," Lauren says. "All this time she knew. She knew you and I were brother and sister. She never told either of us. Why?"

"Don't try to make sense of it, Lauren. You won't be able to."

I sit next to my father in a wingback chair, and Jack and Brendan join us in chairs across from the couch.

"Would you two like some time to talk?" I ask.

"No, please stay," Lauren says. "Seems we're all related, one way or another." She turns to Brendan. "I guess now that she's dead, we'll never know exactly what my mother hoped to gain by impregnating me with your great-uncle's sperm."

"No," Brendan says. "We will never know. But at least we know a little. We know she's the one who orchestrated the deaths of Sean Murphy and Patty Watson. She took the best friend of Brad and the best friend of Daphne away."

"According to Brock," I say, "the one she hurt most by taking Patty Watson was her boyfriend, Ennis Ainsley."

Dad nods. "He was the first winemaker at Steel Vineyards. An Englishman."

Jack widens his eyes. "An Englishman who knew about wine?"

"Yes," Dad says. "He was the best in the business. He breathed life into Steel Vineyards, and once I took over, we went to the next level."

"Still so many unanswered questions," I say.

"Yes," Lauren says. "I want you all to know that you're welcome to look through any of my stuff. Brendan, I know you, your dad, and Ruby found that decoy refrigerator down there. Did you ever have those specimens analyzed?"

"No," Brendan says. "There was no reason to. If they are

indeed sperm samples, they would not be viable at this point. But we did find the actual samples. We decided the most ethical thing to do was to leave them there. They're over fifty years old and probably not viable."

Lauren nods. "I agree."

Dad rises. "We don't want to overwhelm you anymore today, Lauren. But we would like you to meet the family. Could you come to dinner at our house this weekend? Gina will be home from school, and Rory Pike, who's engaged to my nephew Brock, is putting on a holiday concert at the cinema in Snow Creek. You and Jack should come."

Lauren smiles. "I believe I would like that. But it's a huge undertaking. You have a large family."

"We can start with just my family. You already know Ava, Brendan, Ruby, and me. So you'd just be meeting my daughter Gina this weekend for dinner."

"All right. I would like that a lot."

"Mom," Jack says. "We may as well go all in. These people are our family."

"I don't know, Jack."

"It's up to you, Lauren," Dad says. "But if you choose to meet all of us, then Brendan, you should invite your parents as well. One big family."

Lauren smiles, and I see Wendy Madigan in her. But it's the good part of Wendy Madigan. The part that made my father and Lauren. The part that helped make Gina, Jack, and me.

"Please come," I say. "Our family can be overwhelming, but we're also full of love. Full of light. We want you to be a part of that."

Lauren meets my gaze, and that connection I felt to my

grandmother surges through me, but this time it's all positivity. All light. My aunt and I will be close. Close like Grandma Didi and I were.

"All right," Lauren concedes. "I'd like that."

"Wonderful," Dad says. "An early dinner at Ruby's and my place with the extended Steels, and then the holiday concert."

Brendan takes my hand and squeezes it, and then he slips something on my finger.

I look down and smile.

A diamond sparkles.

And in my mind's eye, the rubble from the falling tower is being swept away by a soft breeze.

Morning has come.

*

DESTINY

EPILOGUE

Sixty years ago ...

"It's priceless," my mother says. "But I'm giving it to you. I don't have any daughters, and one day you'll find a woman you'll want to marry."

"Not anytime soon, Mum." I shake my head.

Not that it's something a guy talks to his mother about, but I've got a lot of wild oats to sow before I even think of settling down.

"I never liked the color," Mum continues, "but it comes from somewhere in Australia. Your grandmother came from there."

She hands me the burgundy velvet box that houses her treasure. The ring she never wears. The ring that—if it's indeed priceless—should probably be locked in a safe somewhere.

Which is exactly where it's going now.

I won't be using it for at least ten years.

ACKNOWLEDGMENTS

And so another Steel trilogy ends—this one with a lot of answers I know you've been waiting for. Who's up next in *Melody*? Wait and see!

Huge thanks to the always brilliant team at Waterhouse Press: Audrey Bobak, Haley Boudreaux, Jesse Kench, Jon Mac, Amber Maxwell, Michele Hamner Moore, Chrissie Saunders, Scott Saunders, Kurt Vachon, and Meredith Wild.

Thanks also to the women and men of Hardt and Soul. Your endless and unwavering support keeps me going.

To my family and friends, thank you for your encouragement. Special shout out to Dean—aka Mr. Hardt—and to our amazing sons, Eric and Grant. Special thanks to Eric for helping with *Destiny* before I handed it in to Scott at Waterhouse.

Thank you most of all to my readers. Without you, none of this would be possible. I am grateful every day that I'm able to do what I love—write stories for you!

The Steels will be back soon!

CONTINUE THE STEEL BROTHERS SAGA

WITH BOOK TWENTY-EIGHT

MESSAGE FROM HELEN HARDT

Dear Reader,

Thank you for reading *Destiny*. If you want to find out about my current backlist and future releases, please like my Facebook page and join my mailing list. I often do giveaways. If you're a fan and would like to join my street team to help spread the word about my books, please see the web addresses below. I regularly do awesome giveaways for my street team members.

If you enjoyed the story, please take the time to leave a review on a site like Amazon or Goodreads. I welcome all feedback. I wish you all the best!

Helen

Facebook
Facebook.com/HelenHardt

Newsletter
HelenHardt.com/SignUp

Street Team
Facebook.com/Groups/HardtAndSoul

ALSO BY HELEN HARDT

The Steel Brothers Saga:

Craving

Obsession

Possession

Melt

Burn

Surrender

Shattered

Twisted

Unraveled

Breathless

Ravenous

Insatiable

Fate

Legacy

Descent

Awakened

Cherished

Freed

Spark

Flame

Blaze

Smolder

Flare

Scorch

Chance

Fortune

Destiny

Melody

Harmony

Encore

Blood Bond Saga:

Unchained

Unhinged

Undaunted

Unmasked

Undefeated

Misadventures Series:
Misadventures with a Rock Star
Misadventures of a Good Wife (with Meredith Wild)

The Temptation Saga:
Tempting Dusty
Teasing Annie
Taking Catie
Taming Angelina
Treasuring Amber
Trusting Sydney
Tantalizing Maria

The Sex and the Season Series:
Lily and the Duke
Rose in Bloom
Lady Alexandra's Lover
Sophie's Voice

Daughters of the Prairie:
The Outlaw's Angel
Lessons of the Heart
Song of the Raven

Cougar Chronicles:
The Cowboy and the Cougar
Calendar Boy

Anthologies Collection:
Destination Desire
Her Two Lovers

ABOUT THE AUTHOR

#1 *New York Times*, #1 *USA Today*, and #1 *Wall Street Journal* bestselling author Helen Hardt's passion for the written word began with the books her mother read to her at bedtime. She wrote her first story at age six and hasn't stopped since. In addition to being an award-winning author of romantic fiction, she's a mother, an attorney, a black belt in Taekwondo, a grammar geek, an appreciator of fine red wine, and a lover of Ben & Jerry's ice cream. She writes from her home in Colorado, where she lives with her family. Helen loves to hear from readers.

Visit her at HelenHardt.com